Christmas at the Castle

Christmas at the Castle

An Ever After Romance

Melissa McClone

TULE
PUBLISHING

A royal wedding. A meddlesome mother. An unexpected union.

A European getaway during the Christmas holiday is exactly what veterinarian Katrina "Kat" Parsons needs. She can't wait to be a bridesmaid in her childhood friend's royal wedding, but she hopes to steer clear of the bride's arrogant older brother.

Crown Prince Guillaume wants his younger sister's wedding day to be perfect, but he's suspicious of Kat. He and his mother on are on high alert, afraid Kat is not just there for the wedding, but also to find a prince of her own.

But when Kat's kindness and generosity prove them wrong, the prince realizes there's more to her than he ever imagined. Can he trust his heart or will he lose the one woman he can't live without?

Prologue

June – Fifteen Years Ago

KATRINA PARSONS STOOD on the edge of the dock at Camp KooKoRomo. She'd left her fishing gear—borrowed as an excuse to check out the lake—near the tall grass. If she jumped into the water and pretended to drown, would the counselors send her home?

Camp will be good for you, Kat. You're too young to be stuck on the farm with a couple of old fogies.

So instead of being with her grandparents, whom she loved, or visiting her parents in Africa, whom she missed, she was stuck spending eight weeks of her summer vacation with kids who thought farting was a group event.

She groaned. Her angst and frustration carried across the mirror-flat water.

This was a ginormous mistake. She was going into eighth grade and should have known better than to agree to come, but she'd been swayed by the glossy brochure with pictures of fun in the sun, s'mores by the campfire, and cute boys.

Especially the cute boys.

The ones at her middle school wanted only to copy her homework. They ignored her otherwise.

But so far, in the two hours since she'd arrived, she hadn't seen one cute boy. She'd looked. Twice.

How many others had fallen for the brilliant marketing scam?

"Help! Someone, please!"

A panicked voice came from somewhere on shore. The tall grass and reeds blocked Kat's view, so she ran off the dock.

"Where are you?" Kat yelled.

"Here," a girl called. "Please help my brother."

Kat tromped through the grass and saw two teens.

The girl was around the same age as she was. She had shoulder-length blonde hair and wore a flower-print sundress and white sandals.

The boy looked to be a couple of years older. He lay on the ground and clutched his leg. He was dressed in khaki pants and a navy polo shirt.

Odd clothing choices for summer camp compared to Kat's jean shorts and tank top. Maybe they'd come straight from church.

"What happened?" Kat asked.

"My brother got caught on something and fell." She spoke with a slight accent.

English, maybe? Kat couldn't tell.

The girl stood a few feet away. Her face was pale, and she wrapped her arms across her stomach. "There's…blood."

Blood didn't bother Kat. Last week, she'd helped Dr. Monroe deliver a colt at the next-door neighbor's barn. So cool.

She kneeled on the ground. "Let me see."

The boy grimaced. "Who are you?"

His accent was stronger than his sister's.

"It's okay." Kat placed her hand on his shoulder the same way she comforted an injured or sick farm animal. "I know first aid."

The tension on his face remained, but his green eyes didn't look nearly as dark. He raised his pant leg as much as the fishing line tangled around his calf allowed. Blood streaked the skin. A hook was caught above his ankle.

Not any hook, either. The one from the pole she'd borrowed and left on the ground when she went to the dock.

"I'm so sorry." Her throat thickened. "You tripped on my fishing pole. But I'll fix this."

"No." The lines around his mouth deepened. "Go get help."

"I can do this." Kat removed her pocketknife from the back pocket of her shorts.

He flinched. "What are you doing with a knife?"

"I live on a farm where carrying a knife comes in handy."

This one had been a birthday gift from her parents when she turned eight, though she had a feeling her grandparents had purchased it. Her mom and dad were too busy with their research on primates to remember special dates and holidays. Sometimes, Kat wondered if they remembered they had a daughter. Too bad spending the summer with them hadn't been an option.

She opened up the knife. "When you're in the wilderness, you should always be prepared."

"We're at a summer camp with a ridiculous name." He spoke through clenched teeth. "Not the *Białowieża* Forest."

Kat had no idea what or where that place was, but the exotic name conjured up images of a grand adventure. Someday, she'd travel to places like her parents did and see the world.

"True, but I can use the knife to remove the fishing wire so you won't stumble again." Sunlight glinted off the silver blade. "If you stay still, I won't cut you."

His clear, green eyes turned cold and looked like frozen peas. He must be in pain.

"Go ahead," he said finally.

He didn't sound happy. Kat didn't blame him.

Blood seeped through his pants. A large red spot covered his knee.

Ouch. He must have hit the ground when he fell.

She cut away the fishing line and then closed the blade. "I'm going to pull out the hook. This might sting."

His jaw tensed. "Get it out now."

She was tempted to salute but thought better of the idea.

He didn't seem like he was in the mood to laugh or smile. She didn't blame him.

Kat pulled on the hook.

He grunted.

His sister shrieked. "Oh, please, be careful."

Kat was. She tried again. Each time she worked to dislodge the hook, the boy's face reddened and the girl's paled. Finally, it came out. "Got it."

He squeezed his eyes closed.

Kat placed the hook on the fishing line she'd cut off.

The boy opened his eyes. "Thank you."

"You're welcome."

"You shouldn't leave your things unattended."

"I didn't think anyone would be out here." She gathered the fishing gear, stood, and extended her arm to help him stand. "We need to get back to camp and clean you up. You don't want your wounds to get infected. And someone should check your knee."

The boy hesitated and then slowly, as if he wasn't sure he wanted to touch her, grabbed hold of her hand and stood.

His strong grip surprised her given he was so thin. In spite of his cold gaze, his skin was warm. He was taller than she expected, and she had to look up at him, which was nice. She towered over many of the boys in her class.

She couldn't tell if his light brown hair was curly or messy. The wild style might look good on him if he smiled, but his lips pressed together so tightly she could barely see them.

He must be in pain.

Kat slipped her arm around his waist.

Brushing her hand away, he stared down his nose. "This was your fault, and I am capable of walking on my own."

"I said I was sorry."

Silence.

His I'm-better-than-you glare prickled. So not polite.

She'd tried to help after her mistake, but if he fell again, that would be on him this time. "Let's go then."

He limped.

"Thank you for helping my brother." Color had returned to the girl's face. She fell in step with Kat. "I'm Sophie von Strausser."

"Nice to meet you. I'm Kat Parsons."

The boy made a face. "You're named after an animal?"

"Kat with a K. It's short for Katrina. But I wouldn't mind being named after cats. I love animals."

The boy rolled his eyes. A reaction she knew had nothing to do with his injury. As her grandmother would say, he had an attitude with a capital A.

"You're American," Sophie said in a pleasant singsong voice that belonged in a cartoon.

Kat smiled. "Well, this camp is in America."

"Oh, yes. I forgot amid all the excitement." Sophie grinned. "This is my brother Gee—"

"Gill." His harsh glare traveled from Kat to his sister and

sharpened along the way. "My name is Gill."

The sooner Kat could leave Gill with those in charge at the camp's office, the better, but Sophie seemed friendly. "Nice to meet you."

"The pleasure is mine." Sophie walked with a bounce to her step. Not quite skipping, more like a hop. "I'd be delighted to be your friend."

Sophie was bright and cheery like a meadow of wildflowers, as pretty, too, but Kat wasn't used to anyone wanting to be her friend. Well, except the animals at the farm.

"Sure. You can never have enough friends."

"Who is your BFF?" Sophie asked.

"I, um, don't have a best friend." Kat left off that her closest friends had four legs and were covered with fur. Well, except the chickens and ducks. Only two feet and feathers for them.

Sophie hooked her arm with Kat's. "Now you do."

That was easy.

"I'm from Palouse." Kat supposed BFFs should know something about each other besides their names. "It's a small town in Eastern Washington. Where are you from?"

"Europe," Gill answered.

Kat could relate to his want-to-be-anywhere-but-here look given her mood less than ten minutes ago, but he didn't have to act like a jerk. Gill reminded her of the popular kids at school who looked down on everybody else unless they wanted something, but she knew better than to say anything.

On second thought… "An entire continent is a bit general, don't you think? Or are you nomads?"

Sophie giggled. "Nomads. I love it."

The lines on Gill's face deepened like canyons. "We live in a small place that's virtually unheard of outside of Europe."

His authoritative tone reminded Kat of the school's new vice principal, who passed out detentions like Halloween candy. Best to stay far, far away from Gill. That should be easy to do.

"But I'm assuming an American might know the continent," he added.

Gill not only thought he was better but also smarter than everyone else. The urge to brush him away like a swarm of gnats was strong.

"Don't mind my brother," Sophie said before Kat could respond. "He's always moody and wanted to spend the summer at boarding school instead of camp."

Boarding school? Kat had never met anyone who went away to attend school. She couldn't imagine what that must be like.

"So Kat from Palouse, have you seen any of the cute boys from the brochure?" Sophie asked.

Kat hadn't been the only one who'd fallen for the sales pitch. She glanced at Gill. He could qualify as cute if you liked the tall, silent, hates-everything type.

She didn't.

She focused on Sophie. "No, I haven't, but I'm hoping not everyone is here yet."

"Unbelievable," Gill said. "The two of you are the same."

Kat took that as a compliment. She straightened.

"Which is why we'll get along splendidly." Sophie stuck her tongue out at Gill before turning her attention to Kat. "My brother is going to be miserable the entire time he's here, but I promise I won't let him ruin our summer."

Our summer.

A warm feeling flowed through Kat, as if liquid sunshine poured through her veins. She couldn't help but smile.

Maybe Camp KooKoRomo wouldn't be so bad after all.

Chapter One

December – Present day

"DR. PARSONS...KAT. WAKE up."
The familiar voice of Jojo, a vet tech at the Cedar Village Veterinary Clinic, cut through Kat's sleep-fogged brain. She'd been making one last round before heading home. She must have fallen asleep.

Kat stretched her arms. Something scratched her hands. Hay.

She opened her eyes.

Sunlight filled the stall.

Uh-oh. She scrambled to her feet. "What time is it?"

"Seven-thirty." Jojo, a forty-three-year-old woman who had blue-streaked black hair, petted the sick calf. "I came in here to check on Mabel. Found you asleep."

Mabel needed more care than the farm where she lived could provide. Earlier, the calf had been restless, so Kat had wanted to calm her. Not fall asleep.

"Don't you have a plane to catch?" Jojo asked.

"Yes, but my ride isn't picking me up until eight-thirty." And they had a two-hour drive to reach an airport that offered commercial flights.

She brushed hay from her scrubs. "I have time to get home and shower."

And finish packing for her European vacation.

Sophie might be her summer camp BFF, but she was also a princess. More than yoga pants and T-shirts—Kat's typical attire at home—was required. Although, she did plan to wear those on her flight across the Atlantic so she could be comfortable and sleep.

Kat grabbed Mabel's chart and jotted down notes for the other vets who worked at the clinic. "If you need anything—"

Jojo raised her hand. "This is your first vacation since you started working here. Forget about this place, enjoy your time off, and catch the bridal bouquet."

"I don't know what wedding traditions they have in Alistonia, but if there's a bouquet toss, I'll go for it."

Kat wanted a family more than anything, but she had zero hopes of getting married in the near future. Not only did she have to fulfill a three-year commitment at the rural clinic as part of a veterinary school loan repayment program, but her work schedule made dating difficult, if not impossible. Being the newest vet on staff meant her shifts consisted of late nights at the twenty-four-hour hospital, weekends in the mobile clinic, and holidays.

Not that she minded. She loved her job, but she couldn't

wait for this trip. She'd been saving up vacation time and trading on-call shifts so she could be in Sophie and Bertrand's wedding.

A princess marrying a duke's second son on the twenty-third of December.

A royal Christmas wedding.

A sigh welled.

This would be the best wedding ever.

Kat brushed off more hay. "I have to keep pinching myself that I'm really going on this trip."

"Just don't forget your bridesmaid dress," Jojo said.

"It's in Alistonia along with my shoes. I'm taking three flights today. No one wants to chance my suitcase getting lost."

"Be sure all the hay is out." Jojo picked out a piece from Kat's hair. "A shower won't do that."

Kat touched her head and poked her finger. Oops.

She put Mabel's chart back into place and then reached out to the calf. "Good morning, beautiful girl."

"Oh, no, you don't." Jojo dragged Kat out and into the clinic. "Get your stuff and go. The clock is ticking."

Jojo was right, but leaving was never easy for Kat. This morning was no different. Dogs barked from the treatment room. A cat yowled, not a patient, but a border in the kennel. Sasha, part Siamese, did not like being away from home.

The sounds weren't unusual for the small animal section

of the clinic, but Kat's chest tightened. Fighting the urge to take one last look at their patients, she touched Jojo's arm. "Promise me—"

"I'll check on Sasha as soon as you leave." Jojo placed her hand over heart. Amusement twinkled in her eyes, but her voice was sincere. "I'll take good care of Mabel and the rest who are here, too. We all will. Promise."

Everything would be fine while Kat was away. She knew that. Jojo and the staff had been caring for animals long before Kat had started veterinary school, and they'd be here long after she left.

"Thanks." She grabbed her tote bag. "Merry Christmas."

"You, too." Jojo hugged her. "Take advantage of any mistletoe you see."

Kat grinned at the thought. She hadn't kissed a guy in way too long. "Definitely."

"And I hope Santa leaves you a hot European under the tree."

"Wouldn't that be nice? I have been extra good this year."

Boringly so.

She almost laughed at how her life consisted of two things—work and sleep. Her biggest social interactions were an occasional happy hour with coworkers and video chats with Sophie, but Kat had plenty of time for romance in the future.

Jojo gave Kat a slight push toward the exit. "Take lots of

pictures. I'll want a full report when you get back."

"Will do, but I hope you're not too disappointed. Nothing exciting ever happens to me."

"Being in a royal wedding and going to Europe is the definition of exciting. Enjoy yourself." Jojo pulled another piece of hay from Kat's hair. "And remember, Christmas is a time of magic and miracles."

"I hope so." Kat glanced at the clock on the wall and then reached for the door. "I may need a Christmas miracle to make my flight."

EIGHTEEN HOURS, THREE flights, and too many time changes to count later, Kat arrived in Alistonia, a small country located on the eastern side of the Alps. The view of the snow-covered mountains and lakes, some blue and others frozen white, during her flight's approach had been picturesque, and the decorated-for-the-holidays airport with Christmas carols playing from overhead speakers and twinkling lights hanging everywhere only added to the postcard-perfect charm. Cedar Village was a blink-and-you'll-miss-it small town, but something about this place felt downright cozy.

She adjusted the strap of her tote on her shoulder.

An airport valet placed her luggage on a wheeled cart and rolled that outside to a black limousine. Two tiny blue, yellow, and red striped flags on the hood fluttered in the breeze.

A uniformed driver, an older man with gray hair, greeted her by bowing. "Welcome, Dr. Parsons."

He must have been told what she looked like.

"Hello." She stifled a yawn. Traveling had sapped her energy, but the cold air might give her the boost she needed. She hoped so. The cup of coffee on her last flight hadn't done anything but make her sleepy. She wanted to wake up. "Please, call me Kat."

The chauffer bowed. "I am Claude. If there's anything I can do for you while you're in town, please let me know."

"Thank you."

Sophie had said she would take care of all the details once Kat arrived, but she hadn't expected this kind of service—even though Sophie was royalty.

Kat rubbed her tired eyes. She still had a hard time reconciling her friend's title with the woman who seemed so grounded and had gone into social work as a profession.

Claude opened the limo passenger door. "Make yourself comfortable."

If Kat did that, she would fall asleep. The car ride might do the same thing. "Is the drive far?"

"A few kilometers away," Claude said. "We should be there in less than ten minutes."

Good. Kat shouldn't be lulled to sleep in that short amount of time. She slid into the backseat.

Instrumental Christmas music played. A full wet bar was

at her disposal with crystal decanters and bottles displayed. Panels of buttons and switches glowed. She had no idea what they all did, but she was too tired to experiment. Maybe another day.

Claude closed the door, placed her luggage in the trunk, and then got into the driver's seat. He glanced back. "The town will be on your right as we leave the airport."

She glanced out the window and nearly gasped.

Forget the word *town*. Village better described the narrow streets decorated with garland and the quaint buildings with wreaths hung on doors. A church steeple was the tallest building. The others were two, maybe three stories. Small, yes, but with so much character.

The scene resembled a Christmas card, one she would keep out all year. This might be her first visit to Europe, but this place seemed so welcoming. She had a strange sense of coming home.

"Charming," she said.

It was just as Sophie had been describing for over a decade. Hard to believe they'd been friends for the past fifteen years. Sophie had wanted Kat to visit since they'd met, but the airfare had been prohibitive. Each year, another invitation was extended, but she'd had to say no. With her first paycheck from the clinic, Kat had set up a travel savings account.

And here she was.

Her first time out of the United States. Her first time on

a different continent. Her first time being in a wedding.

She pressed her nose to the window. "It's as pretty as a postcard."

"Just wait until we have snow again. Warm temperatures melted everything a few days ago, but the weather forecast predicts heavy snow will fall this weekend."

"That would be wonderful." Her breath fogged the glass. She leaned back against the seat. "I love snow."

Having snowball fights, making snow angels, and building snowmen had been favorite wintertime activities as a child. She sighed at the memories of growing up on her grandparents' farm. She missed those times, and she missed them.

Her nana and papa would be tickled that she was finally in Alistonia to visit Sophie, who they'd loved like a granddaughter and treated like one during her visits to the farm.

Yawning, Kat blinked. Her eyelids felt so heavy. She shook her head. She needed to stay awake…

"We're here, Miss Kat."

Huh? Kat opened her eyes to find the driver standing outside the limo with the door opened.

She straightened. "Sorry, I must have fallen asleep."

"Jetlag." The driver extended his hand. "You'll need a day or two to adjust to the time change."

Stifling another yawn, she climbed out of the limo. The cold air made her shiver. She stood on a stone-tiled driveway and faced a tall, wrought iron gate with uniformed guards standing watch.

This must be a fancy hotel if they kept security at the entrance. Unless the guards were there for show and photo opportunities with guests.

Claude closed the car door. "I'll take your luggage to your room."

She removed dollar bills from her wallet and handed the tip to the driver. "Thank you."

He placed his arms behind his back, so she couldn't see his hands. "I appreciate the sentiment, but tipping is not necessary during your stay. Liv will help you get settled in your room."

Who was Liv? And where was Sophie? At work?

Kat hadn't spoken to her friend this week other than a few texts. The last one had been right before Kat boarded her first flight. She would text Sophie from the hotel room.

Kat faced the hotel.

Her mouth gaped.

No way. This was a…a…

"This is a castle," she said, forcing the words from her tight throat.

"Yes, Miss Kat. Fortunately for guests, the interior has been remodeled and upgraded several times over the centuries. You should find the accommodations most comfortable."

She stared in disbelief.

Talk about fairy-tale worthy.

Turrets jutted into the sky. An image of a beautiful princess standing at one of the windows in the tower formed in her mind. She could be waiting for her prince to arrive or, as Sophie had, making a mark in the world on her own.

Against the gray sky, the spires sparkled and the roof tiles gleamed as if sprinkled with pixie dust. The sight made her think of a fairy tale with a happily ever after ending. Perhaps her once upon a time wasn't as far away as she thought.

Unbelievable and so unexpected.

She didn't see a sign or placard anywhere. "What's the name of the hotel?"

"This isn't a hotel."

Sophie had never mentioned anything about a castle in Alistonia. That was something Kat would have remembered. She had a soft spot for Cinderella movies.

"I think there's been some kind of mistake," Kat said.

Claude opened the trunk. "No mistake. Your room was chosen by Princess Sophia herself."

No mistake.

The two words echoed through Kat's head.

She should be excited—Jojo was going to love hearing about this—but the hair at the back of Kat's neck prickled. She straightened her tote bag. Alistonia was a more formal country than the US. She'd packed accordingly, but she felt underdressed in her black yoga pants, oversized turtleneck, and long sweater. Comfortable clothes for the flight. Not appropriate attire for a magnificent castle.

She swallowed.

"Is there a problem?" Claude asked.

"No problem." Not really. Just surprised.

Kat had imagined staying at one of the picturesque inns on the hillside that Sophie had described during their six summers together—the first four as campers and the last two as counselors.

Not…this.

If staying here was supposed to be a surprise, Sophie had succeeded. Kat was speechless.

Her friend had never spoken much about being royalty. They'd known each other a full year before Sophie confessed she was a princess. They used to joke about marrying princes, but that was in fun. Kat had never wanted to pry and ask her friend too many questions about royal life. She still didn't.

Claude picked up her luggage. "I'll take you inside where it's warmer."

She followed him.

Up ahead, tall Christmas trees decorated with red ribbon and white lights flanked the entrance. As if on cue, the imposing arched wooden door swung open.

A man in his late twenties or early thirties walked out. His tailored gray suit showed off wide shoulders and an athletic build. His yellow-and-red tie bounced slightly against his white button-down shirt. Light brown hair curled at the ends and framed a handsome face with high cheekbones, a straight nose, and full lips.

Looking at him made her feel warm and tingly inside.

Who was she kidding?

She was downright toasty now.

His lips looked like they would be perfect for under-the-mistletoe kisses.

And more.

She had no idea who he was, but this hottie had just taken over the top spot on her Christmas list. She would have to write Santa.

The man's long strides cut the distance between them quickly. He looked at Claude. "Have you seen Maximilian?"

"No, sir. As soon as I take Dr. Parsons inside, I'll phone the groundskeeper. One of his men will track him down again."

A stunning, green-eyed gaze collided with hers. Sharpened.

Kat sucked in a breath. She knew that color. Knew the man.

Or did.

Prince Guillaume von Strausser.

She'd been fifteen the last time she saw him at camp. Sophie's brother hadn't been drop-dead-gorgeous back then.

Okay, forget about writing Santa. Kat would need to find another hottie to go on her Christmas list. Sophie's brother was off-limits. Kat never wanted anything to come between her and her camp BFF. Not that Gill had given her anything but grief at camp.

Still, unexpected nerves made Kat's muscles twitch. She forced a smile. "Hi, Gill."

Surprise flashed across his face. "Kat?"

"It's good to see you." She sounded breathless. The way she felt.

Whatever shock he might have felt, however, disappeared. His lips pressed together, and his gaze narrowed. "I didn't think you were coming."

That wasn't the reply she'd expected. "Why wouldn't I?"

"You've never been here before."

He spoke with the same authoritative tone she remembered, but Kat thought she heard a touch of accusation, too. Weird since they hadn't spoken in so long, but he'd always been protective about Sophie and thought Kat interfered too much in his sister's life.

"Lack of time and money," she admitted.

He raised a brow. "And now?"

"I need more of both, but I wouldn't miss Sophie's wedding for anything."

He studied Kat. Not as a friend looked at someone they hadn't seen in a long time—thirteen years to be exact—but as a stranger, trying to determine if the person was safe or dangerous.

Her heart sank. Even after all these years, he still didn't like her.

He started to speak but then stopped himself.

CHRISTMAS AT THE CASTLE

She raised her chin instead. "What?"

His gaze darkened to a forest green. "Are you here for my sister's wedding…or have you set your sights on finding a royal for yourself?"

She wanted to believe he was joking, but his tone matched the serious look in his eyes.

Same old Gill. Imperial and pompous.

No doubt, Claude heard the implication in Gill's voice that she was nothing more than a royal groupie.

Great way to start off her trip.

Squaring her shoulders, she took a step back. "I'm here because I'm Sophie's friend and one of her bridesmaids. No other reason."

"Sophie mentioned finding you a husband."

When they were teenagers, she'd wanted Kat to marry one of her brothers so they could be sisters. "Sophie's always kidding around about setting me up on a date."

Emphasis on *kidding around*.

Kat's ordinary life growing up on a wheat farm was so removed from Sophie's world that her being royal had never been much of a curiosity. Perhaps something to daydream about when Kat was caring for her aging grandparents while attending college at the same time, but not enough to warrant an Internet search. Kat had had too much to do back then. She still did.

Watching Sophie on the reality TV show *The Search for Cinderella* had been the closest peek into her friend's life, but to be honest, that had seemed more fantasy-for-the-cameras than reality.

Suspicion filled Gill's gaze, but he didn't say anything.

Words weren't necessary. Kat could tell what he was thinking.

"You don't have to believe me," she said. "But it's true."

He wouldn't change his mind no matter what she said. Gill's behavior had always been consistent—the definition of arrogance. No problem. The castle looked big enough for her to keep her distance.

Just like their old camp days.

"Claude called you doctor," Gill said.

Kat wasn't surprised he knew nothing about her. He'd never been her friend. Gill had tolerated her—for his sister's sake—but that tolerance seemed to have disappeared.

Kat wouldn't let him get to her. "I'm a veterinarian."

"You always had a soft spot for those who were injured or not feeling well."

"You were one of my first patients."

Lines creased his forehead. "From humans to animals."

"What can I say?" she joked. "Animals don't talk back."

She thought Gill might crack a smile. He didn't.

Maybe not having a sense of humor was a prince thing. He was the only one she'd met.

"I don't remember saying much that day," he said finally.

"You grunted more than you spoke."

"Did I? I don't remember." His brows furrowed. "But I

have a scar on my leg from your fishing hook, and I recall you had a knife."

"I still have one. It's in my suitcase," she admitted. "Airport security frowns upon knives in carryon luggage, so I packed it."

His gaze raked over her again. Only this was faster than the last time. He studied and surmised judgement in a brief pass. Not a positive one either based on his expression. The only thing missing was a judge's gavel.

His mouth slanted into a lopsided frown. "You must want to freshen up."

Oh, boy. She must look a mess for him to say that. His looks had changed for the better, but his personality and manners hadn't. How did Sophie put up with him?

Kat nodded. "It's been a long day."

"I won't keep you." With that, Gill walked past her and Claude.

Feeling dismissed, she glanced over her shoulder at him.

He walked at a brisk pace as if he'd forgotten about her. He probably had.

Kat inhaled deeply. She let the cold air fill her lungs and cool her down.

From what she could see, Gill still acted like the moody, arrogant teen he'd once been.

No biggie.

She and Sophie had never let him ruin their time together at camp, and Kat wouldn't let that happen now. She would enjoy being a member of the royal wedding party and make the most of her vacation. If Prince Annoying had an issue with her, that was his problem.

She was going to have the best Christmas ever.

Chapter Two

WALKING AWAY, GILL forced himself not to glance back if only to prove seeing the American had been a figment of his imagination. What was going on? He'd been told a distant cousin would be one of Sophie's bridesmaids and Kat wasn't attending the wedding.

Yet, here she was.

Not his imagination.

Gill would have never pictured her growing so nicely into her model height, or that her fresh-faced farm girl look would be so pretty with dark circles under her eyes, or that her mussed dark brown hair would be so sexy—like she'd just crawled out of a lover's bed. One thing had stayed the same. Her wide blue eyes still pierced him to his very core.

But he wasn't impressed.

Gill preferred women with flawless makeup, hair, and clothing. Kat was the antithesis of flawless.

He needed her gone.

From the castle and from Alistonia.

For the past fifteen years, she had caused nothing but trouble by leading Sophie astray. Kat's advice had put his sister at odds with the family's wishes and her royal duties. He wouldn't let Kat cause more problems.

And she would if she remained.

Gill needed to keep his sister safe.

Circling through the garden so he could enter the castle through another door and avoid Kat, he pulled out his cell phone and called Sophie. His sister owed him an explanation.

She answered on the second ring. "What is it now, Your Serene Royal Highness?"

Her nickname for him bristled. He'd been content as the spare heir. He'd never wanted to be the crown prince or the future king, but when his older brother Jacques renounced his title to become a priest, Gill had no choice. He'd been twenty-two when his plans for the future disappeared, and duty took over.

Daily itineraries ruled his time. His mother's requests—more often demands—determined his priorities. His mother had even asked to approve any woman he dated because the queen was legally required to consent to whomever he married.

He wanted to be the perfect crown prince and son, but balancing his responsibilities and royal duty while trying to find time for himself was a continuous struggle that left him feeling torn between what was required and what he wanted to do. His life was no longer his own. Unlike his younger sister, who was able to do whatever she wanted.

"Are you still on the line?" she asked.

"Your friend from camp has arrived," Gill said.

Sophie screeched, a sound full of delight and anticipation. "I can't believe Kat's finally here. I have one meeting to attend, and then I'll be home straight away."

As she spoke about her plans for Kat's visit, Sophie's excitement poured through the phone. Normally, he would smile and join in her bubbliness. He loved Sophie and would do anything for her, but her American friend was a bad influence.

While the family had wanted Sophie to focus on her royal duties, Kat had encouraged Sophie to follow her heart and become a social worker. When Sophie was asked to be on a ridiculous reality TV show, the family had said no. Kat, however, convinced Sophie to participate.

With disastrous results.

Sophie fell in love with the rakish Prince Luc of Alvernia. When he decided to marry someone else—an American— her heart was broken. Granted, Sophie had met her fiancé Bertrand because of that show, but still…

Had Kat come to console Sophie after the trouble she'd caused?

No.

Helping Sophie through her heartache had been left to Gill and her circle of friends. That only reaffirmed what he'd always known to be true.

Kat Parsons was trouble.

"Won't this be fun?" Sophie asked.

Gill hadn't been listening. "You said *she* wasn't coming."

Silence.

Of course there was. His little sister had been caught.

What was the word the Americans used?

Busted.

"Sophia Elizabeth Marie Louise von Strausser." He used his sister's full name. "Why did you tell me Kat wasn't attending your wedding?"

"Because you can be such a pain." Sophie sounded like she was twelve, not twenty-eight. "I didn't want to deal with it."

"What *it?*"

"You." A beat passed. "You treat all American women with disdain because of Clarissa."

Hearing the name of his ex-girlfriend, the woman he thought he would marry, put a foul taste in his mouth. "I do not."

"Yes, you do," Sophie countered. "Even before Clarissa, you were rude to Kat. You've always disliked her, even when we were kids, so I figured if you knew she was coming, you'd find a way to have her banned from entering the country."

"You're being melodramatic." A good idea though.

"I'm being honest," Sophie said sincerely.

The last thing he wanted to do was hurt his sister's feelings. "I'm only looking out for you. That's all I've ever done because I don't want Kat filling your head with inappropriate ideas."

"Such as?"

"Whoever heard of a princess becoming a social worker?"

"You wanted to be a professor. The two fields aren't that dissimilar."

"That's different."

"Why? Because you're a man?"

Whatever Gill said would be taken the wrong way, so he kept quiet.

"Bertrand says my job attracted him to me," she added.

"He's going to let you continue working after you marry?"

"Of course. I would never marry a man who would force me to stop doing what I love. I have a new position lined up in Darbyton, though I'll miss my job here."

Gill would have to speak with Bertrand. Maybe he could limit Sophie's interactions with Kat. If not before the wedding, then afterward as her husband.

"I'm good at what I do." Confidence filled Sophie's voice. "I'm making a difference in people's lives and you, as our future ruler, should pay closer attention to what our subjects need."

"I know what my people need." He imagined Sophie sticking her tongue out at the phone. A childhood gesture she hadn't outgrown.

"They don't need any more trade agreements," she countered.

"Those will secure everyone's future, including yours."

"I'm securing my own."

"By working?"

"Yes." Sophie sighed. "This call is exactly why I didn't tell you Kat was coming."

"She's a danger to you."

"You only think that because the two of you always disagree about me, but Kat has my best interests at heart."

"And I don't?"

"It's different with Kat. To her, I'm just Sophie, not Princess Sophia Elizabeth Marie Louise."

Gill had his doubts. "Don't be so sure."

"So ominous sounding."

"Kat says she's here for your wedding, but what if she has an ulterior motive?"

"Oh, this should be good," Sophie muttered. "Tell me, oh wise brother, what other reason could Kat possibly have for coming to Alistonia?"

"To find a royal to bed or wed, possibly both."

Sophie burst out laughing.

"I'm serious," Gill countered. "For years, I've heard you talk about wanting her to marry a prince. I heard her say she wanted to be a princess."

"We were teenagers. I had a mad crush on William. I told her she could have Harry."

"No doubt she planted the idea of making her a princess in your head. Look at the timing of her visit. She couldn't bother to come any time before this, but now that that there's a royal wedding, she finally shows up. Two weeks early."

Sophie sighed. "How many times do I have to tell you Kat's nothing like Clarissa?"

His ex-girlfriend had only been interested in snaring the royal with the best title. She'd dumped him so she could date the future king of a much-larger country. "You don't know that for certain."

"I know Kat. I've known her for fifteen years and tried to fix her up with men before. Royalty doesn't impress her. She knows little about our lives. Besides, she doesn't date."

An image of Kat flashed in his mind. She might not be his type, but an attractive woman like her did not stay home alone. "I don't believe that. She isn't telling you what she does."

"I know everything about her. Kat had a serious boy-friend in college, but that ended when she started vet school. Her grandparents needed her help at the farm, and the guy wanted more time than she could give him."

"He must have been a commoner, or she would have given what he asked and married him."

"I feel sorry for the woman who falls in love with you."

"Why is that?"

"Because you don't listen. Kat isn't after a royal or any

other man, including you. But that doesn't mean I won't try to fix her up while she's here. I worry about Kat because all she does is work. I doubt she'll find a man she loves more than animals."

"That's her problem, not yours."

"Of course, it's my problem. She's my friend."

"Family and duty first."

"It's terrifying how much you sound like Mother right now."

He knew that wasn't a compliment. "Sophia…"

A noise sounded in the background. Someone was calling for his sister.

"I have to go," she said. "Promise me you'll be on your best behavior around Kat and remember she's our guest. Don't be rude, and please keep your beastly side hidden."

"I'm never beastly."

"You walk a fine line. And if you hurt my BFF's feelings with your crazy accusations, I'll turn into such a nightmare bridezilla that you'll have to call in the royal guards."

Sophie's words were proving his point about her friend's negative influence. "You never spoke to me like this before you met Kat."

"I did, but blaming Kat for everything you don't like about me is easier. Fortunately, she doesn't mind."

"I have no idea what you mean."

Sophie sighed. "I need to go. Be nice."

"I will be on my best behavior."

The line disconnected.

Gill didn't like how quick Sophie was to defend her friend. His sister wouldn't listen to reason, but the American with the stunning blue eyes would never charm him into thinking she wasn't a threat. He would not put the people he cared about at risk.

Kat Parsons might be his sister's BFF from camp and her bridesmaid, but if the woman showed any signs of hurting Sophie or chasing after a royal, Kat would be on the first plane back to the States.

THE CASTLE'S FRONT door wasn't far away, but each step took effort. Kat's feet dragged as if she were wearing cement blocks not comfy, slip-on suede boots. Her tote bag slapped against her hip. Nothing inside was heavy—her wallet, tablet, pen, lip gloss, and a paperback book about being a good bridesmaid, but she might as well have been carrying a thirty-pound bag of dog food.

Jetlag was defeating her, but she didn't want to surrender yet. Coworkers had recommended staying awake after she arrived to adjust to the time change quicker. She hoped she could, but traveling was affecting her worse than working crazy hours ever had.

Claude walked ahead of her, and then he slowed. "A nice cup of black tea will refresh you."

"Tea would be wonderful." She wouldn't fall asleep

drinking. At least, she hoped not or that would make a mess.

The front door opened again. This time, a group of women exited, but not Sophie. Each positioned themselves as if their placements had been choreographed. Claude went inside with her luggage.

The three women wore gray dresses with starched white collars and aprons. Their nude-colored pantyhose brought back memories of 4-H competitions at the county fairgrounds before school started each year. That was the last time Kat had worn a pair.

A gray-haired man with silver, wire-rimmed glasses followed. He wore a black suit jacket with long tails, a gray vest, a white starched shirt, a fancy black tie, and white gloves. His posture was impeccable, as if he'd practiced by balancing books on his head, and not a single motion looked wasted.

"Welcome, Dr. Parsons." He stood with one arm across his stomach and the other behind his back. "I am Jennings. You'll meet the kitchen and dining staff later. This is our house staff. They will be assisting you during your visit. Liv has been assigned to you."

A young woman in her early twenties with red hair twisted in a tight bun stepped forward. Her face was pale with no makeup or lip gloss, and her eyes were a pretty jade green.

"Welcome, Dr. Parsons." The woman curtsied. "I'm Liv."

"Hi, Liv. Please call me Kat." She extended her right arm to greet the woman.

Liv stared at Kat's hand as if she didn't know what to do.

Oops. Kat pressed her arm against her side. She wasn't in America any longer. "Is Sophie here?"

"The princess will be arriving shortly, Miss Kat." Liv motioned her inside. "I'll show you to your room. You can freshen up while I unpack your luggage."

"Thanks." Although, Kat wasn't so sure she wanted *that* much help. She'd never had anyone unpack her things.

She stepped inside the castle and found herself in a massive foyer that was bigger than her apartment. The floor looked like marble, and an elaborate rug had been artfully placed in the center.

A faint pine scent hung in the air. The smell of Christmas. Two topiaries decorated with red ribbon and gold stars flanked each side of a curved staircase. A plush carpet ran down the center of the marble steps.

The staircase was also decked out for the holidays.

Garland decorated with red ribbon, holly berries, and white lights was strung along the carved wooden bannister and lit the way even during the daytime.

Decorator perfect.

And this was the place she'd call home for the next two weeks.

Butterflies took flight in her stomach.

She forced herself not to spin around to take in the museum-quality artwork—tapestries and paintings—on the walls. A huge crystal chandelier hung above the foyer, and ornate gilded molding formed patterns on the ceiling.

"Wow." Kat didn't know how many times she'd said the word. Probably a dozen, but she hoped only once. Doubtful since this was the most wow-worthy place she'd seen, let alone stayed.

And this was where she would wake up on Christmas morning.

Let the pinching begin.

"Please follow me upstairs, Miss Kat," Liv said from the first step.

Kat climbed the staircase.

"You'll be staying in the family wing." Liv led her down a hallway with many doors that looked the same. "Princess Sophia's bedroom is two doors down from yours."

Kat froze. "Wait. Sophie lives here?"

"This is the family's residence."

That was news to Kat. She'd known Sophie came from money. She'd seen the fancy furniture and artwork in the background during video chats, but Kat had never thought her friend lived in a castle.

Liv stopped in front of an open door. "You're staying in the blue room."

The door didn't have a plaque that said "blue" or look any different from the other doors. Kat wondered how she'd find the room again if she left unaccompanied. Or maybe she wasn't supposed to wander around the castle alone and similar-looking doors were the deterrent.

She stepped inside. Blue room, indeed.

Air rushed from her lungs.

The color was her favorite and not only because the color matched Kat's eyes. Her papa had once told her that her father—his son—had loved blue, too. That was one thing she had in common with her dad, and she clung to the color blue like a lifeline.

Leave it to Sophie to pick this room for Kat.

So elegant and royal.

The walls were painted a robin-egg blue with a white chair rail. Pairs of gilded-framed oil paintings of landscapes hung on either side of a four-poster queen-sized bed with a mountain of pillows in every shape and size. Above the headboard, heavy blue fabric, white lace, and gold tassels provided a regal canopy fit for a princess.

Or a houseguest.

Kat smiled.

The blue, white, and gold color scheme was used throughout the décor. Fancy lamps set on tabletops, and a chandelier hung in the center of the room. A large armoire was in one corner where Claude had set her luggage—the only things in the room that didn't coordinate. Logs crackled and flames danced in the fireplace in the other. She couldn't wait to try out the comfy, overstuffed reading chair. Off to the far side of the room was a round table with a small Christmas tree centerpiece on top. Two upholstered chairs were pulled out from the table, waiting for occupants.

Decorator magazine perfect.

Kat forced herself not to touch anything in case her hands were dirty. She was so tired she might break something. "It's lovely." She could add twenty-five adjectives that were more glowing, and that wouldn't be enough to describe the beauty of the room.

Liv motioned to a doorway on the right side. "The *en-suite* has towels as well as a robe for your use. If you need anything during your stay, please let me know."

Kat continued to look around the room. "I will."

"Would you like me to draw a bath for you?"

"No, thanks." Kat needed to stand if she wanted to remain awake. "I'm going to take a quick shower if that's okay?"

"I will have your suitcase unpacked by the time you finish."

"Oh, you don't have to do that."

Liv smiled. "It's my job."

"Okay, then." Kat didn't want to get anyone in trouble, especially the person who was supposed to be helping her. She unzipped a suitcase and removed her cosmetic bag. "I'll, uh, be out soon."

"Would you like a cup of coffee and a snack when you're finished showering?"

Kat remembered what Claude had said. "Black tea would be great. No snack right now. Thanks."

A burst of caffeine and a hot shower would have her feeling as good as new. Many times in college and at work, she'd survived longer with no sleep. She would do it again today.

For Sophie.

An image of her pretty friend formed in Kat's mind. The sooner she adjusted to the time, the bigger help with the wedding she could be.

The picture of Sophie slowly morphed into one of Gill with his disapproving gaze and the harsh set of his mouth.

If Kat was staying in the family wing, did that mean his room was nearby?

If so, avoiding him might be harder, but she could figure something out. She would do anything for Sophie. That included putting up with her brother.

AFTER SHOWERING, KAT dried off with a fluffy towel and then put on the luxurious white robe she found hanging on a hook in the bathroom. The thick, soft cotton made her feel like she was wearing a cloud. She'd been at the castle less than thirty minutes, but she was getting a taste of how royalty lived.

Talk about being spoiled.

In the bedroom, a tray with a teapot, creamer, sugar dish, and cup set on the round table. "I could get used to this."

Except she couldn't stop thinking about the animals at the hospital. Was Mabel eating better? Had Sasha stopping meowing? The list of patients scrolled through Kat's mind.

She should call.

No, because she remembered two things—the time difference and what Jojo had said about leaving work behind, so instead of phoning the clinic, Kat poured herself a cup of tea. She added two sugar cubes. The first sip warmed her insides. The second made her feel less drowsy.

Kat wiggled into a pair of dark blue jeans, and then she put on a pretty green sweater that reminded her of Christmas. The clothes had been purchased for this vacation. Casual, but a step up from what she normally wore.

The door to her room burst opened. Sophie ran inside, squealing in delight. "You're really here."

Six summers at camp together, and Sophie had never learned the fine art of knocking. Kat didn't mind.

She hugged her friend and then stepped back.

With hazel eyes, a clear complexion, and long, blonde hair, Sophie looked stunning. Even in December, she had color on her face. Not from makeup but natural, as if she'd been spending time outdoors.

"You're positively glowing," Kat said.

Sophie struck a pose. She wore a plain gray skirt, a red sweater set, and tall black boots. Work clothes, Kat imagined, but these looked like high fashion on her friend.

"Thank you," Sophie said. "How do you like this room?"

"Love it. The blue is perfect," Kat said. "But did you just forget to mention you lived in a castle?"

A sheepish expression formed on Sophie's beautiful face.

"I didn't tell you on purpose."

"Why?"

"You've always acted so normal with me. Even after you found out I was a princess. I didn't want that to change, so I downplayed a few things."

"I'm not upset, but is there more than this castle? I'd rather not be blindsided again."

"I understand. Let's see…" Sophie walked toward the bed. "My late father was the king consort. My mother is the reigning queen."

"Queen," Kat repeated. "As in the ruler of Alistonia?"

Sophie nodded. "That's why I said I'd RSVP for you and give you the wedding invitation after you arrived. I didn't want you to get wigged out. That's the correct word, right?"

"Wigged out definitely applies here." Not just royalty. The ruling family. Kat had to laugh.

"I'm so glad you can see the humor in this." Sophie tilted her head. "There's one more thing. Gill is crown prince."

Crown prince meant he would be king someday. That explained his superior-than-thou attitude.

In America, a man his age who lived at home with his mother would be considered a failure, but here in Alistonia, he would one day be crowned king.

Sophie held Kat's hand. "I'm sure you're tired and everything must be overwhelming, so perhaps think about this castle as being nothing more than a great, big house that gets cold in the wintertime so it has lots of fireplaces. And there just happens to be staff and a dungeon."

The sincerity in Sophie's voice endeared her that much more to Kat. "I've never seen a dungeon."

"I'll show you ours. I can't wait to show you everything. I have a feeling you'll love the town. Not as small as where you grew up, but it oozes charm."

Feeling tired, Kat sat on the edge of the bed. "I can't wait, but there's a wedding to work on."

"Which is another reason I'm so happy you're here. I'm about to lose my mind." The way Sophie sat next to Kat reminded her of summers spent in their cabin at camp. "I never understood the logic of eloping until planning this wedding."

"That bad?" Kat asked.

"I'm trying to emulate Switzerland and remain neutral." Sophie leaned back on her hands. "My mother and my future mother-in-law don't agree on anything. We're on the fourth wedding coordinator. Bertrand's mother, the Duchess of Darbyton, is American, and she wants to incorporate some of your country's traditions. My mother says no because the wedding is taking place in Alistonia."

The answer seemed simple to Kat. "What do you want?"

"For everyone to be happy." Sophie sighed. "But I'm not sure that's possible."

Typical Sophie. That brought a smile. "Any chance of the two mothers compromising?"

"They already have. I'll give you one garter toss for a traditional waltz sort of thing. The last wedding planner was about to bring in a mediator to see if that would help, but then she quit."

"Yikes."

Kat remembered the duties of a bridesmaid from the book she'd brought with her. She wanted to do her part. Not just make sure the train of Sophie's dress didn't get stepped on by the children in the wedding party as they walked down the aisle.

"I'm here now, and I can help you," Kat said.

"Good because Heloise—she's Bertrand's sister and the other bridesmaid—won't arrive until right before the wedding, but I fear she'll just agree with whatever her mother says."

"I'll take over as Switzerland."

"Thank you." Sophie leaned against Kat. "I know we video chat each week, but it's not the same as being together in person."

"I know."

"If you're up for a tour, I'd love to show you around the castle."

"Sounds good." Kat would be less likely to nap that way.

Sophie studied her. "You're so pretty. Pictures and video don't do you justice."

Kat's cheeks warmed. "Thanks, though I don't think your brother was impressed."

"I told him to be nice."

Maybe the way he'd acted had been his version of nice. A scary thought. "Gill was being himself. I don't know what I did all those years ago, other than leave my fishing gear out, but he still doesn't like me."

"You did nothing except be yourself," Sophie said. "Unlike the females from our country, you didn't fall at his feet and treat him like a demigod. Granted, you had no idea he was a prince that first summer, but once you knew, you still spoke your mind. No one has done that to him other than family members."

"I hoped time would have mellowed him."

"He's only gotten worse, but in his defense, that's not all his fault." Sophie toyed with the lace on one of the bed pillows. "When our brother Jacques joined the seminary, Gill became the heir to the throne. He was twenty-two, and his plans took a one-eighty. I don't know that he's forgiven our parents—well, Mother since Father died three years ago—or even Jacques for abandoning him. Giving up his dreams was hard on Gill."

"Dreams?"

"Of teaching. Gill had planned to go into academia. He thought being a professor would allow him the flexibility to do his duties as second in line to the throne until a new heir was born but also enable him to have a fulfilling career."

Kat tried to picture Gill forming the minds of young adults. Tried and failed. He didn't seem like he'd have the necessary patience, but then again, she hadn't seen him in

46

years. "You'd think he'd want to be crown prince and the future king."

"Even future kings have desires. Some that don't align with their duty." A soft smile appeared on Sophie's face. "I give Gill a hard time, but he'll be good for Alistonia. He's smart and knows economics better than most. He also has a kind and caring heart. He just doesn't show that side too often."

Pride filled Sophie's voice. She loved her brother.

"Maybe things will be different after he gets married." Gill might not be friendly to Kat, but she only wanted the best for Sophie's brother.

"I hope so," Sophie admitted. "But he doesn't seem to be in any rush to wed. Being dumped by Clarissa hurt him. My mother was so angry, but I was secretly thrilled."

Kat remembered the long conversations they'd had about this. "You never liked her."

"No, I didn't. If he was going to date and then marry an American, he should have picked you."

"So we could be sisters."

That had been Sophie's teenaged dream when they'd been at camp. Kat had to admit she liked the idea of the two of them being sisters, even though she hadn't been too thrilled with the thought of Gill as a husband.

"Let's hope you like the next woman he dates," Kat added.

"I don't know when that will be. Gill hasn't been interested in dating anyone since Clarissa, so Mother has set out to find him a wife."

"Someone nice." Maybe that quality would rub off on Gill.

"Being nice isn't one of the prerequisites for being Gill's wife. Mother will look for a royal with the right pedigree and breeding who offers something Alistonia currently lacks."

That was what dog and horse breeders did. "What about love?"

"Not a requirement." Sophie sighed. "I'm so happy I'm getting to marry for love. I often wonder if my brother rushed into a relationship with Clarissa to heed off Mother's matchmaking."

Not matchmaking.

Ordering.

But Kat didn't need to point that out to her friend.

Sophie hopped off the bed. "Enough about Gill. Grab your coat and gloves, and put on your shoes, so we can go for a walk outside."

Kat opened drawers. Everything was neatly folded. The non-clothing items were in a drawer by themselves. In one, she found her socks. In another, she found her hat and gloves. She sat on the blue-and-white chair to put on her shoes and yawned.

"If we don't get moving, I fear you'll fall asleep," Sophie said. "I know. We'll visit the stable first. You can admire the beautiful horses, and I can steal one of their apples."

"Hungry?"

"Famished. This wedding diet is so hard."

Kat studied Sophie's trim figure. "You don't need to diet."

"The diet is the one thing my mother and the duchess agree upon. They don't want me to look fat in wedding photos so I'm to lose at least twenty pounds by the twenty-third. I've been trying to trick them by using a weight belt that Bertrand bought me. He doesn't want me to lose any weight, so I wear the belt for weigh-ins, and the scale says I'm losing pounds."

"Crafty."

"So long as I don't get caught."

"I'm relieved you're not listening to them." Sophie was healthy and fit. She'd never looked better to Kat. "You'd look like a lollipop if you lost that much weight."

"That's what I told them, but they didn't care."

Kat placed her coat on the bed, went to the dresser, and pulled out a gift bag from a drawer. "I have something for you."

Staring at the gift bag with longing, Sophie wet her lips. "Is it what I think it is?"

"Look inside."

She did. "Cherry Pop-Tarts®. And there are sprinkles on the frosting. You remembered."

Every summer, Kat had brought boxes for Sophie. "I ran out of time, or I would have gift wrapped it."

"No need. This is perfect. I will savor each one." Sophie clutched the bag to her chest. "Who am I kidding? I'm going to eat them like there's no tomorrow. If my mother sees me, she'll banish me to the dungeon."

"Then you'd better not get caught."

"Let's go," Sophie said. "I can hide in a stall and eat."

Kat frowned. "A princess shouldn't have to hide to eat."

"Tell that to the two momzillas."

Sophie headed to the door. The usual bounce to her step was gone. Maybe she'd outgrown it or maybe the wedding was dragging her down.

Kat followed. She was concerned for her friend.

Being a princess who lived in a castle seemed magical—like a storybook come to life—but being hungry all the time and having to sneak food in order to look better in wedding photographs sounded more like a horror story.

Maybe the upcoming royal wedding was causing everyone added stress. Not just the bride, but the two mothers and Gill. Kat hoped so, but she had to wonder.

Would Christmas at the castle be more like a fairy tale, a nightmare, or somewhere in between?

She wasn't sure she wanted to know the answer.

Chapter Three

TWO HOURS LATER, Gill stood outside the stable where a horse groomer had seen Maximillian. That had been ten minutes ago. Enough time for his dog, who loved to run, to be on the opposite side of the grounds. Still, Gill wanted to look.

Not because he was that concerned about Maximillian.

The dog had a habit of disappearing lately, although he always returned in time for dinner. But because Gill had needed a reason to step out of this afternoon's conference call.

His assistant Frederick was listening, and both of them didn't need to waste time hearing the head economic advisor drone on about currency valuation. Especially when the man had given this same talk two years ago—only with the dates and interest rates updated. Very shoddy work especially when Gill's interest in economics was well known throughout the council. He would have to seek a replacement in the new year. No one should lose their position during the holiday season.

"Maximillian?" Gill called.

No paws sounded. No barks, either.

The dog enjoyed roaming the grounds, but he wasn't a miscreant. If he were around, he would come when Gill called. Unless the dog was taking a nap inside. The facility had been built because his mother loved riding. No expense had been spared making the stable more like a house for her beloved horses.

As soon as he entered, the heated air cocooned him in warmth. Yes, the stable would be the perfect place for Maximillian to sleep.

One of the stall doors was open. The horse must be in the arena or pasture.

Gill looked inside. No dog. But there were twelve more stalls to check.

"Maximillian," he called.

"Who are you looking for?" a female voice asked. An American one.

Muscles bunched. Gill glanced over his shoulder at Kat.

She'd changed clothes and put on a heavier jacket, jeans, and tennis shoes. With her hair tucked inside a beanie and gloves on her hands, she looked ready for a blizzard, though snow wasn't predicted for two more days. She must not be used to cold temperatures where she lived.

"I'm looking for my dog," he said.

She took a step forward. "Is he lost?"

"Not lost. He can't get out of the castle grounds."

"That's a relief."

Her concern sounded genuine. Not surprising.

He remembered how Kat would head out at dawn each morning at camp to tend to any injured birds or animals she'd found the previous days. More than once, he'd followed her to make sure she remained safe since she was his sister's friend. Gill had liked watching how kind Kat was to the animals, and she was braver than he would have been with some of the wilder ones.

But that had been so long ago.

Time changed things and people.

Sophie had mentioned something about Kat's college student loans. That was before he'd known Kat attended veterinary school. That explained the lack of money she'd mentioned to him earlier today. One more reason why she could be here for more than just the wedding. Marrying a wealthy royal would get Kat out of debt quickly. Was money her motivation and not a title?

"What does your dog enjoy doing?"

"Exploring," Gill said.

"Many dogs do. It's nice he has a large, enclosed area to investigate, but you must worry when you can't find him."

"Maximillian doesn't stay away that long, so I don't have to be concerned about him."

Kat didn't seem like the worrying type. She took charge and fixed what was wrong. She was the most self-sufficient female he'd ever met, even more so than his mother.

At camp, he'd watched her take care of herself and Sophie. For the first time, his younger sister hadn't needed him because she had Kat. That had made him feel useless. Not an unusual feeling when he'd been the "spare" heir back then, but he hadn't expected to feel that way an ocean and a continent away from home due to a girl with a pocketknife.

He hadn't liked that.

And by default, that meant he hadn't liked her.

He still didn't like Kat.

For other reasons now.

Kat peered into a stall as if she was joining in the hunt. She seemed to make a habit of getting involved where she wasn't needed.

"What kind of dog?" she asked.

"A Brittany."

"They are loyal, intelligent, and energetic dogs."

Those adjectives described Maximillian perfectly. "You know dog breeds."

"I'm a vet, and I was also in 4-H through high school." She walked to the next stall. The horse inside neighed. "We learned everything from anatomy to obedience and were required to know the various breeds."

Alistonia didn't have a program like that for their youth. Based on her smile, she seemed to have liked 4-H. Maybe that was something he should look into for the kids in his country.

"Maximillian enjoys duck hunting, but Sophie's asked us not to do that anymore. You've turned her into an animal advocate."

"Not me," Kat countered. "I'd say your sister's social work is the cause. She's an advocate for the underdogs."

"That is not how I'd describe a duck."

"You might if you were a duck."

"Point taken."

She went to another stall. "Does your dog run away often?"

"He doesn't run away." Gill didn't appreciate the way she made his purebred dog sound like a mutt. "Maximillian is from a line of champion bloodstock."

"Breeding doesn't curb the tendency to roam." She peeked into another stall. "One of our clients has a champion Saluki who takes off the minute she's off-leash."

"Maximillian only recently began his...excursions."

Walking to the next stall, she glanced over her shoulder at him. "Is that what you call his disappearing acts?"

Gill remembered his promise to Sophie and gritted his teeth so he wouldn't say anything that might be considered unfriendly. "You don't have to look for the dog."

"I don't mind."

He did. "Maximillian is likely far away from here."

"Looking for him will keep me awake. He could be sleeping."

Gill had thought of the same thing.

Kat checked inside another empty stall. "Behavior changes can be related to something that's happened to the dog
himself, his environment, or even his diet."

He didn't need her playing doctor with him. "A few out-
buildings and landscape features have been added over the
years. This stable is the newest addition, but otherwise, the
castle grounds have remained the same for centuries. Maximillian's diet hasn't changed since he outgrew the puppy
stage."

"He doesn't seem to be in any of the stalls."

"I'll check the riding arena before I head back to my office, but if he were here, he would have heard me calling
him."

"Does he come when called?"

"Yes."

She looked around the stable as if trying to figure out
where the dog might be. "Will Maximillian obey or do tricks
in the hopes of getting food?"

"He likes both treats and attention."

Kat reached into her coat pocket and crinkled something. The noise sounded like a candy wrapper. "Some
animals associate sounds with food and come running."

No dog appeared.

She continued the crinkling and then stopped. "Looks
like he's somewhere else."

That was where Gill wanted to be. Somewhere else. Far
away from her.

Seeing Kat put him on edge. He didn't like the feeling. Nor did he like her walking around the grounds by herself. She had just arrived. She couldn't know where she was going and would only end up lost or getting in the staff's way.

"Where's Sophie?" he asked.

"Around."

"Where?"

"Somewhere."

Kat's evasive answer added to his suspicions. The woman was definitely keeping secrets.

Sophie stepped out of the last stall on the end. "I'm right here."

Gill couldn't remember the last time his sister had been to the stable. She no longer rode horses. She'd taken up mountain biking because of Bertrand. "What were you doing in there?"

She touched her left earlobe. "I was showing Kat around and thought I'd lost an earring."

"Gill's dog is missing," Kat offered.

Sophie shook her head. "Maximillian is always running off. Thank goodness the castle is walled or he'd be long gone."

"You said this is a new habit?" Kat's voice sounded different, almost clinical. "Have you taken him in for a checkup recently?"

Gill balled his hands. "Maximillian is up to date on his visits and vaccinations."

Kat rubbed her chin with her gloved hand.

"He's a healthy dog who gets plenty of exercise and attention," Gill added.

"A little defensive, are we?" Sophie teased.

He didn't need both of them getting on him the way they used to at camp. "I'm going back to the castle."

"If we find Maximillian, we'll let you know," Kat said.

Sophie nodded. "Otherwise, we'll see you at dinner."

"Thanks for the warning." Gill noticed Kat staring into the riding arena. "See something?"

Her gaze narrowed. "An orange-and-white dog ran across the arena with an apple or ball in his mouth. I think it might have been yours, except…"

"What?" he asked.

"Maximillian wasn't alone." Lines formed above the bridge of her nose. "There was another dog following him. A smaller yellow one."

She didn't know what she was talking about. Gill rocked back on his heels. "Maximillian is the only dog who lives here."

Sophie beamed. "Unless Maximillian made a doggy friend."

A wry grin formed on Kat's face. "Or if he found himself a doggy girlfriend."

"No." The word shot from Gill's mouth like a bullet. "You're tired from traveling, and your eyes are playing tricks on you."

"Maybe," Kat admitted. "But if Maximillian did befriend another dog, that would explain why he disappears for chunks of time."

"What you're suggesting implies a dog, most likely a stray since no one else lives out here, arrived at the castle gate and asked the guard to be let in." Gill shook his head. "Not possible."

"There's no other way inside the grounds?" she asked.

"None." He stared down his nose at her. "The grounds are walled. There is only one entrance."

"Then maybe I did imagine it." She didn't sound angry, only a little tired. "Which is too bad because they looked like they were having fun."

"You most certainly are imagining it then." Sophie winked at Kat. "I forgot to tell you that having fun is forbidden at the castle. Or rather, it will be once my brother is in charge. He's so proper and strict about following rules. Way more so than our mother."

Women were nothing but trouble whether they were relations or not.

"How long before your wedding day, so I'll finally be able to live in peace?" he asked his sister.

Sophie grinned. "Not soon enough for you or for me. But after I leave for my honeymoon on the twenty-fourth, you'll still have Kat here to keep you company on Christmas day."

Gill was afraid his sister would say that.

He couldn't wait for the new year to arrive.

THAT EVENING, KAT couldn't wait to crawl between the sheets. Exploring the castle with Sophie had been fun. Laughing with her tonight even better, but jet lag had finally defeated Kat.

Breathe, yawn, repeat.

She wanted to stop the pattern. That meant no more putting off sleep.

The bed beckoned like a lighthouse.

She was dressed in a new pair of warm and comfy flannel pajamas. Her bare feet sank into the plush carpet. Liv had turned down the sheets and left a chocolate on her pillow and a glass of water on the nightstand.

Kat appreciated the gestures. She hadn't been here long, but felt totally pampered as if she were a princess. Weird and enjoyable at the same time.

A dog barked. The sound came from outside her room.

Kat stared longingly at her bed. Yes, she was tired, but sleep could wait another minute or two.

The bark had to belong to the missing Maximillian. Unless he'd snuck his partner in crime inside the castle.

She hadn't imagined that other dog, but she'd relented. Getting into an argument with Gill in front of Sophie would have stressed out the bride. Kat didn't need her bridesmaid book to tell her that was the last thing she wanted to do.

Kat opened the door.

A dog stood in the hallway.

A castle didn't seem like the kind of place for a dog to roam free, but then again, neither did having full range of the palace grounds seem that safe, either. Wall or not.

The Brittany, however, didn't seem to care what she thought. He stood there as if he owned the place.

Which he probably did.

The gorgeous dog had orange-and-white markings that defined his breed. A bright blue collar with a gold tag contrasted with his coloring.

"Hello there, handsome," she said.

Beautiful amber eyes met hers. His head tilted as if he were curious.

Of course he was. He didn't know who she was.

"I'm Kat. You must be Maximillian."

His tail wagged.

"Are you back from your escapades? Where is your friend?"

He trotted over to her.

The dog showed no sign of anxiety or aggression, so she held out her hand. "You're a handsome fellow."

He sniffed with an adorable pink nose. Once, twice. Everything in him seemed to relax.

"Nice to meet you."

He sat at her feet and raised his front right paw.

She shook it. "The pleasure is all mine, but you

shouldn't run away so much. People worry."

Not people. Person. At least she thought Gill looked concerned, even if his words suggested he wasn't.

Maximillian rubbed his muzzle against her hand.

"You're a sweetie."

Unlike his owner.

Still, a man with a dog couldn't be all bad. Gill cared about this dog and his sister. That told Kat there had to be some piece of human left inside the robot. That was what he was—a royal automaton.

"Between you and me." She scratched behind the dog's ear. "I think the prince likes you, but I wouldn't push him too far. He doesn't seem to have much patience."

At least not with her.

Maximillian responded with a lick to her cheek.

She laughed. "Aren't you a love?"

The dog stood and trotted past her into the bedroom.

"Make yourself at home."

He jumped on the bed and sat.

She walked toward him. "Are you allowed on the furniture?"

He lay on top of the duvet and rolled onto his back.

"I have a feeling you've done this before."

Kat reached the bed and realized she'd left the door open. Closing anything, other than the refrigerator, was something she never had to worry about living alone.

"I'll leave the door open in case you want out."

CHRISTMAS AT THE CASTLE

The dog motioned with his left front paw.

She laughed. "Is that your sign for belly rubs?"

The motion continued.

"Okay, I can take a hint." Kat sat and rubbed his tummy.

The dog looked like he was smiling.

"Aw, you're so cute."

He stretched.

She stopped rubbing to give the dog more room, and he waved his front left paw again.

She rubbed him again. "A little spoiled, huh?"

"Extremely spoiled."

The sound of Gill's voice knotted the muscles at the back of her neck. She looked up. He stood in the doorway with his hands at his side.

Where had he come from?

Kat hadn't heard footsteps or noticed anyone in the hallway, but she couldn't help but stare at him now.

Oh, baby.

A handsome dog for a gorgeous guy.

He wore gym shorts, and his T-shirt clung to him as if he'd been working out. Talk about fit. Not overly muscular. Just right.

Her mouth went dry.

His slightly red cheeks made him seem younger and look like he had at camp after they finished an activity under the hot sun. His damp hair curled more and begged to have

63

fingers run through the strands.

Not her fingers.

Hot, yes, and disappointing that he didn't have a great personality to match his good looks. Still, she couldn't believe how normal he appeared in the workout clothes.

Normal and attractive.

Best part? He seemed almost approachable.

Not that sweat and running shoes made the prince less of a jerk.

She focused on the dog. "Many of my clients spoil their pets."

"Most animals don't have an entire staff at their beck and call. More than a few here treat him as their own."

"Maximillian's lucky to have so much attention."

"Yes, he is."

Gill's gaze was locked on her. Not only that, but he was walking toward her.

Kat's pulse skyrocketed. Cardio workout not required.

The room seemed smaller in spite of the high ceiling. The prince was tall—an inch, maybe two over six feet—but his presence seemed much larger.

The dog waved his paw again.

Maximillian. Her cheeks warmed. The prince wanted his dog. He wasn't here for her.

A twinge of disappointment shot out of nowhere.

Not how she should be feeling about a man like Gill. A man—make that a prince—who didn't hide the fact he hated her.

Must be his hotness factor.

"I'd stop petting Maximillian." Gill came even closer. "Or he'll be after you for rubs while you're here."

"I don't mind."

"Because you love animals."

He hadn't asked a question, but she answered anyway. "Yes."

Gill stood at the side of her bed. A raw, earthy scent replaced his expensive aftershave from earlier. His leg was mere inches from hers. One slight move and she would bump into him. The temptation to do just that to see his reaction was strong.

Bad idea. Best not to agitate the beast.

She *had* enjoyed poking and prodding him when she was younger. Maybe that was part of the reason he acted so annoyed around her.

"You and Sophie weren't at dinner," he said.

That must have made him happy, but he wasn't smiling. "We ate in her room."

"Jennings said you were tired."

"I am."

Kat scooted further toward the middle of the bed to put more distance between her and Gill. Less temptation as well as a lower chance for accidental contact. She didn't want him to think she was attracted to him.

"But I also wanted Sophie to feel free to eat," Kat admitted. "Her diet is stupid. Please tell me you're not in favor of her losing weight before her wedding day."

"You still speak your mind."

He made that sound like a crime. Maybe in Alistonia it was. "Yes."

"The diet is not stupid," he said. "My mother and the duchess are concerned about wedding pictures, even though Sophie looks fine as she is. In my family, you must pick your battles."

Unbelievable. Of any battle, he should pick this one for Sophie's sake. No way would Kat let this go.

"The diet *is* stupid." She leveled a hard stare at him. "Losing twenty pounds would not be healthy for Sophie."

His mouth dropped open. "Twenty? My mother said five."

"The two mothers changed their minds about the amount. It went from five to ten to twenty. This is not only unnecessary, but also dangerous. If I have to steal food for Sophie to eat while I'm here, I will."

"There's no need for you to do that." The words came out quick, as if he knew what to do. "I'll speak with my mother to keep you from having to resort to theft."

"Thank you. Sophie will be happy, and I'm relieved I won't end up in the dungeon."

"We tend to use jails these days."

His playful tone caught Kat off-guard. Maybe he did have a sense of humor.

"Good to know." Kat yawned. "Excuse me."

"You should be asleep."

Nodding, she lay on her side facing the dog. She could reach Maximillian better that way.

"I thought if I could stay awake longer, I'd adjust to the new time zone faster. But doing that has made for a long day." She must be tired to be rambling. Gill didn't care what she had to say. "I was about to go to bed when I heard a bark. I wanted to see if the mysterious Max had showed up."

"His name is Maximillian."

The dog likely had a fancy name that rivaled Sophie's full name, but many dogs—including champion show dogs— had call signs or nicknames. Max seemed to fit this one better than a multi-syllable, pretentious-sounding name. "That's a big name for such a cutie."

"Handsome, not cute."

"Are you going to disagree with everything I say?"

A beat passed. "No."

His slight hesitation made her wonder if he had to think about this answer. Probably.

She had to laugh. "It's okay if you do."

He drew his brows together. "Why is that?"

"Because we're so different. I can't imagine us agreeing on much, if anything."

"We both want what's best for Sophie."

She nodded. "But that doesn't mean you agree with me about what I think is best for her."

"Like the wedding diet?" he asked.

"That's just crazy."

"I agree."

That was a first. She might as well try for more. "Do you agree that Sophie isn't a child?"

"Sophie will always be my baby sister. Age won't change that."

"True. She's young at heart, the kind of person who loves to laugh and have fun, but she's also an intelligent woman. She doesn't need to be told what to do or eat or who to fall in love with and marry."

His jaw jutted forward. "We support her marriage to Bertrand."

Months of long calls and video chats rushed back to Kat. Sophie had been beside herself when Bertrand proposed, yet her family had been indifferent. That was the word Sophie had used while mascara-stained tears streamed down her face.

"How long did it take for that to happen?" Kat asked.

Gill didn't say anything.

She had him there.

But this wasn't a game with a score. He was correct. She only wanted what was best for Sophie.

"Perhaps our support wasn't instantaneous," he admitted finally. "But that's only because she's a princess, second in line for the throne, and Bertrand is the second son of a duke."

"He's a lord."

"That's more of a courtesy title."

"He's a decorated military pilot."

"Yes, and he has land holdings in Darbyton. We did come around to agreeing to the match."

Gill's nonchalance infuriated Kat.

"Waiting for you and your mother's approval was agonizing for Sophie. I'm guessing Bertrand owning land wasn't something that happened overnight." She took his silence as an answer. "Did you consider the effect your delay had on Sophie?"

A muscle ticked in Gill's jaw.

Obviously, he hadn't. That surprised Kat because he cared for his sister and his overprotectiveness wasn't an act.

"We are Sophie's family. We look out for her," he announced as if Kat didn't know that. "She might not always agree with us, but she doesn't need to have you lurking in the distance making decisions for her."

Kat raised her chin. "I don't lurk. My friendship with Sophie has never been a secret, and I don't make decisions for her, either."

Only took the blame.

But she understood he didn't know that. Neither did the queen. But that was for Sophie's sake.

When they were sixteen, she and Sophie had decided to blame Kat or use her as the excuse for whatever Sophie wanted to do that went against her family's wishes. Kat never thought she'd meet Sophie's family, so what did it matter?

But that would explain why Gill didn't like Kat.

He didn't say anything, but the disbelief in his gaze spoke volumes.

Max rolled against her.

She rubbed the dog.

"Looks like you have a new friend," Gill said finally.

"You can't have too many friends." Kat stifled a yawn. Keeping her eyelids open was getting harder to do.

The dog waved his paw again.

"You've mastered that trick." She rested on her elbow. "I'll be your pillow, but I'm getting too tired to rub you."

"I'll take over." Gill sat on the bed and rubbed the dog's stomach.

She couldn't remember the last time a man had been on the same bed with her. Inches separated them. The temperature in the room rose. An unwelcome awareness of him buzzed through her.

Tiredness would explain what she was feeling.

All she wanted to do was sleep, but now she had both a dog and a prince in her bed on her first night at the castle. And not any man. The last one Kat wanted near her.

She yawned again.

His gaze lingered on her. "You need sleep."

"I don't think Maximillian is ready to go."

"He isn't." Gill kept staring at her, but she was too tired to feel self-conscious. "I appreciate your honesty about my sister. In return, I'll give you a word of advice about my mother."

Kat wasn't used to seeing this side of Gill. She liked it. "Please. I've never met a queen before."

"Pick your battles with her carefully. Trust me, there will be some. That's her nature. She isn't one who loses often, and when she does…there's fallout, so plan accordingly."

"I appreciate the warning."

Kat would be better prepared when she met Queen Louise. The woman sounded…interesting. If not intimidating.

"What about my battles with you?" Kat asked, half-joking. "Should I pick and choose those, too?"

"No need with me. I enjoy our…skirmishes."

He would. A part of her did, too.

Curiosity got the better of her. She had to ask. "Why is that?"

"I appreciate how much you seem to care about my sister."

"She's one of my closest friends."

"Perhaps, but no one is as kind and selfless as you appear to be. Animal lover or not." His tone was even, and his voice remained steady. "One of these days, I'll find that chink in your armor and expose the real you underneath."

Kat nearly laughed. He was as far off as a lost penguin ending up at the North Pole. What-you-see-is-what-you-get summed her up. But then again, Gill had never viewed her as anything other than his sister's annoying, opinionated American friend.

Still, his belief that Kat had ulterior motives offended her. She'd done nothing to make him think that way other than be Sophie's scapegoat. Kat had never hurt his sister. She wouldn't do that. Ever.

Nor would she back down from a challenge.

She would prove him wrong. Not because she wanted an apology. This was for Sophie.

Kat stared down her nose like the prince had done with her. "What if you don't find a chink?"

"I will. Like my mother, I always win."

He was so full of himself. But that made him Gill. In a strange way, his confidence appealed to her even though he considered her the enemy.

"Give it your best shot, Your Serene Highness." She used Sophie's name for him. "The game is on."

Gill's rich laughter collided into her like a stolen kiss, unexpected and unwelcome, but not unattractive.

"Shakespeare must be rolling in his grave. The game is not on." Gill stood, and the bed suddenly felt huge and cold. He towered over her. "The game is afoot."

So what if the man was good looking with a heart-melting laugh?

He wasn't nice.

"No matter which phrase you use, you're going to find out just how wrong you are about me." She didn't appreciate his accusation. Nor would she surrender without a fight. "But you might learn something about your sister, and that will make this *mêlée* totally worthwhile."

He stepped away from the bed. "Come, Maximillian."

Max snuggled against her.

She gave him a kiss.

Kat didn't have to look at Gill to know he was frustrated. She could hear his nostrils flare. Okay, not really, but the thought made her tired lips want to smile.

"Go with the prince," Kat whispered in Max's ear. "Tomorrow, we'll play and I'll give you more rubs."

Max gave her another lick before jumping off the bed.

"What did you say to Maximillian?" Gill asked.

"Ask him," she said and then smiled.

Chapter Four

*A*SK HIM. AS if the dog could talk back.

The woman was incorrigible. Nothing but trouble.

And what twenty-eight-year old wore purple polka-dotted flannel pajamas?

Gill walked to the door with Maximillian at his side.

The dog glanced back.

He understood why Maximillian wanted to stay with Kat. Gill had enjoyed the feeling of companionship himself. He missed having someone special in his life—someone who wasn't covered in dog hair—but Kat wasn't the woman he should be spending time with.

He urged the dog forward.

This would be Gill's first and last visit to the blue room while Kat was here. He didn't trust her and had said as much to her face, but their discussion hadn't gone as he'd expected.

You're going to find out how wrong you are about me. But you might learn something about Sophie and that will make this mêlée totally worthwhile.

He didn't know whether to respect the way Kat had

picked up the gauntlet he'd tossed or be annoyed that the pretty American might be a worthy opponent by using her quick intellect rather than her female charm with him.

Was she trying to throw him off?

He was a single royal. She might have him on her list. Unless her loyalty to Sophie prevented Kat from going that far.

Gill glanced back at the bed.

Kat lay strewn across the mattress. She'd lost her fight against jet lag.

Would he be able to win his battle and expose the real her as easily?

He hoped so.

The room was heated, but he couldn't leave her uncovered. Kat was a guest and deserved to be treated as such, no matter what he thought of her personally. A blanket would give her extra warmth.

Holding onto Maximillian's collar, Gill walked back toward the bed and grabbed a throw off the back of a chair.

The dog pulled away.

Gill tightened his grip on the collar. Using one hand, he covered Kat. He doubted she would move until morning given how tired she was.

Maximillian whimpered.

"Shhh."

A book about being a bridesmaid sat on the nightstand with a colorful bookmark sticking out. Maybe she was taking her role in the wedding party seriously.

He stared at her.

Sound asleep, Kat looked harmless. If only she were…

The slight smile on her face made him wonder if she was dreaming. Was a man starring in her dreams? Or, if Sophie was correct about Kat, an animal?

Maximillian had gotten a goodnight kiss.

Not that Gill had wanted one, but a hug might have been nice.

What was he thinking?

Gill shook the thought from his head. He didn't want anything from this woman. He turned off the lamp on the nightstand, walked back to the door, and flicked the light switch.

Darkness flooded the room.

He stepped into the hallway, closed the door behind him, and released the collar.

Maximillian stared up at him.

"Let's go see Sophie." Gill walked the short distance down the hall and knocked on her door.

"Come in."

The dog ran to Sophie, who sat at a table with her laptop open and a stack of papers at the side. She hugged the dog, and then Maximillian sat at her feet.

"Wedding planning?" Gill asked.

"Work." She closed her computer. "I'm trying to clear my desk over the next two weeks."

Before her wedding day.

Gill wanted to know more about the diet. "Does Mother want you to lose twenty pounds by your wedding?"

"You've been talking to Kat." His sister sounded more resigned than upset.

"So it's true."

"Yes, but I told her and the duchess no. That didn't stop Mother from ordering the chef to prepare only low-carb dishes for me. Or had you not noticed my meals were different than everyone else's?"

"I'm sorry. All the wedding talk makes it easy to tune out things at dinner." He sat in the chair across from his sister. "I haven't noticed."

"You've been preoccupied, but I'm eating only a few meals here these days."

"You shouldn't go hungry."

"I eat at work, and I've got the fine art of snacking on the sly figured out. This is what I was munching on in the stable earlier." She reached below the tablecloth and pulled out a box of Pop-Tarts®. "Want one?"

Sophie had been obsessed with those when she was younger thanks to a certain American friend. "Kat brought those for you."

Nodding, his sister opened a silver pouch.

No wonder Kat seemed evasive in the stable. She was running interference while Sophie ate.

His sister handed him a Pop-Tart® covered with pink

frosting and red sprinkles.

"Kat knows me so well."

"Better than those of us here?"

Sophie ate instead of answering.

She was avoiding his question. Fine, he would give her a pass and get back on the original subject. "You shouldn't sneak around to eat."

"That's what Kat said."

"She's correct."

Sophie's eyes widened. "You agree with something Kat said?"

"Yes."

"I didn't think the temperature was going to drop low enough for hell to freeze over, but wonders never cease."

He laughed. "I'll talk to—"

"Mother won't listen to you. I tried, and the awful meals keep being served," Sophie interrupted. "My losing weight is the one thing she and the duchess agree upon. It's reaching the ridiculous level with the wedding only two weeks away."

"How?"

"Mother has me using an app to log food, and then she checks my calorie intake each night. Of course, I'm only entering what the chef cooks for me. None of my outside food. I'm also faking my weigh-ins, so she can't understand why I don't look thinner."

He remembered what Kat had said about Sophie not being a child. He'd always been quick to help his sister out of any situation because he loved her, and he wanted to help her with this, but perhaps he should do something with her, not for her.

"Tomorrow, do you want to speak with the chef together?" Gill asked. "He's a reasonable man who adores you. He'll find a way to appease our mother and make sure you don't have to eat on the sly until your wedding day."

"Yes, please." Sophie studied him. A smile spread across her face. "You've not only been talking to Kat, but you're also listening to her."

"I listen to you. All you need to do is tell me what you want."

He took a bite of his Pop-Tart®—a guilty pleasure he'd looked forward to eating at camp. Not that he'd admitted it to his sister. Or Kat.

"What I want…"

A faraway look appeared in her eyes. Not the wistful one he was used to seeing. "What is it?"

"This is going to sound ungrateful given how much I have, and when I know others would love to be in my place, but I just want to be…normal."

"You mean a commoner?"

"I want to be like Kat." Sophie sighed. "No title. No protocols. No pressure of living up to the expectations of both a family and a country."

Gill understood. He'd felt the same way, but he needed to choose his words carefully. Kat would know what to say.

He pushed that thought from his mind.

"Has Kat's life been that perfect?" he asked finally.

"No, not at all," Sophie admitted. "Her life's been a struggle."

That was news to him. "In what ways?"

"She's never had much money. She's had to work for whatever she wanted, including going to college. Her parents dumped her at her grandparents' house, so they could do research in Africa, and they both died there. Her grandparents loved her and were the most amazing people. They passed two weeks apart. My favorite times as a teenager, other than camp, were when I stayed at their wheat farm."

"You were a child."

"I was seventeen the last time I was there. Old enough to know what I was doing and feeling. We worked so hard in the fields during that harvest, and I've never been more exhausted, but it was so…satisfying."

"You never said anything."

"Yes, I did, but no one heard me. Not that anything could have been done." Sophie leaned back in her chair. "When I wanted to mention it a few years later, Mother and Father were so torn apart after Jacques renounced his title, I couldn't. Granted, he had the best reason ever. But I never wanted to put our parents through that kind of pain again, so I didn't say anything more. And after Father died and Mother was so on edge all the time…"

Sophie had always been so cheery, and nothing seemed

to bother her. Their own personal sunbeam to light their lives. He hated learning she'd been hiding so much.

But not from Kat. He was thankful his sister had a confidant, even if it was the American. Something, however, didn't make sense.

"If you've felt this way, why did you go on that reality TV show?"

Sophie half-laughed. "So I could get away from all this."

"By marrying a prince?"

"Luc was considered the black sheep of Alvernia's royal family, and he was so far down the line of succession that he would never rule. Scandals plagued him, so no one expected much from him other than to mess up again. I thought if I married Luc, I wouldn't have so much pressure bearing down on me."

Prince Luc's reputation was common knowledge among the royalty in Europe. "I thought going on the show was an act of rebellion."

Sophie grinned. "Becoming a social worker was my rebellion, but that worked out better than I expected. I love what I do."

"And you love Bertrand."

"I owe Luc for that," Sophie said.

"He broke your heart."

"Yes, but he also opened my heart."

"I don't understand. You cried for days. You were miserable. If Kat hadn't—"

"Not her fault." Sophie rushed to her friend's defense, as usual. "When I went on the show, I'd bought into the media's portrayal of Luc as a hot prince who liked to party. But the real prince—the man behind the tabloid fodder—showed me I could be royal but also have that feeling of normalcy I craved. I was devastated when I was sent home, but being on the show helped me see the possibilities for my future. Kat was the one who encouraged me to attend Luc and Emily's wedding, so I could move on, and that's where I met Bertrand."

Of course Kat did.

"Now I've figured out a way to have the kind of life I've dreamed about," Sophie continued.

Gill envied the contentment in Sophie's voice. He longed to feel that way about his life. "With your job."

"And Bertrand."

Sophie seemed so grown up. Yes, she was an adult and had been for years, but she'd seemed younger with her sunshine-and-flowers attitude. No longer.

"Bertrand knows how you feel?" Gill asked.

"Yes, and he agrees. If not for our mothers, we wouldn't be having such an extravagant Christmas wedding. But we shall do our duty. After that, we'll ride off into the sunset and live as happily and normally as possible as the Lord and Lady of Darbyton."

"You'll still be a princess of Alistonia and second in line for the throne."

"Shhh." Amusement twinkled in Sophie's eyes. "This is my fantasy."

"It's your life."

"And a very good one. I'm not blind to that." She leaned toward him. "So why don't you tell me what's going on with your life? Particularly your love life."

That part was nonexistent, and he planned to keep it that way for now. "Nothing much to tell at the moment."

"Are you going to start dating again so you can change that?" She sounded hopeful.

He didn't want to disappoint her. "Let's get through your wedding, then I can worry about my social life."

She made a face. "As soon as my wedding is over, Mother will be on you to marry. She wants to give you the throne as soon as you wed so she can retire and enjoy her horses."

He'd heard the mumblings and rumors about potential bride candidates. "No one is picking out my wife."

Even though his mother would have to approve her.

Sophie straightened. "So you plan to marry?"

"Someday." A king needed an heir, but if Sophie and Bertrand had children… "Unless you'd rather rule instead."

Sophie held her hands up in front of her like a shield. "No, thank you. Just the thought makes me want to break out in hives."

Gill laughed. "Then give me another Pop-Tart®."

She did, but she also stuck out her tongue at him. "This could be considered extortion by the Council of Justice."

"Or the council could decide this is simply a sister sharing with a brother."

"They would. You always win. Like Mother."

He did. And he would with Kat.

They both had Sophie's best interest at heart, but that was the only thing they had in common.

A win for Kat meant her finding a wealthy royal to pay off her debts and give her a title. A win for him meant she returned to America alone with no romantic attachment left behind here.

Gill took a bite. He couldn't wait to see her lose.

KAT WOKE TO the scent of bacon and pancakes. She opened her eyes to sunlight and the elegant furniture of the "Blue Room." Her bridesmaid book lay on the nightstand next to a glass of water.

Not a dream.

For a moment, she'd wondered.

The throw from the reading chair covered her.

Strange. Kat didn't remember bringing the blanket to the bed. She was also on top of the covers not underneath them. The last thing she remembered from last night was…

Gill and Maximillian.

She glanced around the room. They weren't there, but Sophie was. She stood next to Liv, who held a tray containing breakfast.

Kat's sense of smell hadn't been affected by jetlag.

Sophie's grin lit up both her face and the room. "I thought food would wake you better than an alarm clock."

"Good morning?" Kat asked. "Or is it afternoon?"

"Morning and an early one at that."

Sophie wore brown pants tucked into leather ankle boots, a coordinating turtleneck, and a multi-colored sweater that fell to mid-thigh. Clunky earrings dangled from her earlobes. Very different from the conservative clothing she'd worn yesterday.

"I'm sorry I couldn't let you sleep longer," she continued. "But we have a dress fitting to attend with my mother and the duchess."

Nerves rattled. Kat remembered what Gill had said about picking battles with his mother. She wanted to get along with Queen Louise. The same way Sophie had gotten along with her nana and papa.

Liv moved the tabletop Christmas tree toward the far edge of the round table, and then she set the contents of the tray down. "You fell asleep so quickly you never made it under the covers."

"Thanks for getting me the blanket," Kat said.

"That wasn't me." Liv poured coffee into two cups. "I'll make a note to check on you tonight."

If Liv hadn't covered Kat, that meant Gill had.

A chill shivered through her. The thought of falling asleep in front of him made her feel exposed, and the idea of him doing a thoughtful gesture went against everything she imagined the man to be.

Sophie carried the two cups of coffee toward the bed. "I had Liv ask the chef to make your favorite breakfast. I thought you could eat up here while you get dressed since we're in a bit of a rush."

Kat bit back a laugh. First, Sophie had never rushed anywhere when they were at camp. Being on time hadn't been a priority. And second, bacon and eggs were Kat's favorite breakfast, and though she noticed scrambled eggs on the plate, Sophie was the one who liked pancakes.

But Kat would play along, so her friend wouldn't go hungry. Gill had better take care of ending the diet ASAP. "I hope the chef made extra because I'm hungry."

"Looks like there's enough for two." Sophie sat on the edge of the bed.

"Will there be anything else, Princess Sophia?" Liv asked.

"No, thank you," Sophie said. "Enjoy your day."

Liv curtsied and left the room.

Kat laughed. "You're not only crafty, but also sneaky."

"Better than being hungry. And since I have the morning off, I needed to improvise from my usual routine."

She sipped from her cup. The castle must order prime coffee beans. This was delicious.

Sophie stood. "Let's eat."

Kat sat across from her friend at the table, and they ate off the same plate. Something they'd done at camp over a decade ago. "Just like old times."

"Except we're more confident and beautiful than we were then, but I'm still shorter than you."

"I won't hold it against you."

Sophie raised a forkful of pancake. Syrup dripped onto the plate. "Are you happy?"

"I'm with you. How could I not be happy?"

"I didn't word that right. Are you happy at how things have worked out for you?" Sophie clarified.

"As in life so far?"

Sophie nodded.

Kat sipped her coffee. She needed a moment to think. "Yes, I am."

"You had to think about it."

"It's a loaded question with many parts."

"Break it down."

She set her cup on the table. "The work part is the easiest to answer. I've wanted to be a vet since I was a kid, and now I am one, but the other stuff, particularly my grandparents, is harder to answer."

"You miss your nana and papa."

"I think about them every single day." Kat picked up the spoon since Sophie was using the fork. "All I ever wanted was a family. I used to think how much better everything would be if my parents came back. After my grandparents were gone, I realized I had a family, a really great one."

"You'll have another family."

"Someday."

Kat sounded more confident than she felt, but she kept her daydreams about having a family to a minimum. No reason to set herself up for disappointment with wanting something she couldn't have right now.

She scooped up a spoonful of eggs. "I'm thrilled to be here with you."

"Me, too." Sophie shimmied her shoulders. "I want you to have the best time."

"I'm sure it will be."

"Anything you can think of that will make it better?"

"Someone to kiss under the mistletoe," Kat said jokingly.

Sophie's mouth formed a perfect O. She jumped up from the table and nearly knocked over her coffee cup. "Mistletoe."

"What about it?"

"I forgot to tell the new wedding planner about hanging mistletoe at the royal wedding ball. I must call Talia. Do you mind?"

Even in a panic, Sophie considered others. Kat motioned toward the door. "Go. I'll get dressed while you do that."

"Meet me downstairs when you're ready. Claude is driving us to the appointment with the dressmaker."

Coffee and pancakes forgotten, Sophie walked out of the bedroom at a brisk pace. But then again, mistletoe at a Christmas wedding, even a royal one, was important.

Though kissing under the mistletoe at the castle seemed

unlikely to Kat. She knew three men at the castle—Claude, Jennings, and Gill.

An image of the prince's handsome face appeared.

He had nice lips, but he scowled more than he smiled when she was around. They didn't get along well enough to kiss. Even if she wanted to kiss him—which she didn't—he would never want to kiss her.

Maybe Sophie could introduce Kat to someone at the wedding who might want to kiss under the mistletoe at the royal ball.

Was a kiss too much to hope for before the proverbial clock struck midnight and her fairy-tale vacation ended?

One kiss—a peck would do—to take back to reality, to her small, one-bedroom apartment and her job caring for animals.

A good life. One she loved.

Just a world away from this castle and Alistonia.

SITTING IN THE back of the idling limousine, Gill tapped his foot to the beat of the Christmas carol playing and hummed along to the tune. Most holidays seemed like a waste of time, but he loved everything about Christmas—from the decorations to the music to the food. Gifts were an added bonus because he preferred to give rather than to receive.

This year, Gill felt torn. He wanted his little sister's wedding day to be perfect, but he didn't want the Christmas festivities to be pushed aside due to the royal nuptials. The fact he hadn't thought much about the holiday season suggested that might happen this year.

Unacceptable.

Christmas at the castle was full of traditions that dated back centuries. The staff deserved the usual celebration and presents, and in spite of his mother downplaying the holiday since his father's death three years ago, so did she.

Come Christmas, Gill wanted to see only happy faces, not disappointed ones. He knew who would make that happen—his assistant Frederick.

Before the second ring, the line connected. "This is Frederick, sir. How may I help you?"

"We haven't discussed Christmas."

"Already on it, sir."

Of course Frederick was. The man never disappointed. "Same as last year?"

"Yes, sir. I've finished purchasing the gifts for the staff as well as their stocking stuffers. I'm only missing the cash bonuses that go in the cards." Frederick's competent tone let Gill know everything was under control.

"I will take care of the bonuses." As well as Frederick's gift. Gill wanted his assistant to be surprised along with everyone else. "Have the cards and envelopes addressed and ready to be filled before the wedding."

"Yes, sir," Frederick said. "Jennings is coordinating with the chef for the staff's Christmas Eve dinner."

"What about the guests staying at the castle?" One particular guest came to mind. Gill would have to give Kat a present. Excluding her would be rude, especially on Christmas morning.

"I have presents for each of the names on the list Jennings provided, and I purchased extra in case of unexpected guests."

"Excellent."

"The plans are in place for the Christmas Eve service at the chapel. The décor will consist of poinsettias and white candles along with the traditional nativity set."

December twenty-fourth was the only time the small church, located on the castle grounds, was used. Sophie had wanted to get married there, but their mother's response had been a resounding no. She'd used the reason of the wedding being on the twenty-third, not Christmas Eve, but both Gill and Sophie knew that was an excuse. The queen wanted the wedding to be a public spectacle, not an intimate family affair.

"Thank you." Gill disconnected from the call.

A new song played. He checked his watch. Laughed.

A good thing he'd sent Claude inside to find Sophie or they'd be even later for her appointment.

Not unexpected.

He couldn't remember when she'd ever been on time. She'd been born a week past her due date.

Poor Bertrand.

Gill had no doubt Sophie would be late for her wedding. Gill's job, as one of the groomsman, would be to keep Bertrand from panicking when his bride didn't arrive as expected. The only question was how late would she be?

Maybe they should place bets.

The passenger door opened. Sophie climbed in, and Kat followed. The two women sat on the back bench together. Both were bundled in thick coats, hats, and gloves.

Sophie blew him a kiss. "Good morning, dear brother."

The circles under Kat's eyes were lighter. He couldn't tell if that was due to sleep or makeup, but her face had more color.

Claude got into the driver's seat and drove toward the gate.

He looked at his sister. "You're late."

"It couldn't be helped." Sophie glanced at her cell phone and frowned. "I would have been on time, early even, except I forgot the mistletoe."

An excuse if he ever heard one. "Mistletoe?"

"To hang at the wedding ball and dinner." She flashed him a don't-you-know-anything look—the kind younger sisters knew how to do instinctively from the age of two. "You can't have a Christmas-themed event without it."

"Call the wedding planner." He'd forgotten the latest one's name.

Working with his mother wasn't easy, but he felt sorry for the women having to deal with both the queen and the

Duchess of Darbyton. Their demands had led to a revolving door of wedding planners. Only one—the first—had been fired. The rest had quit. He hoped this new one lasted until Sophie's wedding day.

"Talia is speaking with the florist today to make a mistletoe plan."

Talia. That was the name he'd forgotten. "You need a mistletoe plan?"

"Mistletoe is important," Kat said.

She would think so. "Funny how people think kissing under mistletoe is romantic when the plant is not only poisonous, but also deadly. Certain types can kill you."

Sophie made another face at him. "No one will be ingesting the mistletoe."

"Just kissing under it," Kat agreed.

Nodding, Sophie touched her friend's arm. "I'm going to find you the most scrumptious man to kiss at the wedding ball."

Kat must have asked Sophie for help. He would put an end to it. "Sorry, but I pass."

"I said scrumptious, not beastly," Sophie teased.

The idea of Kat kissing a man—make that a royal—left a sour taste in Gill's mouth. With the free-flowing champagne at the wedding ball, a kiss could easily turn into something more. Kat could be a seducer, but what if someone took advantage of her instead? This had disaster written all over it.

"Have anyone else in mind?" he asked.

"Not yet." Sophie looked at Kat. "Any requirements?"

Kat shrugged. "Not really."

Gill wasn't buying it. "Come on."

"It's been so long since I've dated that I wouldn't know where to start," she said.

Sophie tsked. "You need to work fewer hours and get out more."

"I did meet someone who fell for me fast," Kat said.

Knew it. His confidence that he was correct about Kat soared. "Who?"

"A two-year-old Doberman Pincher named Felix," she joked. "And because of that, I think I might have some requirements about who I'd like to kiss."

Of course she did. Gill could imagine what they would be—royal title, wealthy, and a marriageable age.

"What?" Sophie asked.

Kat held up three fingers. "Human male, single, and over the age of eighteen."

"Several wedding guests fit those criteria," Sophie said.

Kat seemed to be setting the bar low. Gill wondered why. "Don't you want to kiss a royal?"

"Any man will do," Kat answered.

She sounded believable, but why kiss a commoner when royals would be available? He would play along for now. "So you're not picky when it comes to men?"

"It's one kiss with a stranger," Kat replied. "For fun."

"What part of holiday tradition don't you understand,

Your Serene Highness?" Sophie's words came out sharply, as if each were punctuated with a period. If she was trying to hide her frustration, she wasn't doing a good job. "Pickiness is not required, but my advice to Kat would be to stay away from men who would be king. They are far too much trouble."

Gill wasn't offended since he had no interest in kissing Kat under the mistletoe or anywhere else, but a woman could do much worse than a future king. "You're assuming those men would want a mistletoe kiss."

Sophie stuck out her tongue at him.

"Your brother has a point," Kat said to his surprise. "Some royals won't be interested in a commoner like me."

Gill found himself nodding. "Exactly."

"However, that didn't seem to bother certain princes in Great Britain, Denmark, and Spain," Kat added.

Her smile was half-smirk, half-smile.

Touché.

"You've done your research." The fact she knew what princes had married commoners suggested she was on a hunt for a royal. Sophie should see that, too. "Scouting the field?"

"If you call clicking on a link on my Facebook newsfeed research, then yes, I have." She looked at Sophie. "I wanted to see the dresses the royal wedding parties were wearing."

Sophie rubbed her palms together. That was her I'm-excited gesture. "I can't wait for you to see me in my gown."

Kat sighed. "I know you'll be stunning."

Gill watched the two women. The mistletoe-kissing discussion must be over. A relief. Yet, an image of Kat raising her face for a kiss seemed to be etched on his brain. He wanted the picture gone.

"I hope so." Sophie's smile dimmed. "But I know the momzillas will be on me about losing more weight."

Kat looked at Gill expectedly.

He'd told her he'd do something. And he had.

Not for her, if that was what she thought. He'd done it for his sister.

"Sophie and I are going to talk to the chef about her meals," Gill explained. "I also made a call this morning. I hope you don't mind, Sophie."

His sister leaned forward until her seatbelt stopped her. "Who did you call?"

The anticipation in her voice told him he'd made the right decision. Too bad Kat had been the catalyst for him taking action. He should have done this without prompting.

"Olga." Sophie's former nanny had been mortified to hear what the two mothers wanted. He had no doubt Olga would have Sophie off the wedding diet before the end of the dress fitting. But he needed backup to make sure that happened. "Promise you'll both go along with whatever Olga says during the fitting."

Sophie nodded.

So did Kat. Respect gleamed in her eyes. "Well played."

Her compliment made him straighten. An unfamiliar

sensation bubbled in his gut. Why should anything she say affect him?

He focused on the one person who mattered to him—Sophie. "Anything for my sister."

And Gill would do anything. He looked at Kat. No matter who stood in the way.

Chapter Five

DURING THE DRIVE to the village, Kat stared out the limousine window. The road curved through rolling foothills with the majestic Alps as the backdrop. Sigh-worthy scenery. The only thing missing was snow, but she was hopeful. Not a touch of blue could be seen in the gray sky. Maybe the snow would arrive earlier than the weather forecast predicted.

Sophie handed Kat her cell phone. "What do you think of these?"

A collage of sexy negligees was on the screen—the latest addition to Sophie's trousseau board on Pinterest.

Kat glanced at Gill, who stared at his tablet. She wondered what he would think of the hot pink and dark purple lingerie. Prince Annoying would probably point out something wrong with each item—not short enough, wrong color, cheap fabric.

"Pretty." No traditional white peignoir sets in the bunch. "But if you're not vacationing in a warm place, you might need a robe to wear over the lace and chiffon."

Sophie sighed. "Packing without knowing the honeymoon destination is impossible."

Kat looked at the other pins on her board. The pictures ranged from beach wear to ski clothing. "I'm sure it is, but you've got ideas for every destination."

Sophie nodded. "But I don't want to take clothes I won't need."

Gill's gaze shot up from his tablet. "Ask Bertrand for a temperature range, so you'll know what to pack."

"Great idea." Kat should have thought of that, but she was glad Gill had.

His intense gaze met hers. The way he stared made Kat shift in her seat. She looked at Sophie.

"The temperature won't give away the exact locale, and it'll make packing so much easier," Kat added.

Sophie took back her phone. "I'm texting Bertrand now."

"If he doesn't want to tell you, have him talk to your brother," Kat suggested.

Gill's brows pinched together. "Why me?"

She smiled at him. "It was your idea."

"Yes," Sophie agreed. "Bertrand will be coming to dinner tonight. I can't wait for him to meet the life-sized Kat. He's only seen you on my screen and in photographs."

Kat couldn't wait to meet Bertrand. He and Sophie seemed to be a perfect match. They both gave back to their countries and people in different ways. Sophie through her social work and Bertrand through his military service.

"I've never met a lord before," Kat said.

Gill rolled his eyes.

"You'll also be meeting a marquess tonight," Sophie said. "That's Bertrand's older brother's title. Jamie is joining us for dinner too, but neither is a typical royal."

Gill nodded. "Especially Bertrand."

"That's why I'm marrying him," Sophie announced.

Kat smiled. "He's a lucky guy to have you as his bride."

Sophie raised her hand to stare at her engagement ring— an emerald cut diamond surrounded by tapered baguette diamonds on either side.

"I still can't believe I'm getting married in two weeks." Sophie had a wistful look in her eyes. "If I hadn't gone on that reality TV show, I would have never met the love of my life."

"You don't know that for sure," Gill countered.

"Do you believe in fate?" Kat asked.

"Of course not," he said.

"He's never wished on stars, either," Sophie added.

Kat had, but none of her wishes had come true. Her parents had never came back to get her. They'd died and were buried in some far-off country.

Africa.

That would be her next trip after she saved enough money and vacation time. She wanted to see the place that had meant everything to her mom and dad, along with the animals they'd loved more than their daughter.

"There's a reason I've never done that." Gill smiled at his sister. "I wanted to leave all the stars for you to wish upon."

Oh, how sweet. Kat clasped her hands to her chest. The crown prince flip-flopped between the arrogant man who disliked her and the caring brother who adored his sister. Too bad he couldn't act like the latter to everyone. That would make things more…pleasant.

"Well, I do believe in fate. Being on that show is why I was invited to Luc and Emily's wedding and met Bertrand." Sophie sounded happy and content. "Oh, I almost forgot, Kat. Prince Luc, Emily, a few of the other princesses, and the entire TV crew, will be attending the wedding. The crew wanted to film the ceremony and reception, but I said no because I knew Mother would never agree. But the crew will be doing interviews and vignette pieces beforehand, so you may end up on camera."

"Keep them away from me." Gill held up his hands as if to ward off an imaginary camera. "I have no interest in being asked to be the next prince they showcase in search of a princess bride."

"Puh-lease." Sophie burst out laughing. "I love you, but let's be honest. You'd bore the audience to sleep. The one thing you and Kat have in common is how many hours you work each day. TV audiences don't want to watch that."

"I enjoy what I do." Gill didn't sound offended. "It

doesn't feel like work."

"Same here," Kat agreed.

Sophie pursed her lips. "I know you both love what you do, but I don't want either of you to be lonely."

Gill's brows drew together. "I'm surrounded by people every day. No chance of being lonely."

"I'm too tired to be lonely," Kat admitted. "I work as hard as I can. Sleep as many hours as I can. Sounds boring, but it's exactly what I want to be doing. Establishing my career is my goal right now."

"What about finding a husband?" Gill asked.

His question caught her off-guard. "I'm focused on my career."

"A family would be good for you." Sophie spoke as if Kat could order one online. "You know you want one."

"Yes, but my job—"

"You could do both," Gill said. "My mother has."

Kat didn't hold up Queen Louise as a parenting benchmark given the nannies, boarding schools, and summer camps her children had attended.

"Someday."

Kat's parents hadn't been able to combine a career with having a daughter, and she never wanted to be forced to choose between work and family. She didn't think she could make the same choice as her mom and dad. Kat wouldn't want to do that.

She leaned back against the seat.

"Someday might arrive sooner than you think." Mischief gleamed in Sophie's eyes.

"Huh?" Kat asked.

Gill stared at his sister. "What are you up to?"

"Nothing." Sophie looked at her cell phone with a sly smile on her face.

Kat and Gill exchanged confused glances.

She shrugged.

Who knew what Sophie meant? Maybe she'd thought of someone Kat could kiss under the mistletoe.

She took in the passing scenery. The views coming down the hillside were incredible.

Claude sang along with the carol playing. His lovely tenor voice filled the car and sounded like it belonged on the recording.

"Let's sing along," Gill suggested.

"Oh, yes." Sophie sang a line off-key.

Kat joined in, but she kept eyeing Gill. He didn't seem like the type to be caroling in the car, but a kid-in-a-toy-store smile was on his face.

Weird. She would have thought him to be a modern-day Scrooge given his personality, but he knew the words. His voice was warm and rich and did funny things to her stomach.

Maybe she should have eaten more breakfast.

"Adeste Fideles" came on next.

She knew one verse, but only in English, so she listened

to the others sing in German. Gill knew all the verses.

She was impressed.

When the song ended, she clapped. Sophie and Gill bowed their heads. Claude waved his hand.

A few notes of the next song made everyone laugh. Kat wouldn't be the only one sitting this one out. "Sleigh Ride" didn't offer much in the way of vocals, though humming along was an option.

The limousine pulled to a stop. Claude exited the driver's seat.

Kat peered out the window. They were parked in front of an old stone cottage with empty flower boxes beneath the window and smoke rising from the chimney. A broken gate hung from one hinge.

This didn't look like a bridal shop. "Where are we?"

"The dressmaker's." Sophie wrapped a scarf around her neck and picked up her purse. "Get your things. Claude will drop off Gill and come back for us."

Kat stared at the cottage in disbelief. She'd been measured for her bridesmaid's dress at a local bridal boutique in a nearby town. That place screamed weddings with its pink and ivory décor and racks of poufy white dresses. She'd expected to go to a similar shop, or a nicer one since Sophie was a princess. Not a place that looked like it sold magic wands and potions.

"Something wrong?" Gill's smile had disappeared, and his eyes were dark.

His assessing gaze was on Kat once again. Likely finding something else he didn't like about her.

Too bad—she'd thought he might be warming up to her while they sang. Getting along would be best for Sophie, but Gill would have to agree. That didn't seem likely.

Oh, well. Kat wasn't about to let him continue to make her uncomfortable. She squared her shoulders. "This shop looks different from the bridal stores back home."

Sophie grinned. "We have those here, but this isn't a bridal shop. This is Olga's house. She's making my dress."

Kat stared at the house. Maybe Olga would whip up the dress with a magical phrase and wave of a wand like the fairy godmother in Cinderella. Sophie must have great faith in the woman.

"Olga was Sophie's longtime nanny," Gill said as if reading Kat's mind. "The two are very close."

Kat remembered. "You've talked about her before."

Sophie nodded. "After she retired, she took up dressmaking. She and I have been talking about my wedding dress since I was a little girl. Both Mother and the duchess exploded when I didn't want to use a name designer, but I held my ground on this one."

Kat's gaze met Gill's. He didn't have to say anything. She knew he was thinking the same thing.

Pick your battles.

He smiled at her.

The guy had a great grin when he let it show. Too bad

that wasn't more often.

She smiled back and then looked at Sophie. "I'm glad you did. I can't wait to see Olga's design."

The passenger door opened.

Sophie scooted across the seat and took Claude's hand as she stepped out of the limousine.

Kat hesitated. She knew Gill wasn't coming inside, and she didn't know when she would see him again. "Thank you for calling Olga. That means a lot to Sophie. And to me."

One of his eyebrows shot up. "The wedding diet is a thing of the past."

Cold air streamed inside the car. A popular carol—one Kat knew the lyrics by heart—played on the speakers, but she couldn't recall the title.

Sophie was waiting, but for some odd reason, Kat was in no hurry to get out of the limousine. "I'd better go."

"You don't want to keep my mother waiting," he warned. "I received a text asking the status of our arrival. She's been here for thirty minutes. So has the duchess."

Oops. Kat picked up her tote bag.

He watched her. "Remember…"

"Pick my battles."

He nodded.

"That might not be necessary," Kat said.

His eyebrow rose higher. "Why is that?"

"The queen might like me."

A slow smile spread across his face and crinkled the corners of his eyes. The result—breathtaking.

Her heart thudded.

"She might." He sounded amused, and though that was at Kat's expense, his killer smile more than made up for it. "But I wouldn't hold your breath."

Was she doing that now? She took a breath. Being near him flustered her.

"Kat," Sophie called from outside the limo. "Are you coming?"

"Hurry," Gill teased. "You don't want the queen screaming *off with her head*. Especially since she'd be talking about yours."

Realization hit Kat. "You're not trying to help me. You want to scare me so I'm afraid to meet the queen."

Gill rubbed his chin. If that was him feigning innocence, he was failing. Big time. "You think?"

"I bet your mom is a total sweetheart, just like Sophie."

Wicked laughter lit his eyes. "I may have to skip my appointment."

"Why?"

"So I can hear firsthand about your meeting with my mother." His tone was lighthearted, but Kat wasn't amused. "This has the making of legend or lore."

Taking a page from Sophie's book, Kat stuck out her tongue and got out of the limousine.

Sophie held open the broken gate. "What took you so long?"

"I was thanking your brother for calling Olga."

"He can be a sweetheart when he wants to. I wish you two could get along better."

Kat couldn't miss her friend's hopeful tone. "We're trying."

At least she was, and she would try harder for Sophie.

Part of her job as a bridesmaid was to keep her friend's stress level low.

"I can't believe I ever thought the two of you could fall in love," Sophie said.

"We're very different, and, be honest, you only wanted that to happen so we'd be sisters."

"That's true." Sophie climbed the porch steps. "We might not be related by birth, but we're sisters by heart. Still, I wish…"

The cottage door opened. A woman in her fifties with a chic, jet-black bob hairstyle motioned them up the porch steps and inside. She wore black leggings, a black-and-white striped tunic, and red boots.

Kat thought a retired nanny might look more conservative, but nothing in Alistonia was what she expected—from the castle to Gill.

She stepped inside. The cottage was charming and inviting with no wands or potions in sight. Worn wood planks with more dings and marks than she could count covered the floor. Thick dark beams crossed the low ceiling, and arched wood-paned windows let in natural light.

The woman placed her hands on her hips and gave Sophie a hard stare. "It's about time you arrived."

"Oh, Olga, you know you're not mad at me." Sophie hugged her former nanny and then stepped back. "This is Kat Parsons. My BFF from camp. I've told you about her. Kat, this is Olga. She's creating my wedding dress."

Olga smiled. "So nice to meet you, Kat, but we must hurry."

"Are they disagreeing already?" Sophie asked.

"I believe a six-figure wager may be in the works over whose older son gets married first."

Sophie shook her head. "A bet is better than them starting a war."

"That might be next." Olga lowered her voice. "The queen and duchess are losing their patience with each other."

"I'm sorry." Sophie sounded contrite. "You know how hard being on time is for me."

"Not hard, my sweet girl. Impossible. And your mother should know that by now." Olga pointed to a doorway covered with a patterned fabric. "Wait in there with the two mothers, Kat. I'll help Sophie into her gown, and we'll join you shortly."

Olga took Sophie by the hand and led her down a hallway.

Kat stared at the cloth. The bright colors were inviting, but she had no idea what she'd find on the other side. She took a breath.

No reason to be afraid. Gill had been joking about his mother, only trying to scare Kat.

She took another breath. This one deeper.

Exhaling, she walked through the cloth and found herself in a small living room with mismatched styles of furniture—a Queen Anne loveseat, a wingback chair, a barstool, and a wooden rocking chair.

"Hello," she said to the two beautifully coiffed and fashionable women sitting with their hands clasped on their laps.

Olga hadn't been kidding.

The friction in the room was palpable. If Kat pulled out her pocketknife from her purse, she could slice the tension and serve up pieces.

One woman's stunning features suggested she'd modeled in her younger days. Her blonde hair was pulled up in a French twist. Her gaze studied Kat like this was the first day of sorority recruitment, not a wedding dress fitting.

The other wore a pale green suit and matching jacket. Her light brown hair was pulled back off her face and highlighted her cheekbones, wrinkle-free skin, and impeccable makeup. Her eyes…

Hazel.

Like Sophie's.

With a touch of green.

Like Gill's.

This must be Queen Louise. She was beautiful, and no broom was in sight. Much better than the ugly stepmother or wicked witch that Gill seemed to suggest his mother was.

Kat stood there, feeling on display. Each second her unease quadrupled.

Both women eyed her with wariness as if trying to decide if she should be allowed in their presence. Worse, as when she was with Gill, Kat felt as if she wasn't measuring up to whatever standard the two held.

Her throat clogged.

She forced herself to swallow.

Neither the queen nor the duchess spoke. They didn't move, either, making Kat think of eerie wax figures in a museum.

Unwilling to allow the silence to continue, Kat curtsied in front of the queen. "I'm Kat Parsons, ma'am."

The queen pursued her lips. "You're the American."

The disdain in her voice put her son's attitude to shame.

Kat's stomach sank. Maybe Gill hadn't been joking.

"Yes." She hated the slight quiver in the one word.

"Thank goodness." The other woman, who by default must be the Duchess of Darbyton, spoke with a thick Southern drawl. "I'm so glad I'm not the only red, white, and blue girl here."

"Two against one." Queen Louise didn't sound worried at all. "Whatever shall I do?"

"You have your sweet baby girl." The duchess's smile never wavered, but if her face got any tighter, the skin might shatter like an eggshell. "That'll even up the odds."

The queen's drawn-out sigh could inflate a dozen balloons. "Not quite because my daughter does whatever this one tells her."

Uh-oh. Kat's insides trembled. Whatever words came out of her mouth would likely be the wrong ones, so she kept quiet. But maybe it was time for Sophie to tell her family that she hadn't been doing whatever Kat said all these years.

The queen picked something off the loveseat arm, though Kat hadn't noticed anything there. "We all know this gown will be ghastly, but never fear, I have a gown that was sent from a designer in Paris and is ready for Sophie to try on."

The duchess shook her head. "You leave nothing to chance, ma'am."

The queen's hard gaze narrowed on Kat. "Nothing at all."

Queen Louise seemed so hard-nosed and critical. Granted, Kat had spent less than five minutes in her presence, but nothing about the woman was warm or nurturing.

The queen might like me.

Yeah, right.

Gill had warned Kat, but she hadn't listened. No wonder he'd laughed at her.

Stupid.

But she wouldn't forget his advice now.

Olga held open the cloth door covering. "May I present your bride, Princess Sophia of Alistonia."

A vision wearing white entered.

Tears sprang to Kat's eyes. So gorgeous. And so Sophie.

The style wasn't puffy ball gown with layers of tulle underneath that would make Scarlett O'Hara proud, nor was it a form-fitting sheath that hugged curves like the ones Kat had seen online and in the pages of bridal magazines.

The long-sleeved, A-line silk dress made Sophie look like the ultimate princess bride. An overlay of exquisite lace added the right touch of elegance, as did the crystals and pearls in an intricate design at the waistband.

The duchess clapped. "Just perfect. The high neckline and long train are like the ones from my wedding gown."

The queen harrumphed, yet her gaze remained focused on her daughter. The edges of her mouth curved upward. "Perhaps, but the rest of the bodice is like mine. So is the lace. That's a royal family tradition."

Olga bowed her head. "Sophie brought me pictures of both your wedding gowns and asked me to incorporate designs of each into hers."

"Spectacular." Kat wiped the tears from her eyes. "You are the most gorgeous bride ever. Bertrand is going to lose it when he sees you walking toward him."

The duchess nodded. "He won't be able to take his eyes off you."

Sophie beamed. "Thank you."

"There's one issue," Olga said in a dramatic tone. She hung her head as if for added effect.

"What?" the two mothers said at the same time.

"Sophie has lost too much weight. Any more, and I don't know that the dress will fit as well. I can take it in, but that will take time away from attaching the pearls and crystals to the skirt."

The duchess pressed a hand to her heart. "Pearls."

Queen Louise sighed. "Crystals."

The two women looked at each other. Nodded. "No more wedding diet," they said together.

Sophie bounced, but Olga put a finger on her shoulder to stop her.

Kat was thrilled for Sophie. Gill had put an end to the no-eating insanity without going face to face with his mother or the duchess.

A smart man, even if he didn't want to kiss her under the mistletoe.

Sorry, but I pass.

His loss.

Besides, she didn't want to kiss him.

But she imagined his kiss would taste good for him being, as Sophie called him, such a beast.

"That train will look fabulous as you walk down the aisle." A smug smile settled on Queen Louise's face, but pride gleamed in her eyes. "You couldn't have worn something that long if you'd gotten married at the castle's chapel."

Sophie's smile remained in place. "You're right, Mother."

"Is Crown Prince Guillaume walking you down the aisle?" Kat wasn't about to use nicknames with this crowd.

"Sophia has decided to walk herself down the aisle," the queen answered, and she didn't sound pleased.

"That's progressive," the duchess said.

Queen Louise shook her head as if this was the end of the world. "It isn't proper, but I have relented because Sophia asked your daughter and this American to be her bridesmaids."

Kat had learned from Sophie that they didn't have maid of honors in Alistonia. The bride also went down the aisle first with her attendants behind her. A little different from what Kat was used to back home where the bridesmaids went first and the bride was the last to enter the church.

The queen continued. "That means your older son, and my son, the crown prince, will need to stand with Bertrand. We can't have the wedding party lopsided."

The duchess's fingers touched her gaping mouth. "You cannot. Just imagine. The photos would be doomed."

"Exactly," the queen agreed.

Were these two enemies or twins separated at birth? Perhaps this was how royal mothers acted.

Not that they mattered. Only the bride did.

"You look incredible," Kat said to her friend. "The dress is amazing."

"I can't believe I'm wearing this dream of a dress." Sophie stared down at the dress. "You outdid yourself, Olga.

Just as I knew you would. Thank you."

Olga dipped her head. "The gratitude is mine for being entrusted with your wedding gown."

Sophie squeezed Olga's hand. The look of love that passed between the two brought another tear to Kat's eyes.

And she wondered.

Had there been a caring, loving nanny like Olga in Gill's life when he was growing up? Or was that why he acted the way he did? Because there'd been no one to give him the attention a child needed, the love a child deserved.

The thought tore at Kat's heart. That might explain why Gill had never seemed happy at camp. Caroling aside, he didn't seem much happier now, but for all she knew, he had the most nurturing caregivers in the country.

None of her business.

Except he was part of Sophie's life, and she was part of Kat's.

He'd surprised her more than once today. Maybe there was more to Prince Annoying than she was giving him credit for.

Dare she find out?

Chapter Six

LUNCH AT A café followed the fitting. After that, Sophie had a conference call, so Kat explored the public rooms at the castle. Yesterday, her brief tour had given her a glimpse of the first floor, but she wanted a closer look at where Sophie lived. Walking around with so many paintings, tapestries, and sculptures, however, made Kat feel as if she was touring an art museum, not a home.

Her first stop was the sitting room. The gray and yellow décor was not only inviting, but this room also had framed photographs of the royal family on the walls and fireplace mantle. She enjoyed looking at the childhood pictures of the young princess and princes with their parents. No priceless oil paintings, fragile statues, or suits of armor on display anywhere. This was the only room, other than the bathroom, where she wasn't afraid of breaking something.

The feeling of home flowed through her. Not a way she expected to feel, but she understood why. This room felt the most…normal.

The traditional-style sofa and chairs were contemporary and comfortable looking. She pictured the royal family—any family for that matter—sitting around watching a movie or sporting event. The various wood tables looked sturdier than the antique ones in the music room and parlor. The pillows and throws gave the room a lived-in look. Most of the other rooms seemed more for show than actual use.

Not this one.

A fifteen-foot-tall Christmas tree was positioned against the far wall and centered between tall windows. The castle had more than a dozen trees, but this one was her favorite.

The other trees were decorated by theme or color scheme. Works of art and beautiful, yes, but she preferred the twinkling white lights and the variety of ornaments—blown glass, wood, metal, plastic—hanging from the branches.

Warmth flowed through her.

She walked toward the tree with wide branches and a shiny gold star on the top. The spaces between the branches told her it wasn't a Douglas fir, but she didn't know the type. The scent, however, was familiar.

She inhaled deeply.

The smell brought back fond memories of Christmases past, and she wondered what this year would hold. She pictured colorful wrapped gifts tucked under the tree branches. Pretty packages tied with silver, gold, and red ribbons. Would one have her name on it?

A crystal icicle ornament caught her attention and drew her closer.

Still no snow or icicles outside, but Kat was hopeful the weather forecast of a winter storm would come true.

She touched the icicle. So beautiful and not as fragile as the ornament looked at first glance.

"Looks like you survived meeting my mother."

Gill.

Kat pulled back her hand, turned away from the tree, and faced him. His wool coat from earlier was gone as were his gloves. He wore a navy suit with a light blue shirt and red tie. She'd only been here two days, but he dressed so formally other than his workout clothes. Okay, he was the crown prince, but she wondered if he owned a pair of jeans or khakis.

His suspicious gaze made her feel like a trespasser. Her muscles bunched. She shouldn't feel guilty for being in here—Sophie had said to go wherever Kat wanted.

She straightened. "I did."

"Are you and Mother BFFs now?" The amusement in his voice shone in his eyes.

Heat rose up Kat's neck. Might as well get this over with. "I owe you an apology."

"For what?"

"You weren't trying to scare me. Your mother was exactly as you described." No sense pretending the meeting had gone well. "I didn't have to pick my battles though. She barely addressed me. Which in hindsight may have been a blessing. I doubt she'll remember me if we meet again."

"If?" Gill didn't gloat. Lines creased his forehead. "You're staying here. You'll see her again."

Kat might as well change her name to the invisible American while she was in Alistonia. "Yes, but I doubt she'll see me."

A smile spread across his face. "That sums up my mother perfectly."

Unfortunately.

Kat didn't take any pride in being right. She'd hoped to get along with Sophie's family. The same way her friend had with Kat's grandparents. But that wasn't going to happen.

Not with Queen Louise. Not with Gill.

That stung.

Kat prided herself on being able to fix things, whether a problem or a sick animal. She had no way of making this situation better. That made her feel worthless. A way she hadn't felt since she was younger and needed to know why her parents didn't want her anymore.

She plopped onto an overstuffed yellow-and-gray striped reading chair where she had a perfect view of the tree and not as good of one of Gill.

Kat had no doubt the wedding would be wonderful, but her dream of a fabulous Christmas at the castle was disappearing faster than the dog biscuits they gave out to patients at the animal hospital.

On the twenty-fourth, Sophie and Bertrand would leave on their honeymoon. Kat had planned to stay here for Christmas and then fly home the next day. Now she wasn't sure what she should do. The queen and Gill made Kat feel like an intruder. She might feel less unwelcome and alone spending Christmas in a hotel rather than here where she wasn't welcome.

Gill sat on the couch next to her chair. "What are you thinking?"

She didn't want to tell him because she didn't want Sophie to know. Kat could check into a hotel after the newlyweds took off. Her friend would never have to know she hadn't spent Christmas at the castle. She doubted the queen or Gill would mention her.

But Kat needed to reply now. Something safe and on topic. "That this is where you're supposed to say 'I told you so.'"

His smile widened, and once again, she had to admit he had a nice one. "No need because you admitted I was right."

"You like that."

"Of course."

"Then you should know your call to Olga worked," Kat said. "Sophie's wedding diet is over, and she enjoyed every bite of her lunch."

"What about you?" he asked.

"Delicious." Her entrée had been incredible with spices she'd never considered combining. "Though I couldn't pronounce many of the dishes."

"That's the Eastern European influence."

Kat nodded. "Olga joined us for lunch and gave me a history lesson on food in Alistonia."

His gaze softened. "That sounds like Olga."

This was the opening Kat needed to find out more about his childhood. "Did you have a different nanny?"

"Yes. Freya was British and very proper."

While Olga seemed warm and loving. That could explain a few of the differences between the two siblings.

"Was Freya with you long?" Kat asked.

"Until I was eight and went off to boarding school. After that, her services were no longer needed."

Kat tried to picture a young boy being sent away to school. Home was a place to live, not where a child spent school vacations. "So young."

Then again, she'd only been four when her parents left her with her grandparents, but at least she'd been with family, not paid faculty.

"That was the age my older brother went away to school."

"You followed in his footsteps."

"Tradition." He spoke without emotion.

"That had to be difficult on you and your parents."

"It was," he admitted to her surprise. "My mother thought I wasn't ready, but my father said she coddled me too much and it would be best for me to go away to school."

Kat would never associate Gill with the word coddled.

"Surprised?" he asked.

"Yes. Neither you nor your mom seem like the coddling types."

His smile remained. "That may be true now, but my mother was very hands-on when we were younger, in spite of each of us having a nanny. Lots of hugs and kisses and playing on the floor."

Kat wished she'd had a taste of that from her mom. "Must have been nice."

He nodded. "My mother might not appear to be the warmest person, but she loves us, and I have no doubt she would do anything to protect Sophie and me."

Another warning? Kat hoped not.

She liked hearing there was more to Queen Louise, who appeared so controlling and opinionated. Kat would take a mother like her over one who wasn't around. "You're fortunate she cares so much."

He glanced at his watch and then stood. "I must return to my office."

"I'll go back to admiring the ornaments on the tree."

Gill hesitated. "Those are part of my father's legacy."

"How so?"

"He didn't like themed trees, so he proclaimed no decorators were allowed to hang the ornaments on the sitting room tree. Only family and a few longtime staff members like Jennings and Claude."

"What a wonderful thing for your father to do." Kat remembered Sophie's stories about him. Before he passed and after. Losing her grandparents so close together, and then Sophie's dad dying after that, had brought them closer, even though they lived far apart and very different lives. "That's what makes this tree perfect."

Gill's gaze traveled from Kat to the tree. "Nothing is perfect, but this comes close."

With that, he turned and walked out of the sitting room.

This was the second time he'd walked away without saying goodbye. Third, if she counted last night, except she'd been asleep.

At least they'd spoken pleasantly just now. No disagreeing. That would make Sophie happy. And strangely, that made Kat happy, too.

LATER, IN HIS office, Gill signed documents at his desk, but his mind was elsewhere. He couldn't stop thinking about Kat. She wasn't what he expected, and he was having trouble reconciling the woman he'd spoken with earlier that afternoon to who he believed her to be.

He'd been walking by after playing fetch with Maximillian when he saw her standing at the tree. The backdrop of the lights and ornaments had been picture perfect, and he'd wanted a closer look.

Her apology for not believing him had been unexpected.

Nor had he thought she'd say anything less than flattering about the queen, but he'd appreciated Kat's politeness and honesty.

His mother could stare through a person as if they weren't there. What his mother didn't say often had more meaning than if she'd spoken.

He gave Kat credit. She was both observant and sharp. In some ways, she reminded him of the teenaged girl from camp. He'd tried many times to get a rise out of her, but he'd always failed. No doubt because of Sophie.

But he couldn't decipher who Kat was now, and that bothered him.

The office door opened, and his mother strode in. The skirt of her blue evening gown swished around her legs. She wore a tiara from the royal collection.

"I should have known you'd still be working," she said. "It's almost dinnertime."

He rose from his desk that had once been Jacques'. Before his mother's coronation, when his grandfather was still alive, she'd used this desk, too.

Gill walked around to the front to greet his mother with a kiss to the cheek.

"You look lovely." The scent of her signature perfume—the same fragrance she'd worn for as long as he remembered—hung in the air. "Are you going out?"

"No, I wanted to dress up for dinner." She glanced at the papers on the desk. "You're correct. That American girl is going to be a problem."

He'd heard Kat's take on their meeting. Now he would get his mother's. "Did something happen at the fitting?"

His mother walked to the window that overlooked a three-tiered fountain. "Your sister's wedding gown turned out better than I expected. I'm returning the backup dress. I'm positive your sister would have thrown a temper tantrum had I mentioned the existence of another wedding gown."

"Sophie's always wanted Olga to design her dress."

His mother shrugged, but Gill thought there was more to her feelings about this. He'd always thought she was jealous of Sophie's relationship with her nanny.

"The design is sentimental and not *haute couture*, but your sister has never had much fashion sense."

Sophie had been named one of the *Top 10 Best Dressed Royals* for the past ten years, but their mother chose not to recognize the honors because his sister didn't wear the styles the queen wanted.

"I wasn't asking about Sophie's dress," he said. "I want to know what happened with Kat."

Lines creased his mother's forehead. "Who?"

Gill sighed. "The American."

"Oh, her. I'd forgotten her name."

That seemed unlikely given Sophie had mentioned Kat's name at least twice a day, usually many times more, for the past fifteen years.

"What did Kat do at the fitting to raise your concerns?"

he asked.

His mother glanced up at the tall ceiling. Probably looking for a cobweb the staff had missed. Complaints fell from her lips more than compliments these days. She'd been picky before his father's death, but grief had brought out a bitterness that not even time could ease.

She'd been queen since she was twenty-eight and promised to abdicate once Gill married. The only reason she wouldn't give up the throne until he wed was because, as the reining ruler, she had the authority to approve his bride choice. If he were king, he could approve his own.

"The woman didn't do anything per se, but she acts like she's one of us already. Speaking out of turn. Forgetting etiquette and protocol rules."

"She's American. She may not know them."

"She's in Alistonia. She should act accordingly."

Gill understood his mother's point, but he also knew how Kat had interacted with Sophie all these years—as friends. The same with him at camp.

"The woman is also playing the role of bridesmaid so perfectly that your sister is enthralled by her friend's presence," his mother continued. "When Sophie appeared in her gown, tears filled that woman's eyes, and she lavished praise without a thought to what the duchess or I might want to say."

Gill was not a fan of Kat Parsons. Far from it, but his mother seemed hypercritical, more so than usual. "I believe that's what bridesmaids are supposed to do."

"Yes, but…" Her gaze clouded. "I fear the American has her sights set on you."

He thought about what Sophie had said yesterday and how Kat had interacted with him since she arrived. Granted, Kat could be misleading his sister and him. "I don't know about that."

"Everyone knows you're the best catch among the peerage."

Her words brought a smile to his face. She sounded more like a mother than a queen. "Other princes might disagree with that statement."

"I may have a slight bias."

More than slight, but he knew better than to say that.

"I don't think you have to worry, Mother. Kat hasn't sought me out."

If anything, he was the one seeking her out in her bedroom last night and in the sitting room today.

His mother tapped a finger against her cheek. "The woman could be playing hard to get. Or she could have enlisted Sophie to take part in a royal romance scheme."

"If that's the case, we'll know soon enough. Sophie can't keep a secret to save her life."

His mother sat on the loveseat and patted the spot next to her. "Whatever is going on, I will not allow our family to be the cause of a scandal."

Gill sat. "I'll keep an eye on Kat."

"Not too close," his mother warned. "I must admit she's prettier than I expected. Her blue eyes are stunning."

"Not my type." He did agree about her eyes, though, and she had a nice smile, too. "I'm immune to American women, remember?"

His mother touched his shoulder. "Clarissa wasn't the right one for you."

For so long, he'd disagreed whenever anyone said that to him, but time had allowed his heart to heal. He saw the situation more clearly. "I know."

His mother gave a gentle squeeze. "Your princess bride is out there, my son."

Maybe so, but he was in no rush to find her. He didn't want to be forced to marry for the sake of his country. He wanted to marry for love like his sister was doing. "Whoever she is can stay far away for now."

"Yes, she can." His mother sounded unusually supportive given the subject matter. "Your great grandmother once told me 'Love that is true, always remains.' There's no rush."

Warning bells sounded in his head. This was a complete turnabout from how his mother normally spoke about him finding a bride. He eyed her warily. "You don't sound like yourself. Why the change of heart?"

"I may be queen, but one royal wedding at a time is all I can handle. Another might push me over the edge."

He laughed, but if anyone was capable of having an ulterior motive, it was his mother. "The planning must be a nightmare if you feel this way."

"Not a nightmare, per se, but the duchess is complicating matters. She wants to be involved in every detail. Her ideas are so…so American."

"She's American."

"But she married a duke and should forget the traditions where she came from. Your dear father, God rest his soul, did."

Gill wondered if his mother had given his father a choice in the matter. She'd always been strong-willed and opinionated, but his father had adored everything about her.

"Poor Sophia." His mother shook her head as if some tragedy had befallen her daughter. "She's such a sweet girl, but she needs to stop saying yes to the duchess' demands."

Of course, his mother wouldn't admit to making any demands herself. Gill nearly laughed. He'd bet she'd long surpassed the number of requests made by the duchess.

"You'd rather Sophie say yes to what *you* want."

"Of course," she said, her tone matter of fact. "My ideas are the best ones."

This was one situation where he didn't envy his sister.

His mother stood, and so did Gill.

"I need to speak to Isaac about the seating arrangement for tonight's dinner." She headed toward the door. "I want that American on the opposite end of the table from you."

"Don't be too blatant."

His mother glanced over her shoulder at him. "I doubt

the woman would notice."

Gill had no doubt that anything got by Kat. "She will."

A finely arched brow shot up. "And you know this how?"

"She was sharp when she was younger. She's a veterinarian now. Clearly, she's not stupid."

"Perhaps, but she only arrived yesterday, and we're onto her. How smart could she be?"

"I don't know," Gill admitted. "But I have a feeling we might find out."

KAT CHANGED INTO the little black dress she'd been told by a sales clerk could be worn anywhere and put on her grandmother's pearl earrings and necklace. She pulled out her sling-back heels and held them for five seconds.

No way.

She placed them in the armoire and put on her black kitten-heel pumps instead. She wasn't used to wearing any size heel. Ending up in a heap at the bottom of the staircase would not be good.

Walking down the stairs wasn't difficult, but she kept a hand on the railing just in case.

"You've got this," she muttered.

Kat entered the dining room. No one else was there.

She blew out a puff of air.

Good, she had time to get comfortable.

Not that she would ever be completely at ease in such a

fancy place. The table could seat at least forty guests and was bigger than those tiny houses that were the new home design craze, even in Cedar Village. Two large crystal-and-gold chandeliers hung over the large table covered with a white linen tablecloth. The six place settings barely took up a third of the space. Gold-rim plates sat on gold chargers with five crystal glasses within arm's reach.

Each setting had a place card with a name written on them in calligraphy. The card closest to her had Gill's name on it. His seat was to the right of the head spot. Kat guessed that space belonged to the queen. The card at the place setting to Gill's right belonged to James. That must be Bertrand's older brother, Jamie. The other three place settings were on the opposite side of the table. She must be sitting there.

Staring at the numerous forks, spoons, and knifes on either side of the plates made Kat nauseous. She didn't own this much flatware. Worse, she had no idea when to use each piece. Muscles tightened into melon-sized balls like the ones served with breakfast.

Dinner had epic failure written all over it.

Hers.

What was she going to do?

She didn't want to let Sophie down and add to her stress. Maybe Kat could claim tiredness—not a lie since she was adjusting to the time change—and ask to eat in her room tonight.

Again.

"May I help you, miss?" A waiter dressed in a formal uniform with an easy smile and short, black hair stood in the doorway. He appeared to be in his early thirties and had a friendly demeanor.

A bale of hay seemed to be pressing on her shoulders. No way could she figure this out on her own.

Maybe he could help her. The man's smile looked genuine, but he could be one of the queen or crown prince's minions.

Kat weighed the consequences—make a fool out of herself versus be sold out for needing help. The latter sounded like the better option. She glanced toward the hallway. No one was coming.

"I've never had dinner at a castle before," she said. "Would you mind giving me a rundown on the silverware and what each piece is used for?"

"Gladly, miss." He bowed. "I'm Isaac."

"Hi. I'm Kat."

His grin widened. "You're Princess Sophia's American friend. The animal doctor."

"Yes, I am."

He looked around as if to make sure they were alone. "We don't have much time before the royal family arrives, so I'll give you a short cut to remember for tonight, and we can work more on this another time."

"That would be great."

He joined her at the table and motioned to the closest place setting. "As each course is served, use the silverware from the outside in. Let the utensil be cleared away with the plate or bowl. Don't keep them. And most importantly, follow the queen's lead. She takes the first bite. Don't touch any utensil or food before she does."

"Outside in. Utensils go away. Let Queen go first," Kat repeated. "I can remember that. Thank you so much."

"They're coming," he whispered. "You can do this."

Kat appreciated his vote of confidence. She smoothed her dress, took a deep breath, and prayed she did nothing to call attention to herself.

Chapter Seven

NOT KNOWING WHAT member of the royal family would be entering the dining room first, Kat stepped away from the table. She didn't want anyone to know she'd received a quick lesson on manners. With a deep breath, she forced the corners of her mouth upward.

You can do this.

She hoped Isaac was right.

Sophie entered first.

That brought a rush of relief.

She wore a stylish pink cocktail dress and silver sling-back heels. She held hands with Bertrand, who wore a suit and a big smile. The two looked good together, and Kat had no doubt their future children would be adorable.

"Here you are." Sophie let go of Bertrand's hand and gave Kat a hug. "We went to your room, but you weren't there. I had no idea you'd beat us downstairs."

"I was ready early," Kat said.

"Early," Bertrand repeated. "An interesting concept I'd forgotten about since meeting the love of my life."

Sophie shook her head.

Kat laughed.

Smiling, Bertrand extended his arm toward Kat. "You're taller than I expected."

She shook his hand. A smattering of freckles covered his nose and cheeks. The reddish tint to his blond hair hadn't shown up on screen, neither had the deep blue color of his eyes. But he was as handsome as his pictures. "So are you. It's nice to meet you in person."

"Same, though Sophie talks about you so much I feel like you and I are BFFs, too."

His friendly tone soothed some of Kat's nerves.

"Jamie will be down soon," Sophie said.

Bertrand laughed. "My brother would be here now, except someone told him to put on a tie."

Sophie shook her head. "You know my mother has certain expectations for dinner."

No way could Kat live up to any royal expectations.

What composure she had mustered disappeared. Her mouth was so dry not even a pitcher of water would help. Her fingers and toes tingled. Much worse than the pins and needles feeling when an appendage fell asleep.

"Bertrand." Queen Louise entered the dining with Gill at her side. Her elegant, royal-blue gown and tiara shimmered.

He looked nice in his suit—the same one he'd worn earlier—but he'd changed his shirt, now white, and his tie was red with blue stripes. He looked underdressed compared to the queen, but that didn't make Kat feel any better.

"How delightful to see you," Queen Louise said to her future son-in-law.

Bertrand bowed. "The pleasure is mine, ma'am."

The queen greeted her future son-in-law with a hug.

That was the first public display of affection Kat had seen. A good sign, right?

"We don't see you around here nearly enough," Queen Louise said. "I'm so happy the Air Force let you have a day off."

"Two days, in fact, and I fear that's all I'll get until right before the wedding." He glanced at Sophie with a look of pure adoration. "I flew in as soon as I could. Can't miss an opportunity to spend more time with all of you."

Most especially Sophie, but Kat gave the man credit for being so cool and calm and including the entire family, not only his fiancée. Her insides trembled, but Bertrand seemed to be able to handle the queen without much effort.

Practice? Or a royalty thing?

Maybe commoners didn't stand a chance with the queen. That might explain her antagonism with the duchess. A title by marriage didn't make a person one of them.

Gill shook Bertrand's hand. "Good to see you."

"I appreciate your help with the wedding," Bertrand said to him. "I wish I could do more, but Jamie's here to lend a hand. He should be down any minute."

A third man would be coming, but Kat couldn't help but

compare the two men standing next to each other now. They were the same height with athletic builds. Both had royal titles, but the similarities ended there.

Bertrand was not only good looking, but he also exuded warmth and friendliness. His light hair color and complexion made her think of a white knight—the type you took home to meet your family and married.

Unlike Gill.

Gorgeous, yes. His hair was light brown, not dark, but the contrast with Bertrand's reddish blond was strong and made Gill look black-knight dangerous. More lover than husband material. Not that she was interested in finding either. Or interested in him.

His suspicious gaze zeroed in on her.

A good thing her dress didn't have pockets or he might think she was stealing the silverware. She ignored the urge to hold her hands in the air and proclaim her innocence.

"Sorry I'm late."

A guy with sandy-blonde hair that fell into his eyes approached the table. He moved with the grace of an athlete. His light blue tie was askew, and the top of his dress shirt unbuttoned. He was need-to-catch-her-breath attractive. The kind of man who drew second and third looks and caused women to smooth their hair and pinch their cheeks when he wasn't looking.

She found herself drawn to him. Not only because he was handsome, but also because he had an easy manner about him. He was—in a word—approachable, in a way she'd never pictured Gill.

He bowed in front of Queen Louise. "You look radiant tonight, Your Majesty."

The queen laughed. "Oh, James. You've been missed, too."

This must be Jamie. He was an older, hotter version of his younger brother.

He greeted Gill, and then Jamie's blue-eyed gaze zeroed in on Kat like a laser beam. He sidled up next to her.

Everything about him appealed to her physically, but she fought the urge to back away. He was almost too much. Too male.

Sex in a designer suit was the only way to describe him.

Hot, yes, but no doubt heartbreakingly dangerous.

"Hello, there. I'm Jamie. You must be Kitty Kat." He took her hand and kissed the top. "You are exquisite."

Heat rose up Kat's neck. No man had ever kissed her hand, called her that, or made her feel so desirable. Her throat tightened. She swallowed. "Thank you."

"Love the pearls." Jamie leaned toward her with no regards for personal space. He fingered her necklace. His fingertips skirted over her skin. "So which does Kitty Kat prefer most—purring or meowing?"

He was being so blatantly sexual in front of everyone, including the queen, that all Kat could do was laugh. His flirting was over the top, but he was attractive enough to pull it off. The man had guts. She had to give him that.

"The name is Kat with a K." Gill stepped forward. "Short for Katrina."

"Katrina is a lovely name." Ignoring Gill, Jamie's smile dazzled. "But I prefer Kitty Kat."

"You would," Gill mumbled.

He was so proper that Kat couldn't believe he'd said the words in front of a guest. Maybe he and Jamie didn't get along for some reason. Or maybe Gill considered him family already, so he could be more open.

Isaac, who had been standing by a doorway, stepped forward and pulled out the chair at the head of the table.

Queen Louise sat. She shot a displeased look at Kat before smiling at everyone else. "Please be seated. There is a place card at each setting."

Jamie sat on the other side of Gill. Sophie sat on the opposite side from those two in the chair on the queen's left. Bertrand took the seat next to his fiancée. That left a chair next to the groom open for Kat.

Sitting across the table, Jamie flashed a charming, lopsided grin. The kind that no doubt melted hearts and possibly panties. "My little brother gets to sit between two lovely ladies tonight. He has all the luck."

Gill rolled his eyes. The man looked like he wanted to be anywhere but seated next to Jamie. At least, he wasn't stuck next to her. That would probably make him more miserable.

The queen cleared her throat. She tasted the white wine

and then nodded her approval.

A waiter, not Isaac, filled each of the glasses.

The first course—a soup—was placed in front of them. Kat kept her hands folded on her lap. She could tell everyone was waiting for the queen, but Gill's gaze kept meeting hers.

He looked at her expectedly. And not in a good way.

No way would she screw up with him watching her.

After what seemed like ten minutes, but was probably only one, the queen picked up her spoon and tasted the soup. As if on cue, the others did the same. Kat picked up her spoon.

Isaac gave her a half-nod.

That made her feel better.

Careful not to slurp, she tasted the soup. Butternut squash with a mix of spices she couldn't name. Tasty.

"How do you like Alistonia?" Bertrand asked her.

She wiped her mouth with a napkin. "It's lovely. Sophie showed me a couple of places in town today. I can't wait to see more. The people are so friendly. Everyone is very welcoming."

"Alistonians are friendly and welcoming to all," Queen Louise said. "I don't know why you'd expect them to be otherwise."

What? Kat had been complimentary, not negative, but she didn't know what to say without coming off defensive. Which she was, but that might get Queen Louise more upset.

Jamie picked up his wineglass. "I must have missed part of the conversation because that's not what I heard."

Sophie nodded. "Jamie's correct. That's not what Kat said, Mother."

"No?" The queen sounded surprised. "Well, that's what it sounded like to me."

"Then perhaps Kat should sit in my place so you won't have to strain your hearing," Gill said to his mother, much to Kat's surprise.

He was the last person she expected to stand up for her, but she appreciated the effort, as she'd appreciated his others—covering her with a blanket and stopping the wedding diet. Gill might turn out to be more of a prince charming than she thought.

"If Kat sits closer to me, I can translate if needed, ma'am," Jamie offered.

The queen's lips pressed together. She avoided looking toward Kat's side of the table. "Thank you both, but the first course has been served. I'll pay closer attention to what is said."

"Thank you, Mother," both Gill and Sophie said at the same time.

Jamie winked.

Staring into her bowl, Kat sipped her soup. The less she said in front of the queen, the better.

Bertrand leaned toward her. "I'm close enough to hear you fine. I'd love to know about Sophie's camp days. She says the two of you had so much fun, but she won't share any details."

"I'd imagine pillow fights in T-shirts and panties, reading each other's diaries, and braiding hair." Jamie sipped his wine.

Not bad guesses for the marquess. Kat exchanged a glance with Sophie.

"You imagine girls at camp?" Gill asked with a look of distaste.

"Females are females." Jamie set his glass on the table. "Whether at camp, in a sorority, or at girls' night, only the ages change."

Bertrand shrugged. "I'd still like to know."

"Sophie will have to tell you the specifics," Kat said to him. If Sophie hadn't told him about their times at camp together, Kat wouldn't, either. They hadn't done anything wrong, but that was a time of growing up and sharing secrets. Girl stuff. "My memory isn't what it used to be."

"Mine, either." Sophie didn't miss a beat. "I believe it's called BFF amnesia."

Kat nodded. "Yes, I've heard something about that. A good thing we have pictures or we'd never remember anything."

"We can ask Gill to fill in the missing gaps," Sophie teased. "He used to follow us around."

Jamie raised his wineglass in Gill's direction. "I knew there was more to you than meets the eyes. If I'd been at that camp, I would have followed these lovelies around, too."

Kat hadn't known he'd done that. "You followed us?"

Red tinged Gill's cheeks. The blush was uncharacteristic and cute. "On occasion."

"That was my doing," Queen Louise said. "I asked Guillaume to keep an eye on his sister."

"Why?" Sophie asked.

"Because my little girl was going off to the Wild West in America, and I was worried. That's what mothers do. Worry about our children." The queen held Sophie's hand. "You may be grown up and getting married, but you'll always be my little girl."

Sophie beamed brighter than she had in her wedding dress today. "Thank you, Mother."

A lump formed in Kat's throat. Gill and Sophie had so much patience for their mother. He'd mentioned one of the reasons earlier in the sitting room, but now Kat saw for herself.

Queen Louise sipped her wine. "Enough sentimentality. Who's ready for the next course?"

Beneath the queen's hard edges and harsh words lay a mother's heart full of love for her children. Bertrand was now accepted as someone who loved Sophie. Jamie, too. Kat, however, was as an outsider and, for some odd reason, viewed as a threat.

Not how she'd wanted things to be, but she understood a little better. Maybe by the time Kat left Alistonia, the queen could say she knew more about Kat and, at least, tolerated her.

Kat glanced at Gill. The crown prince, too.

"So Kitty Kat." Jamie stared over the rim of his wineglass. "How about we leave the two love birds alone tomorrow and go sightseeing?"

Sophie and Bertrand held hands under the table. Their gazes had hardly left each other's. The couple needed time alone, but Kat would need to keep Jamie on a tight leash and not let his flirting get out of control. He was a little too out there for her tastes.

"That sounds like fun," Kat said.

Gill wiped his mouth with his napkin. "Yes, it does sound like fun. I'll go with you."

That got Sophie's attention. Her nose scrunched. "You have to work."

"I doubt Mother would want us to leave our houseguests on their own. That wouldn't be polite."

Sophie gave her brother a look. "They don't mind."

"We don't," Jamie offered.

His grin was full of innuendo, which made Kat think maybe Gill should go. She'd never needed a chaperone, but Jamie might.

"I'm happy to offer my services as a tour guide," Gill said.

"Gill knows all the sights," Queen Louise said. "However, Claude could take Kat if you gentlemen would rather tour on your own."

The queen's words weren't lost on Kat. For whatever reason, Queen Louise wanted to keep her away from both Jamie and Gill. Kat didn't want to imagine the reason, but she had a feeling if she wasn't careful that a trip to the dungeon might be in her future.

A one-way trip.

AFTER DINNER, GILL changed out of his suit and into a pair of shorts and T-shirt. He glanced at Maximillian, who was sprawled across the bed. "Want to go for a run?"

The dog sat. His tail wagged like a metronome.

"I take that as a yes."

Good, because he needed to burn off energy. Jamie's flirting had sent Gill's temper spiraling out of control.

Pounding the pavement was better than punching a wall. Or a certain marquess staying in the guest wing. Perhaps Gill should assign royal guards to stand watch in front of Kat's door.

The Marquess of Darbyton knew how to have a good time, and his reputation with the ladies was legendary. Jamie somehow juggled a handful of women without getting caught or burned. His good looks drew women in like a tractor beam. His wit kept them laughing. His awe-inspiring mountain climbing tales had them wanting to be the one he was with before setting off on his next conquest.

Although usually that would be another woman, not an unconquered peak in the Himalayans or Alaska. The man's unfettered life—at least until he became the duke—appealed to Gill at a gut level.

Jamie had been the pursuer tonight, but who knew what Kat might want from the man?

Gill couldn't allow the two to hook up. His mother wanted to avoid a scandal. That pairing would be instant tabloid fodder. He put on his socks and running shoes.

"Jamie isn't going to be happy, but I need to keep him away from Kat."

Maximillian jumped off the bed and sat next to Gill.

He petted him.

Sophie burst into the room without knocking. Her eyes were the color of dark chocolate. That usually meant she was angry.

"I thought you'd be with Bertrand," Gill said.

She placed her hands on her hips. "What are you doing?"

"Getting ready for a run."

She blew out a breath. "I mean tomorrow."

Maximillian trotted over to Sophie, but she didn't bend down to rub him.

"I have no idea what you're talking about," Gill said.

"You can't be Kat and Jamie's tour guide. You'll be in the way. The proverbial third wheel."

"Sightseeing isn't a date."

"But it could turn into one if you're not there." Sophie

paced back and forth. Maximillian followed at her heels. "My plan for tomorrow does not include you being a tour guide."

Her plan? He swore under his breath. This could not be happening. "You want Kat to go out with Jamie."

Sophie stopped pacing. "I want her to marry him."

The words hit like a punch to the gut.

His jaw tensed. He felt sick that Sophie was being dragged into a scheme to snare a royal husband for her friend. "Kat asked you to do this."

It wasn't a question because Gill knew the answer.

"What?" Sophie drew back. "Kat has no idea what I'm doing."

Gill rubbed the back of his neck, but that did nothing to loosen the tight muscles. He was confused. Kat had to be involved. "What exactly are you doing?"

"Playing matchmaker." Sophie leveled a finger at him. "And you'd better not tell her."

He groaned. "Stop. Before this gets out of hand."

"I'm not going to stop. Jamie and Kat are perfect together." Sophie clasped her hands to her chest. "They'll have beautiful, blue-eyed babies."

Gill's stomach churned. He thought he might be sick. "The two just met, and you're already talking babies?"

With a big grin, Sophie nodded.

Time to bring his little sister back to earth. "Not going to happen."

She finally rubbed Maximillian. "Why not?"

"Jamie is a love 'em and leave 'em, delete their contact info from his phone type of guy. Marriage isn't part of his vocabulary. Girlfriend, either."

"Jamie may have been that way in the past." Her tone wavered with uncertainty.

Gill arched a brow. "Kitty Kat?"

Sophie shrugged. "He has a unique sense of humor."

"One that could get him slapped by certain women or arrested in a few countries." Not to mention break Kat's heart. Not that Gill cared.

"He's not that bad."

"Oh, yes, he is."

Sophie tilted her head. "Maybe he was, but Jamie's changed. Or he's in the process of changing."

"How so?"

"Bertrand told me the duke has threatened to cut off Jamie's allowance if he doesn't settle down."

"No more womanizing or—"

"The duke wants him to marry. Jamie has a year to find a wife." Sophie grinned. "The timing couldn't be better."

She made the situation sound so simple. Which it wasn't. "Jamie might need a wife, but Kat—"

"When they get married, Kat and I will finally be sisters. Won't that be fabulous?"

When, not if.

In some ways, Sophie was still a dreamy girl, one who

believed that unicorns lived on the other side of rainbows. Funny considering some of the cases she worked on were heart wrenching and showed the darker side of people. But she never let that consume her. Gill didn't want to burst her bubble—no doubt, it was pink and heart shaped—but she needed to be reasonable and realistic.

"Not sisters, sisters-in-law."

"Close enough." Sophie shimmied her shoulders. "I've dreamed of this happening...forever."

"You haven't known Jamie that long."

She shook her head. "Not with him, silly. I originally wanted Kat to marry you or Jacques. But then Jacques couldn't get married and you can't stand Kat."

Gill stiffened. "I never said I couldn't stand her."

"Actions speak louder than words, dear brother. Not that Kat has ever been interested in you."

That puzzled him. Granted, Kat would have been too young back in camp, but during college, vet school, and now...

"I'm considered as much a catch as Jamie is. Perhaps a better one given my rank and wealth."

"For some women, yes. Not for Kat."

Gill should let this drop, but he couldn't. His ego stung. "Why not?"

Sophie sat on a chair. "You really want to know?"

He needed to know the reason. Not that it mattered. He wasn't getting involved with Kat. "Yes."

"Well, to start with, you're not nice to her. You haven't been nice from the day we met."

He pointed to his calf. "She's the reason I got hurt. See the scar?"

"Which shows you hold grudges," Sophie said without missing a beat. "Another checkmark against you."

He scoffed. "Kat was irresponsible."

"She was thirteen," Sophie countered.

He could picture that day as clearly as yesterday. The touch of Kat's hand as she comforted him. The bravado she'd shown opening her knife. "Perhaps it's time to let what happened by the lake go."

"How big of you."

He deserved that. "Anything else."

"You glare at Kat."

"I do not."

"Yes, you do. You always have, even back at camp. If you're not glaring, you're staring. It's borderline creepy."

Gill wanted to deny it, but he had been trying to figure out Kat. She had the right motivation to be a gold digger, except nothing she'd said lined up with that. She could have easily left with Jamie tonight after dinner, but she hadn't.

Perhaps Gill had gone overboard in his assessment of her.

"I'm not used to seeing her around here," he admitted. "I'll be more careful at how often I look at her."

Maximillian rubbed up against Sophie.

She gave him another pat. "Good, because if I didn't

know better, I'd think you liked her."

"I don't." He said the words quickly. "Anything else?"

"Yes, but this reason is mine."

"Yours?"

Sophie nodded. "I finally realized Mother would never approve of a match between the two of you, so I gave up on the dream."

"A smart move."

"But now that I'm getting married and will have a brother-in-law—"

"You want your dream to come true."

"Very much so. And no one is going to get in the way of this happening." Sophie narrowed her gaze. "You need to come up with an excuse why you can't go with them tomorrow. An illness or emergency at work. Something that sounds plausible."

"Is Kat interested in Jamie?" Gill asked.

"I haven't asked her, but Kat wants me to be happy. I want the same thing for her. Jamie would keep her laughing. He's easy on the eyes, too."

"Kat might want to marry someone she falls in love with."

"She can fall in love with Jamie. They just need time. Alone."

Nothing was going to change Sophie's mind. Gill scratched his chin. "You've got this figured out."

"Please don't get in the way of this falling together."

Falling was the wrong word. She was piecing this couple together like an intricate jigsaw puzzle. Only he had a feeling the pieces wouldn't fit as well as she imagined.

"I'll speak with Mother, but if she wants me to go sight-seeing with them…"

Sophie's shoulders sagged. "You'll have to go. If you do, please give Jamie and Kat plenty of space and time alone."

If Gill did that, he had no doubt Jamie would try to get Kitty Kat to purr. And succeed.

Gill's stomach roiled.

Not happening. The man needed to be kept in line, so did Kat. "I'll see what I can do."

THE NEXT DAY, Kat found herself stuck between two hand-some men at the National Art Museum, an older building with gargoyles on the outside and masterpieces hanging on the walls inside. She should be enjoying the artwork, but she wanted to be anywhere but here. She felt sandwiched like the peanut butter and jelly with Gill and Jamie the slices of bread.

If one was on her right, the other appeared on her left. In the limousine, up in the bell tower, and at the park where people ice skated when the temperature was cold enough. It wasn't today, but given the chilly glances exchanged by the two men, the temperature should hit freezing by early afternoon. The only one who seemed to be enjoying himself was Claude, who was not only their driver, but also Gill's bodyguard. The man used to be in some kind of Special Forces unit when he was younger. He'd been trying not to laugh since they left the castle, sending her sympathetic looks. Maybe she and Claude could sneak off and enjoy the artwork on another floor.

"The colors are so vibrant," Jamie said of a modern art painting. "Alive."

Gill nodded. "Vivid. Invocative."

"Emotional with a hint of anger," Jamie added.

Kat fought the urge to scream. Maximillian behaved better than these two. "You like this painting?"

Both men nodded.

She squinted and tried to see what she was missing. Nope. She had no idea what the artist's intention was other than mimicking a preschooler's artwork.

"What do you think?" Jamie asked.

"There's a cat that comes to the clinic who paints," she said. "I'd pay for one of those canvases. Not this mess."

"It's not that great," Gill backtracked.

Jamie nodded. "Not at all."

Had the two made a bet? Or was this a bizarre, oldest son territorial pissing match? Maybe a game of one-upmanship?

Kat had no idea what was going on, but she didn't like being caught in the middle. They definitely weren't after her because every word out of their mouths made them less attractive. She'd rather spend the day with the queen and duchess than their sons. At least Kat knew where she stood with the women.

She walked away from the painting and from them.

Gill came after her. "Where are you going?"

Jamie quickened his pace. "Wait for me."

She bit back a frustrated sigh. "I'm going to the restroom."

That was the one place the two couldn't follow her.

Inside the bathroom, Kat pulled out her cell phone to call Sophie. She would be able to tell Kat how to handle the two men. Except calling wasn't what a good bridesmaid would do.

Kat needed to lessen the bride's stress. Not add more. She had to figure this out herself.

She placed her phone back in her purse and walked out.

Both men straightened when they saw her.

"Is there something in particular you want to see in the museum?" she asked.

Jamie nodded. "There's an Impressionist exhibit on the third floor."

"The second floor has early Renaissance paintings displayed," Gill said.

"Excellent." An idea formed in Kat's mind. "Go see those, and I'll meet you in the lobby later."

Jamie's face fell.

Gill frowned. "What are you going to do?"

She motioned to the driver/bodyguard. "I'm going to see

if Claude would like to have tea."

Claude grinned. "I'd be honored, Miss Kat."

Kat walked toward him. She didn't need to glance back to see the confused expressions on Gill and Jamie's faces. A bizarre broken mirror collage gave her a perfect view of them.

"Is Kitty Kat ditching us for the old man?" Jamie asked.

"It appears so." Gill stared after her, but surprisingly, he was smiling and she thought she glimpsed pride in his eyes. "Kitty Kat must have lost her patience."

"Meow," she whispered, retracted her claws, and then smiled at Claude. "I hope you're ready for a nice cup of tea, because I am."

Chapter Eight

STANDING AT THE window in Sophie's bedroom, Kat stared at the fat snowflakes falling from the sky. "The weather forecast finally came true."

Sophie sat on a pink upholstered chair and put on her snow boots. The décor of her room was pink and white with touches of silver. A room fit for a princess. "Almost a week later than predicted."

"We've been so busy; I'm glad the snow held off until this morning."

For the past five days, Kat had been helping with the wedding and sightseeing. She'd fallen into a comfortable routine—wake with no alarm, breakfast with Sophie, wedding stuff in the morning, lunch out, sightseeing in the afternoon, and dinner with the royal family and Jamie. Most of it had been enjoyable.

An intricately patterned snowflake landed against the windowpane. Kat had grown up with winter weather, but Cedar Village, Idaho didn't get as much snow, and none had fallen this year.

She couldn't wait to feel the snow against her face. "It's really coming down now."

"We might get enough to last through Christmas."

Hard to believe that was only a week away. "I'd love to have a white Christmas."

"You and Gill both." Sophie smiled. "I'm so glad the two of you are getting along better."

"Me, too."

An unspoken truce seemed to have been reached after the art museum. Whatever competition was going on between him and Jamie had ended, though Gill continued to eye Kat with suspicion. He wasn't unpleasant when they spoke, and he hadn't accused her of anything new, so that was good.

"How are you and Jamie getting along?"

Kat faced her friend. "He's a big flirt, but not as bad as he was those first two days."

"That's because you shut him down at the art museum."

"Did Gill tell you that?"

"Claude," Sophie admitted. "I don't blame you given the way he and Gill acted, but do you like Jamie?"

Kat shrugged. "He's handsome and eager to lend a hand. It's sweet how he's been helping you with the seating arrangement for the wedding dinner."

"And…"

"I enjoy spending time with him."

"Anything else?"

Kat bit her lip. "I get the feeling if I want a kiss that I won't have to wait for mistletoe."

Sophie clapped her hands together. "Wonderful."

"Is it?"

She shrugged. "Who knows what a holiday romance could turn into?"

"One step at a time. Jamie is becoming my friend. There's nothing romantic going on."

"Yet."

Kat shook her head.

"I hate leaving you today." Sophie stood and adjusted the top of her boots. "Are you sure it's okay if I run into the office?"

"Go." Kat understood. Truth was, she'd been tempted to call the animal hospital almost every day since she'd arrived, but she hadn't. The techs didn't need to waste their time talking to her about animals when she was too far away to help. "I know you want your work finished before the wedding."

"Yes, but you've been such a big help. I wish you could have a day full of nothing but fun."

"I've been having lots of fun." The other day, she'd traveled from the west to the east borders of Alistonia. The country might be small, but it was rich in history and tradition. "I've been getting a real feel for your country and people."

"Are you going to meet with Isaac today?"

The kind waiter, who Kat now called a friend, had been giving her royal etiquette lessons. She'd learned how to eat European style with her fork in her left hand, how to wave during the parade that would occur after the wedding ceremony, and how to greet others without shaking hands.

"No, he's off today. Jamie's already gone to town. I don't know what your mother and Gill are up to." Royal duties kept those two busy with ribbon cuttings, groundbreakings, speeches, and luncheons throughout Alistonia. "I'm spending today on my own. Peace and quiet will be nice."

"You deserve it. Acting as the liaison between my mother and the duchess must be draining."

A root canal would be better than spending another day relaying messages between the queen and the duchess, but Kat wouldn't add to Sophie's stress by admitting that.

"They are quite the pair." Kat left out how the two women argued worse than a divorcing couple trying to figure out the medical treatment options for a family pet. "But it isn't long until the big day."

Sophie put on a long down coat. "I keep hoping Talia won't quit."

"She won't."

The wedding planner had been brought to tears two days ago, but Talia had confided to Kat that the crown prince had offered her a bonus if she didn't quit. The amount made putting up with the two mothers worthwhile. Leave it to Gill to take care of his sister.

"Don't worry," Kat said. "Everything's coming together. And Bertrand will be here soon."

"I can't wait." Sophie wrapped a plaid, wool scarf around her neck. She glanced at the clock on her nightstand. "Oh, look at the time. I'm late."

As usual. "Have a great day. I'm going to get ready for a walk."

"If you want company, Gill may be around. He didn't mention going anywhere."

Kat's muscles bunched. Getting along better was not the same as seeking him out. "I'm sure he has work to do."

"Yes, but like you, he needs to work less and play more."

"I'll see if he's taking a break when I head out."

"Do." Sophie hugged Kat. "I'll text you when I'm on my way home."

As Sophie headed toward the stairs, Kat went to her room and put on her coat, gloves, and hat.

Downstairs, she glanced toward Gill's office. The door was closed. She hesitated, but only for a moment. He had work to do. No reason to bother him.

Coward.

She was where Gill was concerned. Her stomach felt funny whenever he was nearby. She didn't feel that way when she was with Jamie.

Kat hurried into the music room and out the French doors onto the patio.

The cold air made her zip her coat all the way to her

chin. Snow fell around her. She couldn't believe how a little white stuff on the ground changed the whole landscape.

Smiling, she tilted back her head and stuck out her tongue.

"Catch any?" Gill asked.

She jumped. "Where did you come from?"

He wore a coat and gloves, but no hat. His leather dress shoes weren't made for this kind of weather, but he didn't seem bothered by that. "I live here."

"I meant just now. Your office door was closed."

His mouth slanted. "You've been checking up on me?"

"No." His suspicious tone annoyed her. "Jamie's spending the day in town. Sophie thought you might want to take a walk, but when I saw the closed door, I figured you were working."

"I was on a call."

"And now?"

He inhaled. "I'm enjoying the snow. You?"

"Same." She shoved her gloved hands into her pockets.

"Cold?"

"I should start walking." She headed down the stairs toward the garden and heard footsteps behind her. Gill was following her.

She glanced over her shoulder. Snowflakes clung to his hair. He looked so adorable.

Wait. Adorable wasn't a word she should use to describe Gill. She faced forward and kept walking. Her boots crunched through the layer of snow on the path.

"You've been keeping busy," he said.

She focused on putting one foot in front of the other without slipping on the snow. That might help her avoid the temptation to look back at him. "The wedding is a week away."

"So I keep being reminded."

She walked through an archway to enter the garden. "You don't sound happy about that."

"Everyone seems to have forgotten Christmas is coming."

The snow gave the garden an artsy feel with the bare branches. Too bad she wasn't a photographer. "Not forgotten, but the wedding is first up."

He walked next to her. "Yes, and the date was selected to allow guests to return home in time for their Christmas Eve festivities."

The concern in his voice surprised her. "You really care about the holidays."

"It's my favorite time of the year."

"Why is that?"

Three snowflakes landed on his nose, but he didn't brush them off. "The castle is so big it can feel more like a museum than a house. But whenever I came home from school for the holidays, the trees and decorations made the castle feel more…homey. Every December, the place feels that way again."

"I'm fortunate to be here during Christmastime then."

Though she imagined this garden—dead during winter—must be beautiful with flowers blooming in the springtime.

"Especially now that it's snowing," he said.

Kat turned onto a narrower path. Her foot slipped. Her leg slid forward, but her upper body went the opposite way.

She held out her arms to regain her balance.

Oh, no. She was going down.

Gill grabbed her. "I've got you. You won't fall."

One of his hands held onto her arm. The other was around her waist. He held her close. His warm breath blew against her head. The scent of his aftershave surrounded her.

"Are you okay?" he asked.

Physically, yes. Emotionally, she wasn't so sure.

Heat radiated from him like a furnace. Whatever chill she'd felt from the cold temperature and snow had disappeared. Being held like this felt way too good.

And it shouldn't.

Not with him.

"Kat?"

She looked at him.

Big mistake.

His face—make that his lips—were right there. So close she could see the lines of his mouth. And boy, did that mouth look good.

Gill stared at her as if seeing her for the first time. No smile, but no frown, either.

Kat had no idea what she was doing, except she wasn't in any hurry to have him let go of her. But they couldn't stand here like this forever.

A few more seconds might be too much.

Too dangerous.

She swallowed around the lump in her throat. "I'm okay. Thanks."

Her voice sounded deep and raw, not normal.

She backed away, but he didn't let go of her.

Gill kept his arm around her. "Make sure you have your balance, so you don't fall."

Kat felt off-kilter, but she had a feeling that had to do with him, not the slippery path. She straightened. "I do."

Gill let go, and she felt a sudden chill.

"Snow turns the grounds into a winter wonderland, but there's still ice to watch out for."

She nodded. "I'll pay better attention to where I step."

"Not just out here," he said. "You'll have to scout out the locations of the mistletoe before the reception starts."

"That's too premeditated."

"And finding someone to kiss under the mistletoe ahead of time isn't?"

"I think I'm going to be more spontaneous about that."

"Spontaneous." He pronounced the word slowly, as if it were a foreign term. Maybe for him, it was.

"Yes. If everything is planned out ahead of time, that will take the fun out of it."

"And the element of fate?"

"Exactly."

"But what if no one else wants to be spontaneous and kiss under the mistletoe?"

"There's always Jamie."

Gill's expression pinched. "Kitty Kat has been kissed by the marquess?"

She flinched. Gill didn't seem the nosey type, especially where she was concerned, but her friendship—and that was all it was—with Jamie wasn't something she wanted to discuss.

"I don't kiss and tell. Or not kiss and tell." Best to change the subject. A gate was ahead of them. "This leads down to the stable, right?"

Gill nodded. "Your nose is turning pink."

"So are your cheeks."

"We should go back inside."

"Go ahead." She let the cold air fill her lungs. "I'm just getting started."

"I'll stay out here a few more minutes."

Curiosity was getting the better of her. She had to ask. "Is this some kind of keep-your-enemy-close kind of tactic?"

His jaw thrust forward. "You see me as an enemy?"

"We've never been that friendly, so we can't be frenemies."

"I've been friendly," he countered. "I warned you about my mother."

"That was a quid pro quo for my mentioning Sophie's wedding diet. I don't need examples. I asked why because I was curious."

"You know what happened to the curious cat."

"Yes, but I'll take my chances."

A cry sounded. She froze. "What was that?"

"What?"

"I heard a noise. It sounded like a child."

"There aren't any children on the grounds or living nearby. I didn't hear anything."

Kat had. She listened. Nothing.

"Are you—"

"Shhh."

Another noise sounded. A cry, no a whimper. Every muscle tensed. Not a child. A dog.

Maximillian.

Adrenaline surged.

Kat didn't need a degree in veterinary medicine to recognize a cry of pain. The anguished sound hurt her heart.

She ran toward the sound.

Something was very wrong.

"WHERE ARE YOU going?" Gill yelled after Kat. He had no idea why she was running, but he followed her down the path and across the lawn. She didn't slow. If anything, she ran faster.

A noise sounded.

That must have been what she heard.

A cry. Or a…

His chest tightened.

Maximillian.

His pulse kicked up. He'd never heard his dog make that sound.

Kat stopped and dropped to her knees next to Maximillian, who lay on the snow with his left front paw caught in a trap.

No. Gill's heart pounded against his rib cage. Traps weren't used on the castle grounds. How could this have happened?

"Don't worry, Max," she said in a comforting voice. "We'll have you fixed up in no time."

Gill's insides twisted. "He's bleeding."

"There's no trail of blood, so that's a good sign." She examined Maximillian's leg. "This trap was loose. Look at the prints in the snow. He was probably trying to make it back to the castle."

She sounded competent and in control.

Gill felt the opposite way. A million and one bad things circled around his mind like speed skaters practicing on the local rink.

He kneeled next to her, but she stopped him from reaching out to his dog.

"Be careful." She touched Gill's arm. "Sometimes dogs

that are injured act differently than they usually do."

"We're here, mate." Gill forced the words from his dry throat. A lump burned, making it difficult to talk. He swallowed, but that didn't help.

An ache spread from his stomach to his heart. He wanted to make his dog better, but he didn't know how. His mother had once mentioned how hard seeing him and Sophie hurt or ill was for her. He hadn't understood until now.

He looked at Kat. "Is Maximillian going to be okay?"

Once the words were out, Gill wasn't sure he wanted to know the answer.

"The damage to his foot could be much worse." Her voice held no worry. She spoke professionally like the veterinarians who worked at the animal clinic in town. "I need to get this trap off before more damage is done."

"Let's call his vet first." The words tumbled out of his mouth before he could stop them.

"Gill, I know what I'm doing. I would never hurt Maximillian." Her tone sounded sincere. "Please, trust me."

That was the problem. Gill still didn't trust her.

The entire royal guard brigade seemed to be standing on his chest. He could barely breathe. Sophie and Maximillian meant more to Gill than life itself. "I—"

"Hold his muzzle and keep him steady." No emotion was in her voice. "Got it?"

Surely, college and work at an animal hospital had only improved her skills with animals.

Gill nodded. He had to trust her.

He held Maximillian's muzzle with one hand and kept his upper body steady with the other.

Please be okay.

"I'm going to pull these levers to release pressure on the jaws." She took a breath and moved the two levers toward her. The jaws opened. Not fully, but enough. "His foot is free."

Gill released the breath he hadn't realized he was holding.

Kat examined the paw. "It doesn't look like he needs stitches, but call your vet. They may want to examine him and put him on antibiotics to ward off an infection."

"But he's going to be okay?"

Smiling, she nodded.

Thank goodness.

"You can let go of him," she added.

Gill did, and the dog stood on all fours, but he seemed to be favoring his injured paw slightly. He'd carry the dog back to the castle to be on the safe side. "Thank you."

"You're welcome."

Max licked her face. She laughed and gave the dog a hug.

One of those might be nice. A hug. Gill wasn't tempted to kiss her.

"You're welcome, too. Such a handsome boy." Laughing, she patted the dog. "But let's not do this again. You might not be so lucky."

"And you might not be here. I'm relieved you were."

And taken charge in spite of his doubts. Gill trusted her vet skills. Yes, he'd hesitated, and he felt bad for doing that, but he didn't trust *her*. Or know if he could. Still, he owed Kat for helping Max—make that Maximillian.

Gill picked up his dog and was greeted with a lick, too. "I'd like to show my gratitude."

"That's not necessary." She stood. Her pants were wet from sitting on the ground, but she looked beautiful with her pink cheeks and warm smile. "I was only doing my job."

"I understand that." He wanted to make this effort, but he needed her to go along. "Please allow me to do this. If not for me, then for Maximillian. And Sophie," he added, to make Kat saying no more difficult.

"Okay."

Uncertainty filled her voice, but she hadn't said no. He needed to set a date and time or she might change her mind about allowing him to thank her.

"Keep tomorrow afternoon free." If his calendar were full, he'd have Frederick rearrange the schedule. And he'd make sure Jamie had something to do, too.

She brushed off her knees and backside. Something Gill would have helped her with if asked. What was he thinking? The last thing he needed to do was touch any part of her.

"What do you have in mind?" she asked.

Gill was about to tell her, but then he remembered her first night at the castle. Had that been only a week ago? It seemed like she had been there longer.

"I'm not going to tell her, but I'll tell you the way she did," Gill whispered into the dog's ear the way Kat had in her room, and then he looked at her. "If you want to know, ask him."

THE NEXT AFTERNOON, Kat checked her reflection in the mirror one last time. She hadn't forgotten to put on makeup or earrings. She brushed her hair one last time.

That was as good as it would get.

The door to Gill's room was open. She peeked inside.

A soccer game was on the television screen. Jamie lay on the floor with a pillow under his head and Max at his side. The two looked comfortable and cozy.

That brought a smile to her face, so did knowing her diagnosis had been correct. Maximillian had been treated by his vet yesterday and sent home with antibiotics, pain medication, a cone around his neck, and a big appetite.

"How's it going?" she asked.

Jamie looked over but didn't move. She had a feeling he didn't want to disturb Maximillian. That was sweet of him.

"He's resting." Jamie kept a hand on Max. "He doesn't like wearing the cone of shame. I wouldn't want to wear, that, either."

"His paw will heal faster without him licking it."

"That's what Gill said, but Max doesn't understand."

Jamie rubbed the dog. "But you'll be better soon."

So cute.

Max's injury seemed to have had brought Jamie and Gill closer. Last night, when Jamie had arrived back at the castle, he'd brought enough treats and bones to feed a dozen dogs. And when she checked on Max before going to bed, Jamie and Gill were in here sitting with the dog and discussing the changes in the European Union.

"Thanks for watching Max," she said.

"Least I can do. He'll be family soon." Jamie blew her a kiss. "Have fun with Gill and be good."

He was such a flirt.

She had to laugh. "Always."

But a part of her was wondering what might happen if she wasn't as good as she usually was.

Chapter Nine

WALKING DOWNSTAIRS, KAT'S emotions bounced from anticipation to apprehension over the outing. She wondered what Gill had planned for his thank you. His invitation appeared genuine, but he didn't seem like the kind of man to go out of his way for anyone who wasn't family. On more than one occasion, Queen Louise hadn't hesitated in letting Kat know she wasn't one of them.

Sophie stood in the foyer. "You look so nice."

"I'm wearing jeans, snow boots, and a parka."

"And you look good in them. Too bad that's wasted on Gill."

"I said goodbye to Jamie."

"Never waste an opportunity when you look hot." Sophie laughed. "Nervous about what my brother has in store for today?"

"A little. I understand your honeymoon-packing dilemma better." Kat's fingertips dug into the fabric of her hat and gloves. "It's hard to know what to wear when you don't know what you'll be doing."

Inside or outdoors? Town or countryside?

The possibilities were endless, but best not to think of this as a grand adventure. Rather, an afternoon one. This was Gill, a man who was as practical as he was proper. Keeping her expectations low was the smart thing to do.

This was his way of saying thank you. Kat hoped she would get to know Gill better without anyone else around.

Strictly for Sophie's sake.

"I'm so happy Bertrand gave me a temperature range. Twenty-two to thirty-one degrees Celsius."

Kat did a quick conversion. That was low seventies to high eighties in Fahrenheit. "Bikini weather."

"No robe required." Sophie straightened one of the garlands on the staircase banister. "I'm thrilled Gill wants to do this for you. I should have known Max would be the catalyst. I always hoped you could be friends."

An outing was a long way from being friends, but Sophie being so pleased made Kat happy. "I just hope Gill knows he doesn't have to do anything to thank me."

"He knows, but you saved his dog."

"I removed a trap, and Max wasn't that injured."

Gill still hadn't figured out where the trap had been placed or why. The groundskeeper and his crew swore none had been used on the grounds. Yet, somehow, Max had found one. That bothered her as much as it did Gill.

"Not injured worse thanks to you." Sophie glanced at the

front door. "I heard what the vet said. Gill has something nice planned."

"A tour of the dungeon complete with torture device demonstrations," Kat joked.

"He loves his dog too much. I'm sure this will be special."

Kat wanted to know what Gill considered special.

The front door opened. He walked in wearing a green parka and black pants. Snowflakes rested on his hat and shoulders.

Wow. She wet her lips. Tailored suits weren't the only things hanging in his closet. The casual clothes suited him. He looked less crown prince and more everyday guy. She liked that. A lot.

He adjusted his gloves. "Ready?"

She pressed her shoulders back. "Yes."

"Have fun." Sophie shifted her weight from foot to foot. Her arms moved back and forth. She acted more excited than Gill and Kat combined. "And no matter what, get along."

"We will," they said at the same time.

Their gazes met, and they exchanged smiles.

Okay. This wasn't so bad. Maybe becoming friends was a possibility. Kat walked out the door.

A shiny silver sports car idled in front of her.

"Where's Claude?" she asked.

"I'm driving today."

That was a surprise. Especially since Claude did more than chauffer the royal family. "No security concerns?"

"We'll be fine." Gill opened the passenger door. "Your chariot awaits."

Chariot was the right word given the engine's horsepower. She got inside, sank into the black leather seat, and fastened her seat belt. Heat blasted her from the air vents. Christmas carols played on the stereo.

She had no idea how the prince earned a living—a salary from the country or if the family was old money—but everything from the dashboard to the armrest screamed luxurious and expensive. The car even smelled rich.

He closed her door, walked around the front of the car, and slid into the driver's seat. Windshield wipers swished away the falling snow.

Gill buckled in. "Sit back and enjoy the ride."

"You're not telling me where we are going?"

"Maximillian didn't tell you?"

"Haha. I suppose I deserve that."

"You do." He grinned. "I will tell you that you're dressed appropriately."

That was a relief. "I'll have to thank Max for the clothing suggestion."

Gill drove past the guard station and away from the castle.

Snow covered the foothills. The tree branches looked covered in thick white icing. She sighed. "Christmas-card perfect."

"Snow makes it feel more like the holidays."

Kat leaned closer to the window. "That's for sure."

Carols had been playing at the castle, but all the white blanketing the landscape made it feel more like Christmastime.

"The scenery is gorgeous." She pressed closer to the window. "I half expect to see Santa and his reindeer flying overhead."

He laughed. "It's still daylight. Santa only travels when the children are asleep."

"It's nighttime somewhere in the world."

"Back home?"

"Yes." Cedar Village seemed so far away from here. She hoped everyone was doing well at work, both her coworkers and the animals.

"Homesick?" he asked.

"More than I thought I'd be."

He glanced at her. "How so?"

From this angle, he looked like his father in the photographs in the sitting room. The late king consort had been an extremely handsome man, tall with curly brown hair and an ever-present smile.

"Cedar Village has a population of less than twelve hundred. I'm halfway through a three-year commitment at a veterinary clinic there, and though I love my job, the town is so—"

"Small."

"Tiny. I grew up on a farm, but there were towns and two universities nearby. I went to school at one of them." Kat had no idea why she was telling him this, but the words kept coming out. "I thought after I graduated, I'd move to a bigger city, but I'm back where I've always been. A rural farm community smaller than the one where I grew up. This is my first time traveling out of the United States."

"You're kidding?"

"Nope. I've dreamed about going on grand adventures my entire life, but my first trip abroad, I'm missing home sweet home."

"It's familiar."

"That must be it."

Gill drove into town. "What other adventures do you have in mind?"

"Africa."

"That would count as a grand adventure. Why do you want to go there?"

She imagined her mother and father. The picture in her mind was from a photograph she carried in her wallet. The last one they'd sent.

"That's where my parents lived and worked."

"Africa is a magical place."

"That's what I've heard." Talking to Gill was easy. More so than she imagined when being around him left her feeling on edge. Maybe Sophie was right, and they were becoming friends. "I told you something about me. It's your turn."

"There's not much to say."

"It doesn't have to be a deep, dark secret."

Gill glanced her way. "I don't have one of those. Do you?"

"No, but this is about you."

He tapped his thumbs against the steering wheel. "My mother didn't want me to get a dog. She actually forbade it."

"Why?"

"The list of her reasons is long and boring and reads like a peerage registry."

Sophie had showed Kat the tome that listed all the royalty. "But you have Max."

"Yes."

She waited for him to say more. He didn't, but Kat wanted to know more. "You didn't listen to your mother."

"The more I thought about her reasons, the more I didn't care."

"Sophie says you're a rule follower."

"I am, but as soon as I saw Maximillian…"

He fell in love.

The words were unspoken, but implied and tugged at Kat's heart.

"The dog is my exception to following the rules," he added. "Bringing Maximillian home was the best decision I've made. I'd do it again in a heartbeat."

"Max is your act of rebellion."

Gill's hands tightened around the steering wheel. "Yes, I suppose he is."

"You did well." Kat never expected Gill to tell her something personal, but she appreciated him doing so and felt closer to him. A way she'd hoped to feel at the end of today, not at the beginning. "Max is a great dog."

"The best."

Gill parked in a lot off the main street. Only a few spots remained, which surprised Kat. She'd never seen this many cars in one spot during her trips to town.

She exited the car.

Snowflakes landed on her face and jacket. Her boots sank into the snow. Another day in winter wonderland. She hoped this one didn't end with any injuries or a trip to the veterinarian's office.

He came around the front of the car and stood by her side. "You're supposed to let me do that."

"Sorry." The condensation from her breath hung on the air. "I'm not used to having car doors opened for me."

"Then you're hanging with the wrong sort."

"Does that make you the right sort?" she joked.

"Today, yes." His tone was light and playful—a way he didn't act around her. "We'll have to wait until tomorrow to see if I still am."

Seeing him act so carefree touched something inside her. Kat had never been able to imagine him being anything other than the sullen teen from camp and the unwelcoming prince she'd seen when she arrived at the castle. But now...

Gill was so different. He was dressed like any other Alistonian, not the crown prince, but more than his clothing had changed. His smile appeared so readily. His voice was softer and gentler. And his gaze wasn't accusing her of anything.

She could get used to this.

The snowflakes became smaller. Not as many fell.

He opened the trunk, removed a red sack with something inside, and swung the bag's strap over his shoulder.

"What's that?" she asked. "Or is that a surprise, too?"

"Patience."

"You're testing mine."

"Not much longer."

"Unless this is all a ruse." If eyes could laugh, his were. Only this time, he was laughing with her, not at her. She liked that. "There could be nothing in the bag, and the only place we're going is around the block and back to the car."

"That's true, but this is not a ruse. I promise. There is something in the bag. And we're going somewhere. Satisfied?"

She winked. "For now."

That made him laugh.

She stared at the footprints in the snow. They went in both directions. "Which way?"

He motioned to a street corner. "Around there."

She expected to follow him so waited for Gill to go first. Isaac had told her about walking behind Queen Louise and

Prince Guillaume, not next to them and never in front of either.

"Waiting for something?" Gill asked.

"You're supposed to go first."

"Let's forget protocol today." He waved his hand toward the sidewalk. "No one will say anything if we walk together."

"You're the prince." Kat fell in step with him.

A school appeared on her right; it was surrounded by a tall, wrought iron fence. The country's flag fluttered from a flagpole near the edge of a playground—one that looked more modern than the old building made of stone. The large, three-story school had to be at least a hundred years old.

Children stood in rows on the front steps. Each wore a blue coat with a red hat and yellow scarf. A few whispered. Some giggled. Several pointed at Gill.

Kat touched her chest. "They are so cute."

"Let's take a closer look."

Gill opened the gate, and she passed through. He closed the gate behind him.

The snow had turned to flurries. Being surrounded by the tiny flakes made Kat feel as if they were standing inside a snow globe. Everything around them looked so Christmassy she could almost believe they were.

The children sang "Welcome Christmas" from *How the Grinch Stole Christmas*. The young voices sounded so sweet, and the lyrics clogged her throat with emotion.

The song transported her back to her childhood and watching the show every year with her grandparents. She had the DVD somewhere in her apartment. Probably packed away with the Christmas stuff she'd left in the closet this year.

Warmth pooled at the center of Kat's chest. "I love this song."

"I know."

Huh? She wanted to ask him how, but not while the children sang.

The song ended, and she clapped. So did Gill, who also whistled uncharacteristically.

The children laughed.

She glanced his way. "How did you know I liked this song?"

"I asked Sophie and phoned the school this morning. Fortunately, the children are singing the song at their upcoming holiday concert, so they included it for you."

"For me?"

Two children climbed down and stood in front of the others. Soloists, perhaps.

"I thought you might like your own mini Christmas concert."

This was all for her. Kat looked around. Her heart drummed in her chest. "Like? I love it."

This might be Gill's way of saying thank you, but his effort made her feel special. A way she hadn't felt in a very long time.

Too long.

She couldn't believe *he* was the one who'd done this for her.

"But…" Trying not to smile too big, Kat stared down her nose at him. "Who are you, and what did you do to Prince Annoying?"

He laughed. "He's around here somewhere. I can find him if you'd like."

"No, thanks. I'd prefer if he not make an appearance today."

The two children in front sang the first verse of "Away in the Manger," and then the rest of the choir joined in. "Deck the Halls" followed, and "We Wish You a Merry Christmas" was next.

The children bowed.

She applauded. "Bravo."

"Now it's our turn to thank the performers." He removed the red sack from his shoulder and opened it. "Grab a handful of candy canes and pass them out."

Bright-eyed, smiling children swarmed like bear cubs to honey. But no small hand reached forward. Each took their turn.

"Here you go." She handed a candy cane to a small boy wearing glasses. "Lovely singing."

"Thank you, miss."

All were so polite. Many seemed to want a minute of

Gill's time. A word, here. A high five, there. Your Highness sounded with every breath.

His laughter grew, so did his smile.

Gill might be Crown Prince Guillaume of Alistonia, but he looked more like a man having fun. And a…

Father.

Kat's mouth went dry. The temperature seemed to warm even though she could see her own breath.

She'd never imagined him that way before.

Okay, he'd been a great doggy dad yesterday and last night with Max. But with the kids hanging on his every word and him doing his best to make sure no one was ignored, she could picture him with curly-haired, smiling children of his own.

Fighting the urge to move closer to him, she handed out more candy canes, but she kept sneaking peeks at Gill. She'd asked the question already.

Who are you, and what did you do to Prince Annoying?

Only now, Kat wasn't joking. She wanted to know the answer so she could figure out who the real Gill might be.

WITH THE CHILDREN inside their classrooms, Gill stood outside in the schoolyard with Kat next to him. Snow flurries continued to fall. But her wide smile was enough to keep him warm.

As he folded the red sack into a small rectangle, his gaze

kept straying back to her.

Kat's blue eyes reminded him of the aquamarine pendant in the royal jewel collection. Exquisite.

But he wasn't here to admire her. He'd wanted to repay her, and he was. But everything he thought he knew about her, everything he believed, seemed…wrong.

Sophie said Kat was a hardworking veterinarian who had no life outside of work. Could she not be trying to find a way to pay off her loans and get out of her contract with the rural animal clinic? Or was she exactly as he and his mother had thought? A woman willing to do anything to get what she wanted.

Africa was next on Kat's list of grand adventures.

That wouldn't be a cheap trip.

She could still have ulterior motives for attending Sophie's wedding, couldn't she?

"The candy canes went quick," Kat said, "but I think the kids love their crown prince as much as they like candy."

An unfamiliar lightness centered in his chest, as if buoyed with contentment. "I enjoy spending time here."

"You come often?"

"I participate in a literacy program. I read to the classes, and they read to me."

"Fun."

He nodded. "My brother Jacques founded a summer reading project for libraries, and then I expanded the program into the schools."

"Sounds like two worthwhile programs."

Gill nodded. "Jacques had so many ideas. Solid ones that could be implemented without costing too much. They called him the people's prince. Now he's known as the people's priest."

"Do you see him often?"

"No." Not much. Gill felt a pang. "He's assigned to Rome, and he and my mother no longer talk."

Swallowing a sigh, Gill tucked the folded sack into his coat pocket.

"I saved a candy cane for you." Kat handed it to him. "It's not much, but I want you to know how wonderful the concert was. Your arranging this was so thoughtful."

Not as thoughtful as her helping Maximillian. "Glad you enjoyed it."

His favorite part hadn't been the concert but Kat's reactions to the songs. Unlike Sophie, Kat didn't show her feelings to the world. She acted so in control at the castle, but not out here today. Watching the different emotions play across her face pleased him and made him want to see more. He wondered what she was like at home.

"It must be time to head back to the castle," Kat said.

She sounded like she wasn't ready to leave. Good, because he had more in store for her. "We're not finished."

Excitement twinkled in her eyes. "Really?"

The anticipation in the one word made him want to tell her what they were doing next. But that would ruin the surprise, one he thought she'd enjoy as much as the concert.

"Of course," he said instead. "A proper thank you needs more than one part. Come with me."

For a weekday afternoon, the streets were crowded more than usual, but he knew others were heading to the same place as them.

Kat stared up at a sign hanging outside a flower shop. The painted plaque hung from a metal scroll. "This street looks like something from a jigsaw puzzle."

"Tourism drives the economy here."

They turned the corner.

She stopped. Her lips parted, and she gasped. "What is this place?"

"Our Christmas Market. Every town in Alistonia has one."

Rows of booths had been set up on the closed-off street. Portable shops were decorated for the holidays with lights and garland. Some sold food. Others offered gift items. Several displayed holiday decorations, including Christmas trees.

Excitement shone in her eyes. She rubbed her gloves together. "This is amazing."

Gill thought she might like this. "Where would you like to start?"

"Let's begin on one end so we don't miss anything. I have a feeling I'll be able to finish all my Christmas shopping tonight."

"You sound happy."

"I am." Her shoulders wiggled. "Thanks to you."

He extended his arm. "Shall we, milady?"

Beaming, she hooked her arm around his. "Let the shopping commence."

Booth after booth, they explored, examined items, and tasted food like the town's famous Christmas cookies. She purchased several handmade Christmas tree ornaments as well as knitted items. Her looks of awe made him feel like a super hero. This was one of his favorite holiday traditions, but seeing the market and his hometown through Kat's fresh eyes made him savor things he'd forgotten and taken for granted.

"There's one final booth," he said. "This one has more Christmas items."

"There can never be enough of those. Oh, look." Kat picked up a large crystal suspended by a red satin ribbon and decorated with mistletoe. "Sophie would love this."

"I'll buy it for her."

"Put away your wallet." Kat removed hers from her tote bag that was crammed with small sacks and gift bags. "I'm buying this for my friend."

A sales clerk in a long wool coat and traditional hat wrapped up the ornament. She handed the bag to Kat and smiled expectedly. "You're standing under mistletoe, miss."

Kat looked up. Her face paled, not snow white, but close. She bit her lower lip. "I'll just pretend I'm not."

The change in her posture and voice bothered Gill. Fun had disappeared, and worry set in. She didn't look like a woman wanting to kiss a prince, a marquess, or any man for that matter. Gill wanted her to relax and have fun. He knew what might do that.

A kiss under the mistletoe would be a nice end to their wonderful afternoon.

He leaned toward her. "You don't want to disappoint the sales clerk, do you?"

"There's no one to kiss," Kat whispered.

Her words stung. What was he? "I'm here."

"You're not interested in mistletoe kisses." She kept her voice low, but he heard the dismissal in her tone. "At least ones with me."

No, he hadn't been, but something about her tempted him now. He was immune to her charm so he wasn't worried. "One won't kill me."

Her nose wrinkled in a cute way. "Gee, thanks."

Gill couldn't tell if she was joking. No matter.

She'd mention a peck the other day. No harm in doing that.

Lowering his head, he brushed his lips against hers.

Soft and warm and…

A lightning rod of energy zigzagged through him.

What was that?

Self-preservation made him jerk back.

But not before his pulse roared through him and reached

his ears.

Gill wasn't sure what was happening, but he didn't like it.

Her closed-mouth smile didn't tell him if she'd felt the same thing when their lips touched. He didn't want to ask because what if she hadn't?

"I hope that wasn't too miserable for you," she teased.

He struggled to calm his heart rate. No kiss had ever felt like that. And they'd barely touched lips. No tongue action.

Strange. He didn't like not being able to explain things.

"Not miserable." He kept his voice steady. "Passable."

She made a face.

"Joking." The kiss had been incredible. He wanted another, but only if she did. "Prince Annoying, however, might say something like that and mean it. Now Prince Charming…"

"If you want the charming title, you'll have to work harder." Her tone teased. She sounded almost flirtatious.

Anticipation roared through his veins, "Really?"

Kat nodded. "But you're on your way."

He grinned. "Thank you, I think."

"No, thank you. Again." The color had returned to her face. Her cheeks looked pink. "Now I can cross a mistletoe kiss off my list."

That wasn't what he expected. "There will be mistletoe at the wedding ball."

"One was all I needed." She sounded certain, and it left

him strangely disappointed. "Now I can work on finding someone to kiss on New Year's Eve."

He didn't have any plans to ring in the new year, and even though he wasn't sure if he could fully trust Kat, he wouldn't mind kissing her again.

Even without mistletoe.

ON THE DRIVE back to the castle, Kat stared out the passenger window. She couldn't see much in the twilight—trees and snow—but that was okay. A blur of passing scenery was better than looking at Gill behind the steering wheel. Her gaze kept straying in his direction. Any more and she'd be leering.

"You're quiet," he said.

Only her voice. Her body and her mind were still going haywire from his kiss. "Thinking about this afternoon."

"A good time."

"Yes, it was."

And his kiss…

One touch of his lips had changed everything.

Okay, not really.

But Kat felt…different. She tried to understand the sensations—the way her five senses felt heightened—but couldn't. She did know there was a new awareness of him that hadn't been there before. She wasn't sure if she liked it or not.

She glanced at his profile. Same strong features. Handsome ones like his father's. But those lips…

Kat faced forward.

A touch of Gill's lips on hers had curled her toes and made her dream of happily ever after.

Bad. Bad. Bad.

The man was no prince charming. Not even close.

Why had he kissed her?

You don't want to disappoint the sales clerk, do you?

He hadn't given Kat time to say no or anything else. Maybe he'd thought this was important to do. A tradition. Not something he craved.

One won't kill me.

She couldn't say the same. Her pulse hadn't slowed yet. Neither had her heart rate. Worse, her lips tingled. And they'd barely kissed.

Yet something had happened.

A shock. A connection.

She didn't know if he'd felt it, but the way he jerked away told her that he might have.

Don't ask.

Don't say a word.

Forget the kiss ever happened.

Being curious was not a smart idea in this situation, even if she wanted to know if he'd felt something, too.

No matter what he felt or didn't feel, nothing more would happen.

He was Sophie's brother and the crown prince, and he

didn't like her.

Kat was an American in town for only one more week and not interested in a one-sided romance. Or a fling.

Best to put this behind her and move on.

As he drove toward the guardhouse, the gates opened. A uniformed guard saluted, and Gill returned the gesture.

He parked. "We're home."

His home. Not hers.

She had a good job, but home was a far-off concept that wouldn't happen until her student loan payments didn't take up such a big chunk of her budget.

"Thanks again. For today." The words sounded disjointed. The way she felt. She pressed her lips together to keep from saying anything else.

He opened his car door. "All that shopping made me hungry. I may have to eat my candy cane before dinner."

His words charmed her. "I won't tell."

She got out of the car.

He did, too, removed her purchases from the truck, and handed her the bags.

Kat reached into one of them, pulled out a smaller bag, and gave it to him. "This is for you."

He stared at the bag with a perplexed expression. "Today was to thank you for taking such good care of Max."

Max, not Maximillian. She wriggled her toes. "Now it's my turn to show my gratitude for you taking me out today."

She'd made the purchase when he'd been talking to a

person at another booth. An impulse buy. She'd bought two. One for each of them. A way to remember the day.

Although, she doubted she would forget. Especially after the kiss.

Gill looked inside. "Lots of tissue paper."

Kat wet her lips. The gift had been inexpensive and was kind of silly, but she wanted to do something after the effort he'd put out for her.

He pulled out the snow globe with a dog, snowman, and Christmas tree inside. His eyes widened. "That looks like Max. I mean, Maximillian."

"I thought so, too. Except the dog is more brown than orange."

Gill turned the knob on the bottom.

The song *We Wish You a Merry Christmas* played.

His mouth opened. "The children sang that song."

She nodded. "A nice reminder of today."

"A wonderful one." He stared at the snow globe. "You didn't have to do this."

She shrugged, though she didn't feel indifferent about this at all. She'd hoped he liked the gift and wasn't sure why it meant so much to her that he did. "I wanted to."

"I'm glad you did." He placed the snow globe back in the bag.

Her gaze zeroed in on his smiling lips.

His kissable lips.

The fluttery feeling she'd experience around him before

returned with a vengeance. So much so she had to force herself not to flee to her room to get away from him.

Confusion swirled. She had male friends from school and ones at the clinic. But none had made her feel this way. Not even close. And she hadn't kissed any of them. Only dates or boyfriends.

What was going on? Kat clutched her shopping bags so she wouldn't drop anything. And how did she make it stop?

Chapter Ten

IN HIS BEDROOM, Gill wound the knob on the bottom of the snow globe. The music made him feel so content, as if Santa would be arriving with everything Gill had ever wanted. As snowflakes fell on the vignette inside, he placed the snow globe on the nightstand.

Maximillian jumped on the bed. The cone around his head knocked into Gill.

"That dog looks like you." He rubbed his dog's side. "I'm glad Kat bought this for us, but I know you'd rather have a biscuit." He reached into the top drawer, removed a bone-shaped treat that Jamie had bought, and gave it to the dog. "Here you go. Don't leave any crumbs on the bed."

That wasn't likely since the dog had the skills of a vacuum cleaner.

The music stopped.

That song would forever remind him of Kat.

And he was more confused than ever about her.

Nothing she'd said or done suggested she had any ulterior motives. Jamie had hardly been mentioned today. She hadn't asked about other royals who would be at the wedding.

Were he and his mother wrong about Kat?

Her actions suggested so.

He stared at the snow globe. Not a sexy gift meant for seduction, but a sentimental one to mark a good time.

She hadn't kissed him. He'd kissed her, thanks to the mistletoe being there. A nice way to end their time together, yes, but there'd been other reasons for him kissing her. Curiosity. Opportunity. And perhaps, a touch of loneliness.

Smiling and laughing with Kat today had made him realize something was missing from his life, something he wanted. He hadn't felt the same companionship with Clarissa. Being with Kat was different.

But he'd never expected that kiss to rock his world. To make him question everything he believed to be true about Kat Parsons. To make him want someone special to spend time with and love.

Someone like her.

He hugged his dog. "I love you, boy."

But Gill needed more. He hadn't realized that until...

Kat.

A knock sounded at his door.

Could that be her? He hurried to the door.

Usually Maximillian would be at his heels, but the dog lay on the bed. His paw? Or laziness?

Gill opened the door.

Not Kat. Sophie. She usually didn't knock.

His sister placed her hands on her hips. "Were you mean to Kat today?

He motioned her inside and closed the door. His room wasn't that far from where Kat was staying. "What are you talking about?"

"Kat wants to eat dinner in her room."

Disappointment shot through him. He wanted to see her. "That's my fault?"

Sophie's hands went from her hips to across her chest. "Well, is it?"

"No. We had a wonderful afternoon." Too wonderful. He wanted more.

"That's what she said, but she wouldn't rat you out if you'd been awful to her."

That surprised him. "Why not?"

"Because she wants to lessen my stress. Something she read in a book about being a bridesmaid."

"You seem stressed out tonight."

"I don't want my brother hurting my friend."

Defensiveness rose inside him. "I didn't. We got along fine." This probably wasn't the time to tell Sophie he'd kissed Kat. There might never be a good time for that. "Kat enjoyed herself."

"That's what she told me. It's just…"

"What?"

"She seems off. Like something is bothering her."

"You naturally assumed that was me."

"Based on your past—"

"We were kids back then. Today was fun." He walked to his nightstand and picked up the snow globe. "If I'd been such a beast, do you think she would have given me this?"

Sophie's mouth formed a perfect O. "That dog looks like Maximillian."

He nodded. "Whatever's bothering Kat has nothing to do with me."

But he wondered what was wrong with her, and if there was anything he could do to help.

Sophie reached for the door handle. "Well, if you're sure."

"I am. See you at dinner."

She opened the door. Gasped. Closed the door so only a crack of light from the hallway showed.

"What—?"

"Shhh." She lowered her voice. "Jamie is at Kat's door."

Gill stood behind his sister. He hated to resort to eavesdropping, but he wanted to know what was going on. *For Jamie's sake*, Gill rationalized, but he knew he was lying to himself. "Let me see."

"Don't open the door anymore or they'll see us," Sophie whispered.

Through the crack, Gill stared over the top of his sister's head and watched the interaction in the hallway. Jamie used lots of hand motions as if he were excited. Kat laughed.

What was so funny? Had Jamie made a joke?

A vise tightened around Gill's heart and squeezed out the last drops of blood. Kat looked so animated, so beautiful. And it was Jamie standing there, not Gill.

Had she forgotten about their wonderful day together?

His muscles coiled tight like springs. He glanced at the snow globe. "Can you hear them?"

"No." Sophie kept her voice low. "But I hope Kat invites Jamie in for a little pre-dinner partying."

Gill's hands curled. "She better not."

Sophie peered up at him. "How come?"

All the reasons had to do with him. But this wasn't about him. He thought for a minute. "Mother would throw a fit."

She shrugged. "Yes, but not as much of one if Kat was with you."

That was true. He pinched the bridge of his nose.

They watched and waited. Finally, Jamie walked away. Kat closed the door to her room.

Interesting. Perhaps Kat was playing hard to get as his mother had suggested. Or perhaps she wasn't interested in the marquess. Gill hoped the latter.

Sophie's shoulders slumped. "No invite inside. No kiss goodbye."

No present in a small bag given like the one Gill had received. His chest puffed up. "It's almost dinnertime, not bedtime."

His sister groaned. "What is it going to take to get those two together?"

He had no idea, but Sophie's words told him nothing had happened between Kat and Jamie yet.

And that made Gill very happy.

THE NEXT MORNING, Kat heard yelling. Female voices. Two of them. Neither was American.

That could only mean one thing—Sophie and her mother were arguing.

Kat slipped on her shoes and hurried out of her room.

Gill stood in the hallway. He wore gray trousers. His belt was undone, and his shirt unbuttoned so she could see his chest. Smooth and muscular.

Oh, my...

She gulped. Heart pounding in her ears, she forced her gaze up to his face.

He shook his head. "Sounds like the cannons are about to be fired."

Not trusting her voice, she cleared her throat. "I'll go so you can, um, finish dressing."

Don't look.

She took a quick peek.

So sexy.

She rushed down the staircase, as much to get away from Gill as to help Sophie. Kat headed along the hallway to the ballroom.

Queen Louise's voice carried like she was using a bull-horn. The woman intimidated Kat worse than Professor Hinkleworth, whose main goal in life seemed to be failing veterinary students. One visit to his office had left Kat shaking and in tears, positive she would be the next one to drop his course, one that was mandatory for graduation.

"You cannot sit Countess Maria Therese next to any of the royal family members from Christonia," the queen yelled. "The countess was banished from her homeland by her own sister. You don't want to cause an incident that will quickly become tabloid fodder."

"This is a wedding. My wedding." The words poured from Sophie's mouth like water from a fire hose. "Guests need to put their personal differences aside for the evening."

Sophie's voice trembled toward the end.

Uh-oh. Kat recognized that tone. Sophie had sounded that way once before—after she'd been sent home from the reality TV show.

Kat ran to the ballroom.

Queen Louise laughed. Though cackle might be a better description. "Step out of your perfect rose-colored world, Sophia. A wedding won't make people behave differently. Most don't care about being civil. Only pursuing their own agendas."

The ballroom doors were open.

Kat stood in the doorway. She took a step and then

stopped. Fear of the queen in the designer red skirt and jacket kept Kat frozen in place.

Queen Louise towered over Sophie, who kneeled on the floor next to the seating arrangement she and Jamie had been working on. "Take these two for example."

The queen plucked two of the toothpick flags with wedding guest names written on them from a cardboard circle representing one of the many dining tables. She waved the tiny flags.

"These two countries have been bitter foes for centuries. If you seat these two leaders together, you'll start a war."

Sophie took a deep breath. And another. "Mother—"

"You don't want your wedding to be known as the catalyst for international unrest."

Sophie stared at the miniature dining room layout. She wasn't a glowing bride now. Lines formed around her mouth. "The guests will be eating. No one is required to speak to each other. All they have to do is swallow, chew, and repeat. International unrest avoided."

Kat's heart told her to barge into the room to support her friend, who looked like she needed a hug, but logic said to wait. Perhaps the situation would calm down on its own. The last thing Kat wanted to do was make things worse, which she feared her presence at the castle had already.

"You're much too naïve, Sophia," Queen Louise said. "Not everyone gets along with others like you do."

Sophie frowned. "It appears the aristocracy cannot be

expected to behave better than toddlers who want the same toy."

"Who's winning?" Gill whispered into Kat's ear. He stood behind her with his hands on her shoulders.

Kat's muscles bunched. The scent of his aftershave surrounded her. She forced herself not to inhale deeply.

"I wish I could say Sophie." Kat kept her voice low. "But I think your mother's ahead right now."

"She never takes on a battle she can't win."

His warm breath against Kat's neck sent her pulse into overdrive. Awareness of him buzzed through her body. The same way it had after he kissed her yesterday.

Kat needed to stay in control. He was just a man, not a slice of calorie free seven-layer chocolate cake. "I keep waiting for the right time to go in."

"I love my mother, but there is never a right time when she's trying to get her way."

With him so close and wreaking havoc with Kat's senses, this might be the perfect time to enter the ballroom.

"There's only one thing you can do," Queen Louise said.

Sophie looked up at her mother. "What's that?"

"Start over."

Sophie's mouth gaped. She rarely seemed caught off guard, but she did now. "What?"

"Redo the entire seating arrangement and take into account political alliances and past love affairs."

Her shoulders sagged. Shook. "Jamie and I have spent

hours on this. Days. I wanted to have everything finished before Bertrand arrives."

"Then it is a good thing you have a few more days until your fiancé is here." The queen's flippant tone wasn't helping matters. "Have your animal doctor friend help you. She seems reasonably intelligent enough to manage searching the Internet for friends and foes of the various countries that will be attending."

"Reasonably intelligent," Gill whispered. "High praise from the queen."

Kat bit back a laugh. The highest praise would be when she left the castle to return home. At least Sophie would be moving out once she was married, but she'd have both her mother and a mother-in-law to deal with then.

"I'm going in," Kat said to him.

"I've got your back."

If only that were true…

Pushing the thought from her head, Kat inhaled deeply and then entered the ballroom. "Good morning. Anything I can do to help?"

The visible relief on Sophie's face made Kat wish she hadn't waited so long.

"I'm happy to lend my assistance also," Gill added from behind Kat. "I believe Jamie is on a hunt to find ice to climb in Alistonia."

"The two of you have impeccable timing." Queen Louise's gaze narrowed on the two of them coming in together. "Help Sophia redo the seating arrangement. I have three appointments in town. I expect to see progress when I return."

With that, the queen walked out of the ballroom with a click, click, click of her heels against the floor and the scent of her expensive perfume wafting behind her.

"Is it too late to elope?" Sophie asked.

"Yes," Kat and Gill said at the same time.

Her gaze met his before he looked at his sister.

"If you and Bertrand eloped, that would cause an international incident." Gill stepped closer. "Mother would blame him. The duchess would blame you. Tempers would escalate, and fashion designers everywhere would be forced to choose sides. I fear the results of that might not be to Mother's liking, which would lead to shoe makers and jewelers being dragged into the fray."

Sophie laughed.

The sound warmed Kat's heart.

Gill not only knew his sister well, but his love for her also shone through. Kat loved seeing his caring big brother side.

"I fear Jamie had fun seating arch enemies together," Sophie admitted and then looked at Kat. "But I don't hold that against him and neither should you."

"Sounds like something he would have fun doing." Kat touched Sophie's shoulder. "What do you need me to do?"

"Us," Gill corrected. "We're both here to help."

Sophie motioned to the miniature seating arrangement

layout. "Help me avert arguments, tabloid fodder, and war."

Gill gave a mock bow. "At your service, princess."

"You have time?" Sophie asked her brother.

He nodded. "If I didn't, I would make time. And with the intelligent doctor—"

"Reasonably intelligent animal doctor," Kat corrected.

The amusement in Gill's eyes made her feel warm all over.

"With the two of us working together," he said to Sophie. "You'll have no worries about progress being made."

Kat nodded. "We make no promises about food fights not happening during the wedding dinner. Some things cannot be avoided."

"That's true. Especially with Jamie in attendance," Gill agreed. "After a couple glasses of bubbly and dancing next to your centuries'-old foes, you never know what might happen when the second course is served."

Sophie sat straighter, but she was smiling again. "Mother would be mortified if food went flying. Could you imagine?"

"Her reaction would almost be worth it." Gill grinned. "Emphasis on almost. She'd likely decide to make sure she never died so I couldn't inherit the throne."

The glow returned to Sophie's cheeks. "You mean she hasn't already done that?"

Kat burst out laughing. "If your mother hears you, she'll have you locked away in the dungeon."

Gill winked at her. "Be careful; she might throw you

down there, too."

Stuck with him in a dark place might not be so bad.

Sophie plucked flags from the cardboard tables. "Let's get busy so that doesn't happen."

Kat sat on the ballroom's hardwood floor.

A moment later, Gill sat. His thigh pressed against her. Heat emanated from the spot, and she fought the urge to scoot closer.

The man was hot.

His kisses, his looks, his body.

Kat had a feeling the seating arrangement wasn't going to be as hard as not being affected by him. She forced her attention on Sophie. "Where should we start?"

TOO MANY HOURS later, Gill placed the last flag onto the cutout cardboard table. He slumped against Kat, both happy to be finished and wanting to touch her. Not that he hadn't while they worked, but an accidental brush of the fingers or a collision of hands wasn't enough.

"We are finished," he announced.

"Finally." Kat raised her palm. "High five."

He did. "No wars will begin or challenges to duels made."

"A romantic duo might emerge," Kat added. "Maybe two couples."

He could see that happening. "Depends on those mistletoe kisses."

Kat's cheeks turned pink.

Sophie's nose scrunched. "What is it with you two?"

"Huh?" Kat and Gill asked at the same time.

"You're getting along so well." Sophie seemed puzzled. "I'm happy that's the case, but it's a little strange to see."

Kat shrugged. "We're just…"

"Getting to know each other," he finished for her.

Sophie narrowed her gaze. "You're completing each other's sentences like an old married couple."

"No, we're not," they said, again in unison.

Kat gave him a stop-doing-that look.

It was Gill's turn to shrug.

A canary-eating grin spread across Sophie's face. "You're acting like brother and sister now. That's cute."

Gill didn't feel that way about Kat. He made a face. "I don't do cute."

"You're so not cute," Kat agreed. "But I agree with Sophie; it's weird."

"She said strange, not weird," he corrected. "But I disagree. Perhaps it's a little odd but not deplorable."

Kat shook her head. "Definitely weird."

"You are too much." Laughing, Sophie stood. "Now that we've figured out the dinner's seating arrangement so a war won't break out, I'm going to call my betrothed and see how he's doing."

"Say hello to Bertrand for me," Kat said.

"Are you going to wait around for Jamie?" Sophie asked Kat with a hopeful expression.

Gill didn't want her anywhere near the man. That gave him an idea. "I thought I might show Kat the dungeon."

"Oh, that would be great," Sophie said. "Kat was too tired her first day here."

Kat didn't say anything. "No" being the most important word he hadn't heard.

He wanted to spend more time with her. "Might be a good idea to show her the escape routes in case she finds herself stuck down there someday."

"Have fun." Sophie headed out of the ballroom.

Kat's brows drew together. "The dungeon? Don't you have work to do?"

"It can wait." He stood and reached out to help her up.

She grabbed his hand and stood. Her skin was soft and warm.

He didn't want to let go, but he did. "You'll enjoy this."

"I didn't think dungeons were supposed to be enjoyable."

"This will be."

Her mouth slanted. All he could think about was kissing her again.

"Why is that?" she asked with suspicion.

He smiled. "Because you'll be with me."

WITH HIM. KAT followed Gill down a narrow circular staircase made out of stone blocks. Since yesterday, that was the only place she wanted to be—with Gill.

Crazy, yes, but being with him felt…right. In a way spending time with Jamie didn't.

Old-looking electrical sconces hung on the wall. Much safer than the open flame torches that were used in centuries past. The lights cast eerie shadows on the staircase and Gill.

Oh, the flirty marquess was good for Kat's ego. She'd never felt more wanted. But she had a feeling he acted like this with many women. She wasn't special to him. She just happened to be staying at the same place and was single.

Still, he was fun to have as a friend. And yesterday evening when he'd come to her door to ask about the best kind of puppy to adopt, she knew she'd made a friend.

Gill was different.

"Be careful." He pointed to a doorway they approached. "You may need to duck to keep from hitting your head."

"Aye, aye, Captain."

He glanced over his shoulder. "Captain?"

The humidity increased the lower they descended. The air smelled dank. "This part of the castle reminds me of a pirate movie."

"If I'd known that, I would have brought rum."

"Yo-ho-ho."

He hunched down and went through the doorway. "Is Captain Annoying expected to make an appearance?"

Captain, not prince. She liked that. "I assumed the dungeon was his favorite place, and he'd be here."

Ducking, she followed him into a small room. The same old-looking sconces hung on the stone walls. The floor was stone, too.

"Careful," Gill teased. "Or you're going to need to invoke the right of parley."

He knew his pirate lore. "But is there honor among pirates when protection is requested?"

"In the original pirate code, there was no such thing as parley, so no. But if you happen to be in a Hollywood blockbuster, you may be in luck."

The fact he knew trivia was a real turn-on. She loved stuff like that.

This place reminded her of a museum exhibit or theme park ride. Too clean to seem real. "You should bring the film crew down here tomorrow. Bet they'd have fun."

Gill's smiled disappeared. "I can't believe Sophie invited them to the wedding and is letting them come to the castle to film ahead of time."

"Too many commoners?"

"Reality TV. It's beneath her."

"Prince Annoying is making an appearance."

"It's the truth," he said. "I know she says that's why she met Bertrand, but I wish you'd never convinced her to go on the show."

"I didn't convince her of anything. I merely presented

the pros and the cons of going on the show. Sophie made the choice, not me."

Lines formed on Gill's forehead. "But she said…"

Kat shook her head.

Sophie was getting married in a couple of days. The time had come for Gill to learn what his family had driven their youngest member to do all these years. "A long time ago, after I found out your sister was a princess, I told Sophie she could use me as the excuse to do something if that would make life easier for her."

Gill opened his mouth and then closed it. He rubbed his chin. "All these years, you've been taking the blame? Been her scapegoat?"

He sounded like he didn't believe her. Kat understood.

She nodded. "Sophie's one of my best friends. It's the least I could do."

"But that made you look…"

"Bad?"

It was Gill's turn to nod.

Kat had zero regrets. "I live thousands of miles away, so what your family thinks doesn't affect me. But your family's opinion matters a great deal to Sophie."

He stared at Kat with an odd expression on his face. "We…I thought you had too much influence over her."

"That's what your sister wanted you to think. In case you hadn't noticed, after she met Bertrand, she stopped using me as an excuse. Again, her choice."

"I hadn't noticed." Gill continued to look at her. "Why are you telling me this now?"

"Sophie. She thought if your mother knew that it might change the queen's opinion of me. You were next to be told."

"Did it help with my mother?"

"No." But Kat hoped it might help with him. "This little room isn't the dungeon, is it?"

He glanced around, as if remembering where he was, and then pushed open a thick wooden door reinforced with iron bars. "The dungeon is in here."

She stepped inside.

Lighting illuminated the space. The ceiling was higher than in the smaller room. The air wasn't as musty, but the temperature had to be ten degrees cooler.

She shivered. Goose bumps covered her skin.

"What do you think?" he asked.

No skulls and bones or blood and guts. She sniffed. "Cleaner than I thought it would be. Smells better than the staircase."

He rattled thick black chains that hung on the wall. "This is where people were kept before being tortured."

"I don't see any awful-looking devices."

"My mother had them removed after Jacques got trapped in one."

"Uh-oh."

"We weren't allowed down here, but Jacques thought it would be a fun place to play. It was, until we couldn't remove him from the rack."

"Ouch."

"That's what Jacques said."

Engraved placards hung on the wall and described what had been there once upon a time. Nearby were photographs or sketches of the devices.

Kat read a placard. The "boot" was used to crush feet and legs. She took one look at the contraption and cringed. "I can't believe people used these things on others."

He was watching her, but the accusation and suspicion she'd grown used to seeing in his gaze had disappeared. That made her happy she'd mentioned what Sophie had been doing all these years.

"Barbaric," he said. "But it's a part of history."

He walked around the area, pointing out scratches on the wall and discoloration in the stone where something had been attached before. "Public tours are given twice a year, and they always sell out. Mother has museum pieces brought in to show. Actors do skits. It's quite entertaining."

"Entertaining torture? You, sir, are a pirate in disguise."

He laughed and then bowed. "Pirate prince, at your service."

She giggled. Something she hadn't done in forever. "Just my luck to be down here with a pirate prince and not a gallant knight."

"Truth be told, I don't own an eye patch or parrot, but I have a suit of armor."

Her attraction quadrupled in an instant. That was what she got from watching all those princess movies. "Do you wear it?"

"I have, but it's uncomfortable and heavy. Hard to move covered in all that metal."

"But armor is sexy."

"If you think so, I may have to don the suit."

Tension crackled in the air. She experienced that same connection she'd felt at Christmas Market. A pulse between them that she couldn't explain, let alone rationalize.

She walked the inside perimeter of the room. All she wanted to do was move closer, but he'd given her no sign he felt the same way. Call her old fashioned, but she didn't want to make the first move without knowing how he felt.

Kat focused on the equipment that still remained. So many chains with thick links. She touched one. Impossible to lift.

"What's this place used for when you're not doing the tours?"

"Nothing except a hideaway." Gill walked over to a lone chair she hadn't noticed. His fingers curled around the top cross bar on the back. "This is the one place where Sophie and I can get away. No cell phone service. No intercom."

"No queen."

Smiling, he nodded. "It's also a quiet place to read."

"Read," Kat repeated.

"I like books."

"Books are good. I don't do that as much as I used to."

"You're too tired."

She nodded. "Are there ghost stories associated with the dungeon?"

"Lots, but nothing that's been proven." He scanned the dungeon. "If any exist down here, they haven't bothered us."

"Says the royal," she joked. "That's probably because they torment commoners."

Gill walked toward her with long, purposeful strides. "I'll protect you."

Anticipation buzzed. She stepped closer to him. "You're not wearing armor."

"How strong can a ghost be?" He stood in front of her. "But I promise to keep you safe."

If only…

A million thoughts ran through her mind, but only one mattered. Kat wanted to kiss him. She wanted that more than anything. And that made her wonder…

She swallowed. "What are we doing?"

"I'm hoping to kiss you."

Good. He wanted one, too. "Like yesterday?"

Mischief glinted in his eyes. "I hope this one will be longer."

Her, too. "And then?"

"One kiss at a time."

One more kiss. She could handle that. "Okay."

He slipped his hand beneath her hair and cradled her

head. A shiver of need raced over her. As he lowered his lips to hers, she rose slightly on her toes to meet his mouth.

Oh! Oh, my. Maybe she couldn't handle this.

Heat was the first thing she felt.

Peppermint was the first thing she tasted.

Hunger was the first thing she experienced.

And she wanted more. Lots more.

Her body quivered with longing. It had been so long since she'd been kissed like this—like the kiss meant something.

And she did, too.

Gill's lips moved over hers. A giving, a taking. He increased the pressure and wrapped his arms around her.

Kat went willingly against him. She held onto his back and arched to be closer. Her body molded to his. Softness against muscles.

Sensations fluttered. Tingles exploded. She wasn't sure her legs were holding her upright or if it was his embrace.

He was a pirate prince. A dangerous one. Because the booty was her heart.

That should have frightened her and made her want to stop.

But she didn't need rescuing. She needed kissing.

Lots and lots of kissing.

Just. Like. This.

Chapter Eleven

A S THEY STOOD in the dungeon, Gill wanted to keep kissing Kat. He'd considered this place the anti-thesis of romance, but no longer. He dug his hands into her hair. The strands sifted through his fingers. Silky soft. His tongue tasted and explored and enjoyed her mouth.

Sweet. Hot. A delicious combination. Addictive.

Holding and kissing her felt so right, but his control was slipping. He didn't want to stop. That told him he should.

This wasn't the time or the place for…more.

More would lead to things he wasn't ready for and places he couldn't go.

He slowly pulled his mouth from Kat's.

Her breathing was ragged. Her lips looked plump from kissing. Her face flushed.

So beautiful.

How could he have thought she was a bad influence? She was willing to bear the blame of his family for Sophie. Kat loved his sister as much as he did. And if Kat wanted to catch a royal, he was willing to be caught.

"Was that kiss long enough for you?" she asked.

No.

"Yes." Gill liked the husky sound of her voice. He tucked a piece of hair behind Kat's ear. "But I believe that counts as more than one kiss."

Her lush lips curved. "You may be correct."

"May?"

She grinned. "We can't agree on everything. People might think something is going on."

"Isn't something going on?" he asked, his voice uncharacteristically low.

She looked up at him. Desire and…trust shone in her eyes. "You tell me."

The electricity in the air evaporated as if someone had flicked a switch and turned off the power.

Unfamiliar nervousness grabbed hold of him. "I like being with you. Kissing you."

"Same," she admitted to his relief. "You're so not who I thought you were."

Her words made him smile. He fought the temptation to kiss her again. "I've been thinking the same thing about you."

"Your mother hates me."

That might be a problem. "She doesn't have to know."

Kat stepped back. "I don't want to be your next rebellion."

He frowned, not liking her words. "You're not."

Another step back created more distance between them. "Sneaking around doesn't appeal to me."

He closed the gap. "There's something between us. I know you feel it."

She didn't move. She'd gone cold. "Whatever it is has nowhere to go. You have responsibilities. I have a life far away from here."

His heart rate ticked up. "What are you suggesting?"

"Friends."

"Friends." He didn't like the sound of that. "I'm not in the habit of kissing friends the way we kissed."

She sighed. "That was great, but…"

Tension tightened his shoulder. "I should have known a 'but' was coming."

"Being friends would be best."

Logically, he knew that, but a knot formed in his chest. An ache he didn't understand. "I wish—"

"You don't make wishes."

This time, he wanted to. "I wish we could forget about everyone else and enjoy the rest of the time you're here."

"We can do what we've been doing…"

That sounded promising. Maybe being friends wouldn't be so bad.

"…except no more kissing."

His lips wanted to protest, but he respected Kat. She was doing what she thought best for herself, him, and his family.

She was correct. He'd miss kissing her, but they couldn't be more than friends.

"When do you leave?" he asked.

"December twenty-sixth."

"Plenty of time for BFFs to hang out." Saying the words was simple. He hoped the execution was, too. "What do you say?"

She took a breath. Smiled. And stuck out her hand. "Sounds great. I could use another BFF now that mine's getting married."

EARLY THE NEXT day, Kat stared at her reflection in the bathroom mirror. Her tired eyes showed her lack of sleep. "BFFs, really? What are you doing?"

No answer came because she didn't know. Oh, she was trying to figure it out. She'd been analyzing every word, every touch, every kiss exchanged with Gill from the day she arrived at the castle over a week ago until last night's dinner where the queen kept watching her with suspicion, but Kat hadn't come to any conclusions.

Only frustrations.

She groaned. Being friends was not going to work.

Her feelings for Gill went so much deeper than the bonds of friendship. Her affection for him kept growing, doubling each of the past two days. Too bad nothing but friendship was possible between them.

"I hate this."

But she never wanted to do anything to hurt Sophie and her family. Kat brushed her hair. The least she could do was look good for her friend.

"If only I felt this way about Jamie."

Sure, the marquess was a giant flirt and big fun. He was also kind and considerate, but friendship was the only thing she felt toward him.

"Life isn't fair."

But she'd known that from a young age.

Her cell phone buzzed. The sign she'd received a text. She glanced at the name on the screen. SVS aka Sophie von Strausser.

SVS: *Where are you? The film crew is setup in the ball-room.*

Kat read Sophie's text. She'd forgotten the reality TV crew would be here. That meant a possible interview. She typed a reply:

DocKat: *Almost ready. Be right down.*

SVS: *Hurry!*

Kat swiped blush across her cheekbones and added lip gloss. A little mascara and she was ready.

Presentable, maybe a touch pretty.

She didn't expect to find herself on camera. The crew would be looking for royals to interview, not Americans, but she wanted to meet Sophie's friends from the show.

Kat went to the ballroom. Cords and cables lay across the hardwood floor. Stands with lights mounted to them were arranged around two chairs and a small round table. Furniture she recognized from the library had been brought in.

"Hello." A beautiful woman with long, brown hair pulled back in a ponytail smiled at her. Strands framed her face. Freckles across her nose and hazel eyes that looked more green than brown regarded her with curiosity. The eye color could be due to the green tunic that showed off her pregnant belly. "I'm Addie Cahill."

"You were on the honeymoon show."

"Yes, with my husband, Nick."

Reality TV shows were one of Kat's guilty pleasures, but she didn't have much time for television these days. "I'm Kat Parsons."

Addie's lips parted. "You're Princess Sophie's American BFF from summer camp."

"That's me."

"So nice to meet you." Addie shook Kat's hand. "I've been living in Alvernia while my husband does security for Prince Luc. It's a lovely little country, but I miss San Diego and the Pacific Ocean. Where are you from?"

"Eastern Washington originally. Now I live in southern Idaho."

"You traveled a long way for the wedding."

"I wouldn't have missed it."

"Nick and I were surprised to receive an invitation, but Sophie's so sweet to include us with the crew."

"That's Sophie. She doesn't like to leave anyone out."

A handsome man with blue eyes and brown hair waved a clipboard.

Kat recognized him. Nick Cahill. He was former military. Army, maybe. He and Addie had grown up with Emily White, the advertising executive who'd married Prince Luc von Rexburg. "I think your husband is trying to get your attention."

"Thanks. I'm assisting the film crew, so I'm sure I'll see you around." Addie walked toward her husband.

"Hello." A man in his twenties with bright red hair stopped at her side. He carried a video camera. "I'm Conrad."

"Kat. I'm one of the bridesmaids."

"American."

"Yes."

"Nice to meet you."

"Hey, Brad," Conrad shouted. "I've got one of the bridesmaids."

The bleached-blond host of the show made his way over. Kat recognized him from the first two shows he'd done. His white teeth gleamed underneath the lights.

"Hello. I'm Brad Hammond with Ever After Productions." He held a tablet but looked like he'd be more comfortable at the beach surfing than filming at a castle.

"Are you Katrina or Heloise?"

"Katrina, but I go by Kat."

He typed on his tablet. "Today, we're going to be taping interviews. I'll ask you questions about Princess Sophie, wedding planning, and being here in Alistonia."

"Sounds easy enough."

"It is." Brad pointed to a man who wore a beanie cap and had a pair of headphones around his neck. "That's Dylan. He's the sound guy who'll get you hooked up with a microphone."

Dylan danced as if music was playing from his headphones. "Okay."

"The other guy with a camera is Wes. You just met the redheaded clown, Conrad. Both will be filming so we get all the angles."

Her palms sweated. "I've never been filmed before."

Brad touched her arm. "You'll be fine. All you have to do is smile and answer my questions. The crew does all the hard stuff."

Kat rubbed her hands against her pants. She hoped so. Because right now, she was the definition of nervous.

She looked around the ballroom.

Where was Gill? She could use a little moral support from her new BFF and a…hug.

Of support.

And maybe a kiss for good luck.

❦

BRAD HAMMOND CLAPPED his hands together once. "That's a wrap, people. Thank you for your time and your patience."

"About time," Gill whispered to Kat, who sat in the chair next to his.

She put her finger to her mouth. "Shhh."

Gill would rather she touch his mouth. His interview had been over an hour ago, but he stayed in the ballroom because Kat was here. He rested his arm on the back of her chair.

Friends did that. If he happened to touch her hair or shoulder, that was purely incidental. And very pleasant.

The film crew milled about and laughed with Sophie. His sister looked so happy to see her friends. Gill had to admit she was a natural on camera. He'd refused to watch the show when she was on it, but maybe he would now.

Jamie seemed taken with Addie, even though the woman was pregnant and her husband watched the interaction from a few feet away. The marquess had better be careful. Nick didn't look like the kind of guy to upset.

Gill enjoyed just being with Kat. He hoped they could sit closer at dinner tonight. A swap of place cards might be in order.

His mother strode into the ballroom wearing her crown. Her shoulders were back and her head held high, as instilled in her since childhood, when manner and etiquette lessons were as important as school. At least they had been for him and his siblings.

"Does she always wear jewels on her head?" Kat asked in a low voice.

The queen hadn't until the past couple of weeks. "Only when we have guests."

"I keep expecting to hear trumpets sound when she enters."

He laughed. "I sometimes hear them in my head."

His mother glanced at Sophie and then made a beeline for his table. "Don't the two of you look comfortable?"

Gill pulled his arm to his side and straightened. "The filming just finished."

"Good, because I need your help." She didn't glance at Kat. "I need you to escort me to the council's dinner."

Something was going on. "You haven't had an escort in years."

"There's a first time for everything." His mother smiled at Kat. "Don't you look pretty today?"

Kat's smile looked unnatural. "Thank you, ma'am."

His mother tilted her head. "Perhaps you and Jamie can keep yourselves entertained while we're away. Enjoy a quiet dinner. Or explore the castle. We have a dungeon."

Gill's shoulders tensed. His mother must have heard they'd toured the dungeon yesterday, but what else did she know?

Kat's cheeks turned pink. Charming, but noticeable. "We'll figure out something, ma'am."

"I'm sure you will. You're quite resourceful." His mother

looked at him. "Meet me in the foyer at six."

She walked out without talking to Sophie.

Underneath the table, Kat touched his thigh. He covered her hand with his.

Concern clouded her gaze. "Do you think she knows?"

"No, but she's curious." And would be looking for any clue or sign that more than a tour went on in the dungeon.

Gill removed his hand from Kat's. "I must go with my mother tonight."

"It must be awful to have no choice."

His situation with Kat was one of those times. "It can be, but that's how it is."

"I wish it could be different for you."

He fought the urge to touch her. Too many people were around. And they were supposed to be just friends, but still… "I wish that, too."

KAT WALKED TO the dining room for breakfast. She hadn't seen Gill last night, but he'd mentioned having her go with him to show the film crew around the grounds this morning.

Yes, they were only friends, but the thought of spending the a few hours with him, even with the others in tow, made her feel as buoyant as a cloud. Her feet barely skimmed the floor. She hoped she would be able to keep her attraction hidden.

Max ran up to her. He'd come from the direction of the

dining room. Gill must already be there. A thrill shot through her.

"Good morning, handsome." The dog looked at her with an expectant gleam in his eyes. She slowed and patted his head. The dog soaked up the attention, as usual. "Enough rubs for now?"

Max panted.

"Let's go find Gill."

When they reached the dining room, Max sat. The queen must be at the table. The dog knew better than to enter when she was there.

Kat entered the dining room. Neither Jamie nor Sophie was there. The chair next to Gill was occupied by a woman she'd never seen before. A beautiful, elegant woman with violet eyes and long, amber hair.

An extended royal family member in town for the wedding? Sophie had said more people would be arriving today, including Bertrand.

"Good morning," Kat said.

Gill rose. He greeted her with a warm smile, but his posture seemed stiff. "I hope you slept well."

She nodded.

"Sit there." Queen Louise motioned to an empty chair on the opposite side of the table.

"Thank you, ma'am." Kat took the seat.

"A surprise visitor arrived this morning." Queen Louise beamed like a cat that'd captured a mouse. Kat was surprised not to see a tail hanging out the corner of the queen's mouth. "I'd like to introduce you to Princess Rowena from Colletto. She and Gill attended boarding school together for many years."

Kat waited for the queen to introduce her, but the growing silence in the dining room prompted her to speak. "Hello. I'm Kat Parsons. It's nice to meet you."

"Kat is a veterinarian from the States," Gill added.

Princess Rowena straightened. "Oh, you're Sophia's so-called BFF from camp."

The use of the word so-called poked at Kat like a large gauge needle, but she kept a smile on her face. "Yes, I am."

"Kat's one of Sophia's bridesmaids," the queen said.

Rowena's perfect smile faltered, but it was back in place an instant later. "How sweet she's included a childhood friend in her *royal* wedding party."

Sophie had warned Kat about women she'd meet who were anything but sweet. Mean girls who also happened to be royalty. A dangerous mix.

Kat had learned to hold her tongue with patients. This would be no different. "Yes. I am honored to be a part of my dear friend's nuptials."

"We're ready for breakfast," the queen said to Isaac. "No one else will be joining us this morning."

Rowena focused her attention on Gill. "Your mother was telling me you've been helping your sister with her wedding."

He glanced at the princess. "Yes, I must admit it's been more enjoyable than I imagined."

Queen Louise leaned over the table. "You sound like you're ready to work on your own wedding plans."

Rowena seemed to be holding her breath based on the fact her face was turning red. Subtlety didn't appear to be one of the woman's strong points.

His gaze met Kat's.

Her heart bumped.

That same energy as before passed between them, and then he looked at Queen Louise. "Remember what you said, Mother, one royal wedding at a time."

Rowena took a breath.

"Of course." The queen picked up her fork. "But there will be many eligible young women attending the wedding, including one who's right here at this table. Isn't that right, Rowena?"

A normal person might blush when put on the spot like this. Not the princess. Her face was returning to its flawless ivory color. "Yes, and I look forward to getting reacquainted. It's been too long."

Too bad it couldn't be longer.

That wasn't the kindest thought, but Rowena acted so differently from Sophie. Kat filled her mouth with a forkful of omelet. Better if she didn't say anything.

But inwardly, she steamed. Oh, she wasn't surprised that Queen Louise forgot about her. Two eligible women were sitting at the dining table—the princess and Kat, but the queen was making it clear that only Rowena had the qualifications to date the crown prince. The fact Gill hadn't corrected his mother about Kat being eligible poked at her.

Friends, she reminded herself.

But it still hurt.

She stabbed a melon ball, but instead of the tines going into the fruit, the ball shot off her plate and rolled to the center of the table.

So much for her etiquette lessons. She was not only proving her ineptitude at interacting with royals, but also proving she didn't belong.

Isaac appeared, as if by magic, and gathered her coffee cup, snagging the stray melon ball without a break to his motion. "I'm sorry, Miss Kat. I forgot that you prefer black tea and served coffee instead. I'll bring you another cup."

She wanted to jump out of her chair and hug her friend, but she forced herself to remain seated and not sigh in relief. "Thank you, Isaac."

Just words, but she hoped he saw her gratitude.

He nodded once, winked, and then walked away.

Warmth flowed through her. She had friends at the castle besides Sophie, Jamie, and Gill.

She ate another bite of her omelet.

"I don't believe Rowena has been to Alistonia before," the queen said to Gill.

The princess wiped her mouth with a napkin. "I haven't,

ma'am."

"I have a wonderful idea." Queen Louise sounded so excited that she nearly sprung out of her seat. "Gill will show you around town today. There are so many sights to see. Who better to play tour guide than the crown prince of Alistonia?"

Rowena nodded so fast she looked like one of those bobble heads given out at baseball games.

Gill shifted in his seat, as if uncomfortable, but he didn't look at Kat. She didn't know if he was ignoring her on purpose or if he was trying to figure out what to say. A good thing her napkin was linen or the thing would be shredded into a million pieces.

"That would be nice, but I have plans this morning," he said.

With me.

Kat was thankful he hadn't forgotten.

"Do you have state business to attend to?" Queen Louise asked.

Gill's jaw clenched. "No, I'm showing the film crew around the grounds."

"Kat and Jamie can do that. They've been here long enough to know their way around," the queen said. "You've been working too hard. A day off will be good for you. And this will give you time to catch up with the lovely Rowena."

"I would enjoy spending time with you." The princess placed her hand on his forearm. "It's been too long since we've seen each other."

"I agree. You've both eaten enough." The queen motioned with her hands. "Go now, so you have time to see everything. I'll keep Kat company while she finishes breakfast."

So much for spending time together, but Kat kept a smile frozen on her face. Doing so wasn't easy, but she had no choice.

Neither did Gill.

The queen had spoken. As he'd told Kat, he picked his battles. This didn't appear to be one he wanted to fight. Disappointment ran rampant in her veins.

Gill looked at her, but she knew he couldn't say anything. Not in front of the queen and the princess.

The last thing Kat wanted was for him to feel bad. Or to have him defy his mother.

"Have fun." She forced a smile. "Make sure you show Rowena the art museum."

"Oh, I love art. Especially modern."

Rowena would. Kat blew out a breath.

The princess ran her French-manicured nails up Gill's arm. Worse, he didn't seem to mind.

Jealousy burned. Kat had never felt this way about any man in her life. She didn't like the feeling one bit.

He stood and pulled out Rowena's chair.

After she stood, Gill extended his arm. "Shall we?"

Huh?

As the princess placed her arm on his, Kat's stomach churned like a tropical storm in the Pacific.

Gill had done and said the same thing with her when they'd been at the Christmas Market. He'd called her milady, but still...

That had made her feel special, but it appeared to be a line he used with many women. Her throat closed. She should have known. Who had she been kidding to think she could mean anything to him other than, well, friends?

Friends had been her idea.

Feeling upset was stupid.

Gill and Rowena walked out of the dining room. The sound of their footsteps faded as they disappeared from sight.

Thank goodness Sophie wasn't here, because this was going to be a rotten day. Kat didn't want to bring down her friend two days before the happiest day of her life.

Emotions ran the gamut. The reason why struck Kat like a fallen hay bale.

She had fallen for Gill.

Head over heels fallen for him.

Nerve endings tingled. Her heart ached. She picked up her orange juice and sipped, afraid the realization would show on her face.

Queen Louise sighed. "Don't they make an attractive couple?"

Kat nearly spit out the liquid in her mouth. She swallowed. The orange juice went down wrong, and she coughed.

"I'm glad you agree," Queen Louise said, even though the only thing Kat had done was nearly choke to death. "I shall leave you to finish."

So much for keeping her company, but honestly, Kat didn't mind. "Have a nice day, ma'am."

"Now that I've seen Gill and Rowena together, I will." The queen stood. "Mark my words. There will be another royal wedding in Alistonia next year. In the spring or summer when the flowers are in bloom will be the best time."

Princess Rowena was the one his mother had picked out for Gill to marry. Kat could barely breathe.

As the queen walked away, Kat slumped in her chair. Her appetite was gone.

Maximillian barked from the entryway. He was still sitting in the same spot.

"You're such a good boy." She rose from the table. "Would you like to go for a walk when we take the film crew around?"

His tail wagged.

"I'll take off your cone since I can make sure you don't lick your paw. Sound good?"

The dog headed to the stairs. At least another member of the royal family besides Sophie wanted to spend time with Kat.

She should stick to loving animals. They didn't require a person to be from a certain country or have the right background. They just loved—openly and unconditionally.

She'd had that from her grandparents but never her parents.

Was that too much to ask for from a man?

From…Gill?

Christmas is a time of magic and miracles.

Kat hoped Jojo was right about that.

Chapter Twelve

TODAY WAS FAR from Gill's worst day ever, but he would rather be back at the castle with Kat doing a million wedding projects than sitting in the backseat of the limousine with Rowena. Time seemed to be going backward. He missed Kat, and every word out of the princess's mouth aggravated him. His shoulders were so tight that he was afraid he'd have a permanent hunch.

Rowena was gorgeous with looks any man would desire, but beyond the outer package, nothing about her intrigued him.

"I had no idea Alistonia offered so much…culture," she said after visiting the art museum where she'd droned on and on about the pieces as if reciting them by rote from a guidebook.

"Alistonians enjoy the arts as much as others." He'd much preferred his visit with Kat and Jamie, even with her calling them out on their acting like schoolboys trying to impress a girl.

"Extraordinary."

It was extraordinary considering many smaller towns in Europe offered similar galleries but theirs was unique because of the special collections. Works that belonged to his family and were on permanent display so all could enjoy. "I'm glad you're enjoying the tour."

"Immensely."

Rowena rested her hand on his forearm. She'd been touching him in some way all day. This type of behavior had been happening since he became crown prince.

Back at boarding school, he'd been the spare heir and his brother Jacque got all the attention. The girls had viewed Gill with little regard. Only the girls back home had been interested in him. As crown prince, however, his worth had risen among the elitist nobles.

"I may have to return for an extended stay." Rowena squeezed his arm. "Your mother said there's an entire guest wing that's rarely used outside of special occasions like the wedding."

Of course his mother would say that. He had no doubt Rowena was being displayed as one of his future bride choices.

His breakfast curdled in his stomach. Not happening.

Claude pulled over to the side of the road.

Gill leaned forward until the seatbelt across his shoulder stopped him. "Is there a problem?"

"A phone call from the castle," the driver answered. He

held his cell phone to his ear. "We're in the car now, Princess Sophia. Of course I will relay the message. Is there anything you need us to bring home?"

That didn't sound like an emergency. Gill leaned back against the seat.

Rowena patted his arm. "I'm sure everything is okay."

He hoped she was right about that. "If not, they would have called me."

She leaned into him. Her chest pressed against his arm. "Where are we going next?"

He wanted to skip the Christmas Market. If Rowena wanted to see that, she could do that on her own. "The waterfalls. James, the Marquess of Darbyton, said they are spectacular-looking right now."

"Oh, I know Jamie quite well."

That didn't surprise Gill.

"That was Sophie, sir," Claude said. "Congratulations, you're going to be a grandfather."

The driver's words didn't register. Gill blinked, though his eyesight had nothing to do with his hearing. "What did you say?"

"When Kat and Jamie were out with the camera crew, they took Max with them. He led them to a hole in the castle wall where they found another dog who is about to have puppies."

There was another dog following him. A smaller yellow one.

Kat had seen a second dog. He should have listened to

her instead of dismissing her words out of hand because he'd thought the worst of her. Foolish. Arrogant. Wrong. Kat was intelligent, compassionate, and competent. A woman worth more than the jewels in the royal collection.

"The dog is in labor. Kat has taken charge, and everything is going well."

The dog would be in good hands with Kat, but Gill wanted to be there.

"She's alerted the veterinarian in case there are complications or they need x-rays to make sure all the puppies have been delivered," Claude continued. "Bertrand and Jamie have constructed a whelping box. The queen thought the stable was the best location for the puppies given the wedding."

It wasn't surprising that his mother would want the dogs hidden from guests. Fortunately, the stable's heating system was first rate and would keep the puppies warm. "Anything else?"

"No, your sister thought you should know."

"Why didn't she call me?"

"Princess Sophia said she tried but was sent straight to voice mail."

"My phone hasn't rung all day." Gill pulled out his cell phone. He tapped his screen. Nothing. His phone had been fully charged when they left. He held down the button on top to restart his phone. It powered up. Full battery. "That's strange. The power was turned off."

Rowena stared out the window. "I wonder how that happened."

"I wonder." He had his phone on the seat next to him when they'd left this morning. He had an idea who might have turned off his phone. "Let's head back to the castle."

"What about the waterfalls?" Rowena asked, her voice rising.

"Claude can drop me off and take you."

"I want to go with you."

Her lower lip thrust forward in a pose that some might consider sexy. He didn't. The exact opposite in fact. He kept his beast mode reined in. Best not to lambast her for turning off his phone and playing the coquette. The princess was a guest. He needed to be polite. "Perhaps another day."

"Yes, please. Find a date on your calendar. My schedule is rather open at the moment due to the holidays."

The time it took to return to the castle stretched in interminable silence.

At the front entrance, his mother welcomed them home. "I'm so sorry your day was cut short."

Rowena curtsied. "It's fine, ma'am. We'll be setting a date to see what we missed."

His mother beamed. "Meet me in the sitting room in thirty minutes. We'll have tea."

"Thank you, ma'am." Rowena smiled at Gill and then went inside.

The door closed.

"I'm going to the stable," he said.

"You should have continued your tour." His mother had that knowing look in her eyes. "You won't find a more suitable princess bride than Rowena."

Unbelievable. Anger simmered low in his belly. "Then you marry her."

She arched an eyebrow and gave him her best intimidating stare down. "Excuse me?"

"It isn't going to work, Mother. Not today. Or ever." He was growing tired of her meddling. A son—man—could only be pushed so far. "You may have the legal right as queen to approve my future wife, but you will not choose her."

His mother sighed. "This is that American's fault. She's filling your head with ideas the way she has your sister."

His fingers curled into fists at his side. He purposely flexed them. "Don't blame Kat for this."

She may be the catalyst, but she wasn't at fault.

Kat made him want to take action, do more, to lead—not only follow what his mother ordered. He'd pushed aside what he'd wanted in life to be the dutiful son worthy of the kingdom, but like Kat dreaming about grand adventures in Africa, maybe he didn't have to give up everything he wanted.

"I'm thirty-one," Gill stated in a matter-of-fact tone. "I respect you as my queen and am more than willing to do my duty for our family and Alistonia, but I don't need my mother micro-managing my personal life."

"Your romantic life—your marriage—will never be your own."

Her tone sounded more like a warning than her trying to control him.

"That may be true, but it's more mine than yours."

"I'm only looking out for you." His mother's voice softened. A closed-mouth smile formed. "You're such a good son, Guillaume. You always follow the rules and do what's required of you, even when you'd rather not. I'm sure doing that gets old, and you get the urge to do something wild or inappropriate. And you want what you can't have."

An image of Kat appeared in his mind. Longing flooded him. He did want the American. For now, for always.

His throat clogged. He couldn't speak if he wanted to.

"You may find this hard to believe, but I've been in your shoes," his mother continued. "I know what it's like to have so many others' expectations piled on your shoulders and want to break free, if only for a day or a few hours, but your infatuation with that American is only going to lead to disappointment."

His mother didn't raise her voice. If anything, her tone was compassionate, even if he didn't appreciate her words.

"That woman will break your heart the same way Clarissa did. You deserve so much better, my son."

"Kat and I are friends." Being friends would never be enough for him. He wanted more with Kat, and he knew she wanted the same.

The question was what.

And how. There was so much at stake. He couldn't picture a future together because of being the crown prince. Yet, that was where his rebellious mind wanted to go.

His mother raised her eyebrows. "Be careful then. The way she looks at you might bring additional benefits soon."

The insulting tone and insinuation made the urge to lash out strong, but Gill pressed his lips together. He flexed his fingers again. Time to retreat before he did or said something he'd regret. "I'm going to the stable now."

The walk there would give him time to cool off, except a quarter of the way down the snow-cleared walkway, he didn't want to take his time getting there. He quickened his pace and reached the stable in less than five minutes.

Inside, lights and cameras greeted him. The film crew had set up around a stall. Voices were quiet, but he counted several people—the four crew members, their pretty pregnant assistant, her husband the security guy, Isaac, Sophie, Bertrand, Jamie, and, of course, Kat.

Her hair was pulled back into a ponytail. Her peaches-and-cream complexion flushed. The concentration on her face was arresting.

No one noticed Gill. All eyes and camera lenses were focused on the stall. He moved until he could see what everyone was looking at.

There was a large box with sides about two feet high and an opening in the front. A yellow dog rolled around inside the box.

Kat kneeled by a basket not too far away from the yellow dog. A blanket or two appeared to be inside wrapped around something. A puppy? The smile on her face sent his heart careening into his rib cage.

Gorgeous.

"Mama dog is having more contractions. This little girl, however, is doing fine." Kat pointed inside the basket. "She has similar coloring to Max."

Jamie laughed. He held Max's leash and patted the dog. "You done good, boy, but I have a feeling you'll be going to the vet soon for a little snip-snip."

Everyone laughed.

Gill cringed. He'd thought about breeding his dog at some point. Guess Max had taken the initiative.

Sophie stood in front of Bertrand; he had his arms around her. She stared down at the basket with a big smile. "When will the next puppy arrive?"

"Hard to say, but depending on the size of the liter, we could be here all night." Kat sounded happy, not worried at all. "This mama dog knows what she's doing. Our job is to assist her. Keep the puppies safe and warm until she stops moving around and can nurse safely. Nursing can help labor."

Gill watched Kat with a sense of awe. Respect and affection for her overflowed. She was a special woman, one he wanted to take into his arms and kiss.

There had to be a way…

Bertrand rested his chin on Sophie's shoulder. "A good thing the wedding isn't tomorrow."

Brad elbowed Nick. "Rating's gold. I'm telling you."

"How will you know if the puppy is warm enough?" Addie asked.

"There's a heating pad under the blanket in the basket, and then you let the puppy tell you how they feel. Usually, crying means too hot. Whimpering too cold. They have similar signs when they're hungry."

Jennings arrived with a stack of folded towels. "In case Mama needs assistance cleaning the puppies, sir."

"Thanks." Gill took the towels from their longtime butler and made his way into the stall. He didn't want to be in the way, but this gave him an excuse to be near Kat. "Where do you want these?"

Kat was already smiling, but her face brightened. "You're back."

An energy flowed between them, once again, and drew him closer. "Jennings brought these out."

She pointed to a corner where other towels, blankets, and supplies were stacked. "Put them over there."

He did. "Puppies, huh?"

"Max is a daddy."

Gill laughed. "I suppose I should have said more about the birds and bees to Max."

Kat's gaze kept going from him, to the mama dog, to the

puppy in the basket, but he never felt like she wasn't listening. "What did you say to him?"

"That birds are for hunting and bees sting."

She laughed. "Well, now you have puppies for Christmas. You're fortunate because I think a couple of people here might want one."

He glanced over his shoulder. Jamie raised his hand. So did Sophie and Bertrand.

"We're discussing it," Nick said.

Addie crossed her fingers.

His fingers itched to touch Kat. "Anything I can do to help?"

"Thanks, but it's up to Mama now. All we can do is wait."

"Then that's what I'll do." He hunkered down beside her.

There was no place Gill would rather be than with Kat.

AFTER MIDNIGHT, WITH the smell of horse and hay in the air, Kat leaned her shoulder against Gill as they sat in the corner of the stall and watched the puppies with their mama in the whelping box. Contentment flowed through her. A sense of belonging, too, that had eluded her since she arrived. But here, in the stable and next to Gill, she felt at home.

She sneaked a peek at him staring at the dogs.

She could never think of him as only a friend.

Yes, they were friends, but he meant so much more, more than she could say. She was having trouble denying her feelings. And pretending.

That wasn't working at all.

He might be Crown Prince Guillaume of Alistonia and the last man she'd ever pictured herself wanting to spend time with, but he was the only one she wanted to be with now. Tingles erupted with the brush of his fingers against her skin or just thinking about him. Gill was far from perfect—she wouldn't kid herself about that—but she saw behind the mask he wore as a crown prince dutiful to his country to the sweet and kind man who loved his family and his dog.

Gill had stayed long after others went for dinner or to bed. He'd helped when two puppies arrived one after the other and Mama needed help removing the membrane and stimulating the second pup. The work was dirty, but he hadn't complained about the mess and helped clean up. And after the last puppy arrived into the world healthy, he'd wiped the tears of joy from Kat's eyes and kissed her. A lingering kiss that had exploded in her heart like a burst of sunshine.

Gill was everything she could imagine wanting in a partner, a lover, a husband. If only…

Best not to let herself go down that heartbreaking path.

Side by side, one tucked under another, the puppies nursed. A few made little noises that broke the silence.

He laughed. "Cute, but they're hungry little devils."

They had one desire—to nurse. If one fell off a nipple, an alarm might as well sound because they would not be quiet about not getting fed. "That's what puppies like to do."

He smoothed back stray strands of hair that had escaped her ponytail. "Well done tonight."

She heard the pride in his voice. Pride for her. His touch was a caress that sent shivers through her. "Thank you."

The only deliveries she saw these days were the ones with complications. To watch the process happen naturally, as intended with healthy puppies, filled her with both amazement and relief.

"You're an excellent assistant," she said.

He met her gaze. His green eyes were soft. Adoring. "We work well together. Make a good team."

She swallowed past the lump in her throat. "Yes, we do."

His expression turned serious expression. "So what do we do about this?"

"About the puppies?"

"About us."

Us. Kat liked the sound of that. A pipe dream, but still…

Her heart rate accelerated. She had no idea what to say. She had no experience with this type of complicated relationship.

"It doesn't make sense to cause problems with your mother when I'm leaving in a few days," she said finally as reality closed in.

The rehearsal was tomorrow. The wedding was next, followed by Christmas Eve and then Christmas. She flew out the next morning. Going back to America. To her apartment, her job, and her friends. Her life. A life that didn't—couldn't—include him.

"I'm not in the habit of wanting to kiss my female friends."

"Me, either." She gave a small laugh. "Male ones, that is."

He leaned over and kissed her softly on the lips. "I keep wanting to do that."

"Me, too."

He blew out a breath. "Do we have to put a name to whatever this is between us? Can't we just be together, enjoy each other until it's time for you to leave? I don't want to worry about what anyone else thinks."

"Yes, but..." Kat was torn. Whatever was between them—even if it turned serious—could go nowhere. She remembered what he'd told her about his mother. If they made the most of Kat's remaining time here, there might be consequences. "You could be left to deal with the fallout."

"I can handle my mother. The time together will be worth it."

But would memories be enough for Kat? She didn't know. But maybe having those was better than nothing.

She took a breath. "So we'll spend time together..."

"Like this. More than friends, but not a fling. Something

in between." He laced his fingers with hers and squeezed. "Of course, no blatant PDA. That's frowned upon no matter what the situation if you're a royal."

That made her laugh.

"We'll be subtle," he added.

She nodded, even though she had a feeling her emotions wouldn't be so easy to turn on and off when she said good-bye and returned home.

Worth it, right?

Kat wished she knew.

She didn't want to leave behind her heart in Alistonia, but with her growing feelings for Gill, that was a big possibility.

DECEMBER TWENTY-THIRD, THE royal wedding day, arrived with snow flurries. The perfect Christmassy day for a princess, or any bride in Kat's opinion, to say "I do." She sat in her room with Lady Heloise, the other bridesmaid. Both wore big, fluffy pink robes with their first initial embroidered in hot pink. A present given to them that morning from Sophie.

Kat studied the morning's schedule. "I knew today would be a big day, but there's a lot of stuff to do."

"Typical royal wedding day prep." Heloise was twenty-four with long, strawberry-blond hair, dark blue eyes, and freckles like her brothers. She resembled Bertrand more than

Jamie. "Knowing my mother and the queen, though, this could be over the top. The boys will have a much easier time."

Gill.

Thinking his name brought tingles.

So far, being together—or whatever they weren't calling this thing between them—was working. Not that they were in anyone's face, but during yesterday's wedding rehearsal, Gill put his arm around Kat and the world didn't end. No one noticed except for Queen Louise. That blood vessel in her forehead didn't actually burst, so Kat called that a win. The queen also didn't say anything, but that was most likely due to the film crew that was there. Those guys, especially the cameraman named Wes, cracked Kat up.

"This looks like the ultimate spa day. Only the spa comes to us." She read the list on her schedule. "Pedicure, mani-cure, hair, makeup."

"Be happy I convinced my mother that spray tans weren't necessary." Heloise brushed her hair. "Otherwise, we'd be orange."

Kat grimaced. "That would stand out in our white dress-es. Especially with the red sashes."

"The pictures would be awful." Heloise made a face. "But now we'll look like princesses in our pretty dresses and sparkly tiaras."

"Tiaras? I thought we'd wear flowers in our hair."

Heloise placed the brush in the cosmetic bag she'd

brought with her to Kat's room. "The tiara was Sophie's ideas, and, surprisingly, neither the queen nor my mother objected."

Growing up, Kat's only tiara had been a pink plastic one with fake jewels glued on the front. Nothing fancy, but she'd felt like Cinderella wearing the crown and drinking tea with her grandfather. She couldn't wait to wear another one today.

There was a little bit of princess still inside her, and tonight she would get to dance with a prince.

"I cannot wait for the wedding ball. We'll be fighting off the eligible bachelors tonight." Heloise picked up her cup of tea. "Is there anyone you want to kiss under the mistletoe?"

Gill's face appeared front and center in Kat's mind. "I'll have to think about it."

"I have my eye on a duke." Heloise drank.

"Good luck." Kat hoped for some herself. She wanted a kiss from Gill, but she also didn't want to lose her heart.

Liv knocked on the door and entered. "Princess Sophia and Queen Louise are finished with their pedicures. It's your turn, ladies."

"Time to get gorgeous," Heloise said.

Kat wanted to look good. And not just for the pictures.

Three hours later, after more pampering and plucking than a show dog went through, Kat's hair had been put in a gorgeous up-do by a fairy godmother of a hairstylist named Melinda and flawless makeup applied.

At least that was how everyone described what she was having done. Kat hadn't been allowed to look in a mirror. Sophie wanted her bridesmaids to be surprised.

Liv helped Kat into the gorgeous white bridesmaid dress. She wrapped the red sash around Kat's waist and tied the ends into a big bow at the small of her back. "So lovely, Miss Kat."

She wriggled her toes—well, as much as she could in her bridesmaid shoes—in anticipation. "I can't wait to see."

"Soon." Liv showed her a pair of pearl earrings. These were also a gift from Sophie. "Would you like me to put these on you?"

"Thanks, but I can do it myself."

A teardrop-shaped pearl hung from posts encrusted with crystals. At least Kat assumed they weren't real diamonds, but she had no idea. She secured the first earring and then the second.

"May I look now?" she asked.

"You're missing one item."

Liv held a silver tiara covered in small crystals.

Kat inhaled sharply. The elaborate design reminded her of filigree, only this was a much larger design. "It's stunning."

Liv placed the tiara on Kat's head and then secured it with hairpins. "That shouldn't fall out."

She wrung her hands. "Can I look now?"

"Yes." Liv removed the sheet covering the full-length

mirror.

Kat turned. Her mouth gaped. She didn't recognize the reflection staring back at her.

"That's me?" She blinked. The image hadn't changed. She squinted to see better. "I look so…different."

Liv smiled. "You look the same. Only the accessories and dress are fancier than you're used to."

Kat gently touched the tiara. "But I almost look like a princess."

"Not almost, you do." Pride filled Liv's voice. "You're stunning."

Kat couldn't believe the transformation. One thought ran through her mind. What would Gill think?

She wanted him to like how she looked. Who was she kidding? She wanted him to fall at her feet with a combination of adoration and desire.

Grinning, she turned side to side. The gown's hem swooshed one way and then the other. She might not have any place to wear a dress like this, but she could do so in the privacy of her apartment.

And would.

She giggled at the thought. "What's next?"

"Photos here at the castle, and then you'll put on the long, red velvet cape with a hood and elbow-length gloves for the ride to the church. You'll wear those home again to keep warm."

"Talia thought of everything." The wedding planner was

waiting downstairs for them.

"This wasn't her idea, Miss Kat," Liv said. "Princess Sophie took care of the bridesmaid details herself. She wanted today to be as special for you and Lady Heloise as it will be for her."

Leave it to Sophie.

"She succeeded." And then some.

Liv carried the outerwear. So festive, yet regal.

Excitement shot through Kat. She hoped Gill was having as good a day as she was. "This is going to be the best royal wedding ever."

Chapter Thirteen

A T THE ALTAR, Gill stood next to Jamie. Bertrand was on the other side of his older brother. The doors at the back of the church were closed to keep people from seeing the bride in the vestibule.

Gill glanced at his watch. The wedding was supposed to have started five minutes ago. "Who bet the wedding would begin on time?"

Bertrand shook his head. "That was me. I thought today would be different."

Jamie laughed. "Set all the clocks ahead by a half hour and you may come close to being on time in the future."

A flourish from the pipe organ sounded.

"Five minutes isn't that bad." Impressive for Sophie, actually.

Gill straightened. He couldn't wait to see his sister walk down the aisle. Kat, too. She'd been on his mind all morning. He'd enjoyed spending time with her these past two days from building snow soldiers in one of the pastures to decorating Christmas cookies with the kitchen staff.

The back doors opened.

"This is it, little brother," Jamie said to Bertrand. "It's not too late to back out."

Sweat beaded at the groom's temple. He shifted his weight between his feet. "Shut up, or I'll tell Mom."

Gill laughed.

Music played. The well-dressed and coiffed guests stood.

Sophie appeared in the center of the doorway in a breathtaking white gown. She wore a tiara and veil. The same tiara their mother had worn on her wedding day.

Instead of stepping into the church, Sophie reached out her arm. A beaming grin lit up the princess bride's face.

A man stepped from behind the door. He placed his hand below hers and faced the crowd.

A collective gasp sounded.

This wasn't any man. This man was a priest assigned to the Vatican. Father von Strausser. Their older brother Jacques. He wore a black cassock and stared at Sophie with the love and adoration of a big brother.

Gill stared in shock, but the relief that flowed through him was palpable. Sophie loved her oldest brother, so did Gill, and Jacques needed to be here.

The organist continued to play.

Jacques escorted her into the church and down the aisle. Exactly what he should be doing according to protocol. As the eldest son, regardless of relinquishing his title, he was the

CHRISTMAS AT THE CASTLE

one who should be standing in for their father.

Sophie had known that. She had wanted to include her older brother in her most special of days. And had.

Little Sophie, their sweet baby sister, had pulled off the unthinkable—a miracle.

A wave of emotion overwhelmed Gill. Pride and respect for the woman she'd become filled him. His eyes stung. He blinked and then refocused on the pair walking toward him.

Jacques had always resembled their father with his lanky build, tall height, and easy smile, but now that he was older, the similarities between the two were more apparent.

No wonder Sophie had insisted on walking herself down the aisle. She'd had other plans for her wedding, ones she knew Mother would never approve.

Gill didn't dare look at their mother. He didn't want anything to ruin this special moment.

Bertrand rubbed his eyes. The emotion—his love—for Sophie was written on his face for all to see.

Gill had no doubt this was the right man for his sister. He was so happy for both of them.

As Sophie and Jacques reached the halfway point, Gill saw Kat.

He gasped.

Something fluttered inside his stomach, and a ball of warmth settled at the center of his chest.

She looked spectacular in her white dress and tiara. She walked next to Lady Heloise, beautiful in her own right, but overshadowed by Kat. The young attendants, children of cousins dressed in fancy white suits and dresses, followed behind. The two women kept the four-to-seven-year-olds from stepping on the bride's train.

He looked at Sophie and Jacques, but Gill's gaze wanted to stay on Kat. She looked like a princess in her dress and sparkling tiara.

His princess.

In that moment, he could imagine himself standing in Bertrand's spot and watching her walk down the aisle toward him.

A weight pressed down on him, so heavy he couldn't breathe.

Kat. A bride. His bride.

He felt lightheaded.

"You okay?" Jamie whispered, putting his arm around Gill's back to steady him.

The support allowed Gill to recover. He straightened. "I'm fine."

He forced his gaze onto the bride and his brother. The two were almost to the front of the church.

But a voice sounded in his head.

You're next.

The two words didn't frighten him the way that they might have a week or two ago. He could imagine a future, a life, with his sister's bridesmaid. His sister's BFF.

Kat could make him a happy man.

But would he be able to do the same for her? Would she want him, too?

OUTSIDE THE CHURCH, a crowd gathered to greet the princess bride and her groom. People shouted and cheered, much to Kat's delight. Wearing the red cape and gloves, she climbed into one of the five horse-drawn carriages waiting outside the church. She dried the happy tears from her eyes.

Such a lovely wedding ceremony.

And now Sophie was a married woman.

Liv carefully placed the hood over Kat's head before covering her with a heavy wool blanket. "It's not that far to the castle. This will keep you warm during the ride."

"Thank you."

"Remember to wave as the queen instructed."

Isaac had taught her that, so Kat had only had to spend an hour with the queen learning to wave. Queen Louise had scheduled three hours of lessons. The woman was meticulous.

"I won't forget."

"I'll be at the castle when you arrive to get you ready for the ball." With that, Liv scurried into the crowd.

Kat had spent the morning getting ready. She couldn't imagine anything else being done.

Gill climbed into the carriage. "Is this seat taken?"

Her heart galloped in her chest. "It's all yours."

She wished he could be hers.

He wore a black uniform with gold epaulets. The fringe hung down each shoulder. A blue-and-yellow sash ran diagonally from his right shoulder to his left side, and medals hanging from colorful ribbons were pinned near his heart.

So handsome.

She nearly sighed. "You look like Prince Charming."

He sat and then settled back against the bench seat. "Is that a good thing?"

"It's not bad," she teased. "Though I don't need to be rescued by a prince."

His thigh pressed against her. The blanket and their clothing was between them, but heat emanated at the point of contact. She fought the urge to scoot closer to him.

"You are more than capable of taking care of yourself and everyone around you."

Did that include him?

She wished.

The crowd shouted, "Kiss, kiss."

A thrill shot through her.

If only the people of Alistonia wanted their crown prince to kiss her, but Kat knew they were calling for a kiss between the bride and groom.

More cheers sounded.

Kat grinned. The newlyweds, who sat in the last carriage, must have obliged the crowd.

Gill's gaze softened. "You are exquisite."

Her cheeks warmed. "So are you. I love your uniform."

"It's only worn on formal occasions."

One of the horses neighed as if anxious to get moving.

She was content to sit beside Gill and never move. "Then as crown prince, you should add more of those to your schedule."

He bowed his head slightly. "I shall do that."

The carriage moved forward.

She waved at the crowds that stood on the street with paper cutout hearts colored like the Alistonia flag.

A child waved frantically at her to catch her attention. She waved back and blew him a kiss.

The young boy jumped up and down. His mother mouthed *thank you*.

Down the road, a group of young girls wearing thick coats over snow pants and boots blew bubbles into the air.

The scene was like something out of a movie.

Christmas magic or wedding magic? Perhaps a mixture of both thanks to Sophie's fairy godmother who must be out there waving a sparkly wand.

"It was a lovely ceremony," she said.

He nodded. "Did you know my brother was coming?"

"Not until we had photographs taken. He surprised us outside while the queen was still inside." Kat hoped he understood what this meant to his sister. "Having Father Jacques walk her down the aisle was important to Sophie. Maybe the most important part of today other than saying 'I do.'"

"I'm thrilled my brother is here, but my mother—"

"Will get over it," Kat interrupted. "Father Jacques is riding in the carriage with your mother."

Gill's face tightened. He looked to the first carriage in the wedding procession. "My brother is in there with her? This could turn into a disaster."

The tension in his voice tugged at her heart. She leaned closer against him. "Or lead to a reconciliation."

He half-laughed. "I wish I had your optimism."

She wanted to make him feel better. Otherwise, he might not enjoy the rest of the day. That wouldn't be fair to him or to Sophie and Bertrand.

"Whatever happened between your brother and parents is in the past. He's still your and Sophie's brother. She wanted him here, and I can see on your face that you did, too."

Gill nodded.

"Your mother knows better than to throw a scene on her only daughter's wedding day."

"As queen, she's aware of the public's perception, but as a mother, she tends to let emotion get the best of her."

"That's because she loves you all so much. Jacques, too."

Gill covered his hand with hers. "I hope you're right."

Kat stared at their linked fingers. Contentment flowed through her.

Someone shouted at Gill.

Smiling, he waved back with his free hand. If he was concerned about his brother and mother, he showed no signs. That made Kat happy.

He also hadn't let go of her hand. She loved that.

Maybe she had a shot at a happy ending like Sophie.

Kat grinned and ignored the warning voice that told her not to hope for what she couldn't have. She couldn't forget about Rowena, who kept trying to get Gill alone or his mother interfering in her son's life. Gill would never be Kat's, but she didn't mind living in a dream for a few more days. Besides, she'd never sent her Christmas list to Santa. Maybe it wasn't too late to ask for a happily ever after.

THE ROYAL WEDDING ball was in full swing. As the orchestra played, Kat danced with one partner after another. Twirling this way and that. Her heart was full of joy. Sophie had given Kat a list of dances to learn months ago, but there was nothing like putting the dance steps into practice. Several of the dances, including waltzing, were new to her.

"Enjoying yourself?" Jamie asked as he spun her around the dance floor.

"Yes." She valued his friendship and how he'd helped with the mama dog and puppies the other day. That had brought them closer. No flirting or fun required. It was nice. "Especially now that we're dancing together."

"I hope you'll save another for me."

"Of course, but I see some beautiful women who would love to be in my place."

"Let them stew a little." Laughing, he dipped her. "Playing hard to get often works in my favor."

"I'm sure it will in this instance."

Not even Jamie's handsome face and witty charm could keep Kat from searching the sea of guests for Gill. She wanted to dance with the prince, too, but she didn't see him in the crowd.

As a song ended, she curtsied. "Thank you."

Jamie took her hand and kissed the top. "My pleasure."

She didn't notice a waiter walking around with drinks so headed toward the bar for a glass of water.

Against the wall, away from others, Prince Luc and his wife Emily talked. The prince still had his trademark shoulder-length wavy hair and to-die-for thick eyelashes, and though his looks hadn't changed, he seemed more focused and centered than when he starred on the reality TV show. He, like Gill, wore an official uniform. His wife looked elegant in a forest-green gown that accentuated her green eyes and blonde hair worn up.

Kat had met them earlier, and they were as personable as on the show and very much in love.

"I thought I'd never find you without a dance partner." Gill appeared at her side and held out his hand. "May I have this dance?"

She had no idea where he'd come from, but she curtsied.

"I would love to dance with you."

As the music played, he led her out onto the dance floor.

She focused on him but sensed others looking at her.

At them.

Only she didn't feel self-conscious.

She felt special, as if this moment had been somehow pre-destined. Maybe from the day she'd met Sophie and Gill out by the camp's lake.

"What are you thinking?" Gill asked.

"How wonderful it is to dancing with you."

His smile reached his eyes, and her breath caught. "I was thinking the same thing."

The two of them moved, their steps in unison, as if they'd been dancing together forever.

Kat couldn't have said what song the orchestra played or who else was around them or what time it was. All she knew was this dance with Gill was perfect.

Her heart seemed to beat in time to the music.

Maybe *her* fairy godmother had waved her magic wand tonight.

He looked at Kat with such affection and made her feel like the only woman present.

Nothing mattered except Gill.

She'd never felt anything like it. She didn't want the song to end.

"Enjoying yourself?" he asked.

"Very much so. You?"

"I am now that I'm with you." His eyes darkened. "This probably isn't the time or place, but I'd like you to do something for me?"

"What?"

"Consider staying in Alistonia."

"I'm here until the twenty-sixth."

"That's only three days away." He twirled her around. "Stay longer so I can spend more time with you."

Her lungs constricted, and she couldn't breathe.

He wanted her to stay.

Kat wanted to scream *yes* at the top of her lungs. She opened her mouth, but no words came out.

She couldn't stop thinking about his mother or what he meant by spending more time together. He hadn't said he wanted her stay to be permanent. Only longer. As in a few days or weeks. But not forever.

"No need to answer now," he said. "But think about it."

"I will."

The song ended.

He kissed her cheek. "We'll talk and dance again later."

The Duchess of Darbyton stood at the microphone. She wore a sparkly pink long-sleeved gown and looked beauty-queen gorgeous. "It's time for one of my favorite traditions. The bridal bouquet toss. Will all single ladies please come onto the dance floor?"

Queen Louise leaned into the microphone. "The lucky woman who catches the bouquet will get a dance with my son, Crown Prince Guillaume."

The duchess pulled the microphone stand toward her. "And a dance with my son James, the Marquess of Darbyton."

As the two mothers sized each other up like professional wrestling opponents, excitement buzzed through the ballroom. Some women whispered. Others laughed. A few put on their game faces.

Kat watched in amazement.

Even royals went crazy over the bridal bouquet toss. Add in the extra reward of dancing with two eligible, titled gentlemen, and the women were ready to rumble.

She caught a glimpse of the film crew. Each was positioned around the edge of the dance floor—Brad in the front on the right, Dylan behind her, Conrad in the back on the left, and Wes in the front on the left. Funny, she'd almost think they were filming except they didn't have cameras. Too bad they weren't taping. Kat had a feeling it would make for entertaining viewing later.

She'd told Jojo she would go for the bouquet, but as women jockeyed for a prime spot, Kat stepped to the rear of the dance floor. Catching the bouquet might give the queen one more reason to dislike her.

She stood far enough away from where the bouquet would be tossed it would never reach her. Sophie had practiced throwing earlier in the week. The bride had never come close to this distance.

Grinning, Sophie stood on the dais in front of the orchestra. "Are you ready, ladies?"

The women shouted and screamed.

Sophie turned her back to them. "1…2…3…"

She tossed the bouquet high into the air. The flowers flew over the women waiting in the front with hands in the air.

Princess Rowena jumped for the bouquet and bumped into a countess, who stumbled and took out a princess and a baroness. The three landed on the ballroom floor with a thud, a grunt, and a squeal.

Rowena reached again for the bouquet only to have a duchess jump in front of her. Their hands collided and hit the bouquet like a volleyball. The flowers continued toward the back, soaring past fingertips and hands, until the bouquet hit Kat in the chest.

"Oh." She couldn't help but catch of it.

Clapping, Sophie bounced up and down.

The queen glared at Kat as if she'd somehow planned this when she'd done nothing of the sort.

Gill, Jacques, Jamie, and Bertrand helped up the pile of women lying haphazardly on the floor. No one seemed to be injured. A few women laughed, but not Rowena.

The princess asked Gill for help, which he gave her.

Back on her feet, Rowena straightened her gown, smoothed her hair, and then grabbed a glass of red wine.

Good idea, Kat thought.

She sniffed the bouquet. So pretty.

Rowena walked toward Kat. "Aren't you the lucky one tonight?"

"I should buy a lottery ticket."

"Or a plane ticket home," Rowena mumbled.

Kat looked around. No one else seemed to have heard that.

The woman had issues with her, but the princess was a guest at the castle, like her, and Kat wasn't going to call her out.

Talia, the wedding planner, had been clear about the wedding party's behavior tonight—*do not drink too much or make a scene.*

But Kat couldn't stay mute. "I beg your pardon?"

"Never mind. I'm just a little green-eyed." Rowena stood in front of Kat. "The bridal bouquet is so lovely. Would you mind if I took a closer look?"

Kat held out the bouquet.

Rowena bent slightly and sniffed. "Lovely. Thank you."

"You're welcome."

As Rowena straightened, a wave of red wine flew out of her glass and hit the front of Kat's bridesmaid gown.

Rowena covered her mouth with her hand. "Oh, no. I'm so sorry. I don't know how that happened."

"Oh, what a shame," Queen Louise said in a compassionate tone as she joined them.

Kat hadn't seen her come up, but she stood next to Rowena.

The queen shook her head. "That was such a lovely dress on you, too."

Emphasis on *was*.

Kat trembled with embarrassment.

Gill touched Kat's arm. "What happened?"

"It was my fault," Rowena said. "Someone bumped in to me and my wine went flying all over Kat. I feel dreadful. The dress is ruined."

"It was an accident." Kat said through gritted teeth and tried to ignore the stares from other guests.

Servers arrived to mop up the floor. One handed her a white towel.

"Thank you," she managed.

Her dress was not only ruined, but also unwearable. The liquid made the fabric see through even though the white was now stained burgundy.

Kat crossed her arms over her chest. Thankfully, the bouquet provided extra coverage. "Please excuse me. I need to change."

"Since Kat won't be here..." Queen Louise said. "Dance with Rowena."

It wasn't a question but a command.

So much for luck.

Kat had lost.

This reaffirmed what she'd already known. No matter how much she cared for Gill or how much he wanted her to stay in Alistonia, Queen Louise would never accept Kat in her son's life. His mother had chosen a woman for her son. And heaven knew Gill would do as his mother decreed.

A weight pressed down on Kat's shoulders. She forced herself to stand tall and not to run out of the ballroom.

Do. Not. Cause. A. Scene.

That had been drilled into her enough times by Talia that Kat managed to say a polite word or two to several guests who spoke to her on the way out of the ballroom. She'd never been more relieved to see an exit.

Driven by the threat of tears, she accelerated. At the curved staircase, she ran. She kept running until she reached her room.

So much for being a princess at the royal wedding ball. She couldn't even pass for Cinderella.

Kat stared at her reflection in the full-length mirror. She looked worse than an ugly stepsister.

Not even the best dry cleaner in the country could salvage the beautiful gown.

But she couldn't sit up here and mope.

This was Sophie's big night.

The gown might be ruined, but Kat needed to put on a smile, a new dress, and return downstairs.

A knock sounded at the door. "It's Liv."

"Come in."

Liv raced into the room. She wore a black dress with a white apron. "Let me help you change."

277

"Thank you." She turned so Liv could unhook the back of the dress. "I have no idea what I'll wear. Nothing I have is fancy enough for a royal ball."

Liv studied her. "I may have something. It's a little out there."

"I don't care," Kat admitted. "Anything would be better than a plain little black dress. That's my only option."

"This isn't plain, and it is…royal." Liv unzipped the bridesmaid gown. "I'll be right back."

As the door closed behind Liv, Kat went into the bathroom. She peeled the wine-soaked gown from her body and then wiped off the wine with a wet washcloth.

Kat waited to hear another knock on the door, but none came.

Sophie couldn't leave her own wedding, but Gill could. She thought he might come to her room to check on her. Wasn't that what people who cared about each other did?

Except…

He would be dancing with Rowena.

Under the watchful gaze of Queen Louise.

Kat's stomach roiled.

I don't need to be rescued by a prince.

And she didn't.

What had Gill said?

You are more than capable of taking care of yourself and everyone around you.

Kat squared her shoulders. She was, and she would.

She would put on Liv's dress, march downstairs to the ballroom, and pretend nothing had happened.

For Sophie. For Gill. And for herself.

Chapter Fourteen

WOULD THIS SONG ever end? Gill danced with Rowena as his mother wanted, but he hated every moment. The woman had completely forgotten what she'd done to Kat's dress. Granted, it was an accident, and she'd apologized, but he thought she might be more subdued or remorseful.

The woman looked ready to party.

With him.

He shuddered. *No, thank you.*

The song ended, and he breathed a sigh of relief. He bowed. "Thank you for the dance."

She ran her fingertip along his arm. "The night's still young; perhaps we can continue our...*dancing* in private."

Just shoot him now.

Out of the corner of his eye, he glimpsed Sophie. She was hard to miss in the bridal gown. She waved to him.

Saved by his sister.

"Excuse me," he said to Rowena. "My sister needs me."

He wove his way through the other couples on the dance floor. As soon as he was within arm's reach, Sophie grabbed his hand and pulled him to the side.

Gill had no idea what was going on, but Sophie's smile had disappeared. "What's wrong?" he asked.

She blew out a breath. "I'm worried about Kat."

"Where is she?"

"Upstairs with Liv." Sophie glanced to the doorway. "Kat will be back after she changes."

"You sound certain." No one knew Kat better than Sophie, though he wished that he did.

"I am, but I need you to make sure she's okay." Sophie's eyes twinkled. "It would seem I picked the wrong brother for my BFF, but I couldn't be happier about that. Just please, don't let Mother ruin whatever is going on between you and Kat."

He didn't want that to happen, either. "I'll do what I can."

A flash of color caught Gill's eye. He looked to the ballroom entrance. Kat was no longer wearing the stained gown, but an elaborate costume that looked like something one of Henry the Eighth's wives might wear. She carried the bridal bouquet.

Gill could barely breathe. His mouth watered.

In the white bridesmaid gown, she had looked gorgeous, but also sweet and innocent. Now dressed in a historical reenactment gown with the bodice a tad too small, she looked take-her-to-bed sexy.

He would start with a dance and hope for a kiss. Anything else…

His mother gasped. "What is she wearing?"

Rowena pursed her lips. "She looks ridiculous."

"She's hot." He gave them both a look that said *back off.* He walked straight toward her, not allowing anyone to distract him.

Earlier today, he'd imagined her as his bride. She was smart, caring, compassionate, and brave.

Not many women would have returned wearing a dress like that.

But she had.

And he knew the reason.

Sophie.

Kat had put her friend—the bride—above all else.

Yes, he could picture Kat on her wedding day, but more so, he could imagine her as his wife. The one who would be at his side and be the mother of his children.

He had met her over fifteen years ago, but he'd been too young to see just how right she was for him. And she was.

Gill bowed and then kissed her hand. "I believe I owe you a dance, milady."

Kat curtsied, giving a glimpse of her chest. "Yes, you do, Your Serene Highness."

Was it wrong that he was hoping for the bodice to experience a fashion malfunction?

Sweat beaded at the back of his neck. "Your dress—"

"Belongs to Liv. She made it for a Renaissance Festival. I had nothing fancy enough to wear."

"The gown is perfect. I'll buy it from her for you to keep. You look amazing."

Kat beamed. "It's not too much?"

"Way too much." He grinned. "That's why it's perfect."

The orchestra played a different tune. Couples filled the dance floor.

"Come." He laced his fingers with hers. "They're playing our song."

"We don't have a song."

He had no idea what this one was called, but he would find out the name from the conductor. "We do now."

SITTING IN THE ballroom, Kat had no doubt in her mind that magic was real. That was how tonight had turned out for her—magical. She lost track of the number of times she danced with Gill. But each time was better than the last.

As Gill spoke to a council member at another table, Kat sat to give her feet a rest from all the dancing.

Queen Louise approached her. "Your costume has mesmerized my son."

Kat knew Gill liked the dress, but she also knew what she wore was only a small part of why he was so attentive.

Something had changed between them—from the way

he looked at her to the possessive touch of his hand at the small of her back. She didn't know what, nor did she mind, but even her nerve endings sensed a difference in both his mannerisms and in him. She was afraid to get her hopes up too high.

"I'm grateful to have a dress I could borrow, ma'am."

"I expect you to dress more appropriately for the wedding breakfast."

She'd brought a dress especially for the breakfast. "I will, ma'am."

"Princess Rowena will be there. I'm sure Guillaume won't be able to take his eyes off her." Queen Louise walked away, and Gill reappeared.

He pulled Kat to her feet. "In less than an hour, it'll be December twenty-fourth. You never told me what you wanted for Christmas."

She wanted him. "The only thing I want, that I've wanted, is to be with you."

"That makes things easy."

She smiled. "It's the truth."

"I know, but you try to make things easy on everybody else, even if that may turn out to be hard on you." He ran his finger along her jawline. "It's time someone did the same for you. I want to be that person."

Her throat constricted with emotion. She tried to speak but couldn't.

Her grandparents had provided her with unconditional

love and support. Sophie did what she could for Kat living with an ocean between them. But she'd never expected anyone to make her feel so loved and special as her grandparents had made her feel.

But Gill did.

"Thank you."

"Anytime." The sincerity in his voice matched the look in his eyes. "And I mean that.

Gratitude brimmed, but so did something else.

Love.

She had been falling for Gill before, but she'd fallen all the way now. Stepped over the edge and crashed heart first.

She loved him.

The realization should terrify her, but she felt nothing but peace. The fairy tale was hers to grab like a brass ring.

If only the situation weren't so complicated with his mother…

They could still make this work. Kat had to try.

She gazed into his eyes. "There is one more thing I would like."

"Name it."

"A kiss."

Kat didn't wait for him to lower his mouth to hers. She rose up on her tiptoes and planted a kiss on his lips.

If Gill was surprised, he didn't show it.

Instead, he pulled her close against him. His lips moved across hers, soft at first, and then harder as if he couldn't get enough.

Kat couldn't. She ran her hands through his hair. Strands curled around her fingers.

Their tongues met and explored. Heat pulsed through her. She arched against him.

He was all she needed.

Time seemed to stop. There was only this moment and him. She wanted the moment to last forever.

Gill drew the kiss to an end and pulled back, then he brushed his lips against her again.

"I want nothing more than to continue this in your room, but we should say goodnight and not rush things." He pushed a piece of hair off her face. "We have plenty of time."

Two days didn't seem long enough, but maybe he was right. She hoped so. The words *I love you* sat on the tip of her tongue, ready to leap out of her mouth.

Too soon.

He was right about not rushing things. Especially tonight after so much had happened today.

"I understand. I need to check on the puppies."

He laughed. "Of course you do."

"Goodnight," she said.

Gill kissed the top of her hand. "I'll see you at the wedding breakfast."

Kat nodded, but she didn't have to wait that long. Anticipation buzzed from the top of her head to the tips of her toes. Because she knew she would see him in her dreams.

AFTER CHECKING ON the dogs at the stable, Kat returned to the castle and peeked into the ballroom. Only a few guests remained. One of them was Emily.

The woman motioned to Kat. "Could I talk to you for a minute?"

"Sure." Kat followed her out of the ballroom to a hallway where the film crew was. "What's going on?"

Brad handed his cell phone to her. "Watch this."

Video from the wedding ball played. "I didn't think you were filming."

Conrad hung his head. "We weren't supposed to be."

"We just wanted a little extra footage," Wes explained. "So we positioned ourselves in four corners during the bouquet toss and used our phones."

"We'd never use anything without permission." Dylan fingered his collar. "This footage was on my phone."

"You'll understand why we want you to see this," Brad added.

Emily stood with her arms across her chest. She wasn't smiling.

Kat watched herself catch the bouquet. She listened to the congratulations and tensed the moment Rowena approached with that glass of red wine in her hand, but wait...

"Who is behind Rowena?" she asked.

"You'll see," Emily said.

Kat took a closer look. "That's Queen Louise."

She watched the queen not only bump into Rowena, but also purposefully push the princess's arm forward. Wine flew out of the glass and landed on Kat's dress.

Kat's mouth gaped. She stared at the screen, not wanting to believe what she'd watched. "Queen Louise did that on purpose."

Emily sighed. "I'm sorry, Kat."

Dread slivered through Kat.

Two things were never clearer.

Queen Louise truly hated Kat. And she and Gill would never get his mother's approval to date or do anything else.

Her breath hitched. Flames seemed to lick her throat. Kat felt like crying, but she couldn't. Not until she did something first.

She looked at Brad and the rest of the crew. "Can I get a copy of this, please? There's someone who needs to see it."

LATER THAT NIGHT, the wedding guests had left the castle or returned to their rooms in the guest wing. Kat waited until Queen Louise was alone and approached her outside the ballroom.

"Excuse me, ma'am." Kat curtsied. "May I speak with you for a moment?"

"Yes." Queen Louise clucked her tongue. "Too bad about your bridesmaid dress."

"About that…"

A steely resolve born out of love for Sophie and Gill gave Kat strength. A mother was important, and Kat never wanted Sophie and Gill to experience the questioning or wondering or hurt as Kat had. She removed a cell phone from her pocket and brought up the video. "Please watch this."

"Watch this, ma'am," Queen Louise corrected.

"Yes, ma'am." Kat hit play.

"It's the bridal bouquet toss. Sophie looks so stunning. Such a beautiful bride."

Kat didn't say anything. She heard the shouts and the clapping during the toss.

"You got lucky," the queen said.

"Yes, I did." Kat hesitated a moment. "Ma'am."

The moment with Rowena and the wineglass appeared on the screen.

Queen Louise sucked in a breath. "Where did you get this?"

"It was given to me."

The video clip made what the queen had done clear.

Anger burned in the queen's eyes. "What do you want?"

"Peace."

"Excuse me?"

"I want a peaceful Christmas. For you, for Sophie and Bertrand, for Gill and me."

"Nothing else?"

"That's all.

The queen's eyes narrowed with accusation. "You're in love with Guillaume."

All Kat could do was tell the truth. She squared her shoulders. "Yes."

"He'll never marry you."

Her heart squeezed tight. "I know."

Queen Louise drew back. "Then why are you doing this?"

"*Because* I love him." Kat took a breath and tried to control her heart rate, which was beating out of control. "Gill loves you and his country, and I would never want to come between you and him. I know what it's like not to have your parents be part of your life. I won't let that happen to him."

Queen Louise scoffed. "You think my son would choose you over me?"

"No, but it's a decision he shouldn't have to make."

"So what do you get from two days of peace?"

"Gill loves Christmas. He'll have an enjoyable one. I get two days with him before I leave on the twenty-sixth."

Queen Louise tapped her finger against her chin. "No matter what happens, you'll leave on the twenty-sixth?"

Not trusting her voice, Kat nodded.

"Fine. You'll have your peace."

She didn't feel any relief.

The queen eyed her. "I never would have expected this from you. You're stronger than I thought."

Kat raised her chin. "It's easy to do when you have nothing to lose."

She didn't.

Because Gill was never hers.

But she would make the most of these next two days…

GILL'S ALARM RANG, but he was already awake.

Knowing Kat was only a few doors away made sleep impossible. She consumed his every thought. More than once last night, he'd walked out into the hallway intending to go to her room, only to turn around and return to his.

He tried to blame the feelings on physical attraction, but this was…more.

Lying at the foot of the bed, Max barked.

"Shhh." Gill sat and touched the top of the dog's head. "People might be sleeping."

Was Kat still in bed? He dragged a hand across his face as an image of her tangled in sheets, her hair mussed from his touch, rose in his brain like fireworks. Razor stubble scratched his palm.

Kat Parsons hadn't gotten under his skin. She was in his blood and on his brain and inside his heart. No woman had made him feel this way. His ex-girlfriend Clarissa seemed like nothing more than an infatuation compared to his feelings for Kat. Feelings that had changed in only two weeks.

Could this be real? Or was he just caught up in the romance of his sister's royal wedding and the magic of the

Christmas season?

"Feels real."

He'd known Kat for fifteen years as his sister's friend, an American teenager, a kind girl. Those things were still the same except she was no longer a teenager. But over the past two weeks—*not long enough* he imagined his mother saying—he'd gotten to know the woman. A beautiful, intelligent, caring woman.

Max rolled onto his back.

"No rubs for you this morning. I need to get ready."

Gill showered, shaved, and dressed for the wedding breakfast. No need to wear a tuxedo. A suit would do. He could change into dressier clothes later for the Christmas Eve festivities.

"Ready for breakfast?" he asked the dog.

Max jumped. Like Sophie, the dog didn't hide any emotion, especially when food was involved. He ran and pawed at the door. Max could be more interested in seeing Mama and the puppies than eating.

Gill opened the door.

The dog ran out.

When he reached Kat's room, he stopped and knocked.

No answer.

She must be downstairs.

Except she wasn't there, either. He headed to the stable and found her sitting with Mama and the puppies.

"I thought you might be out here," he said.

"Just wanted to check on the wee ones." She grinned. "They're doing well. Brad Hammond told me last night the film crew wants to get more footage of them."

"That's fine," Gill said. "I'll have Frederick contact them and let my mother know."

"Can you believe it's Christmas Eve?"

"No. Or that Sophie's married." Gill shook his head. "Did you know Jacques is staying for the holidays?"

"That's wonderful." Kat stared at the puppies. "I want this to be the best Christmas ever."

Gill grinned. "Sounds good to me. How would you like to start?"

She pulled something out of her pocket. "With this."

He took a closer look. Laughed. "Mistletoe. I'm in."

"I thought you might be. But what are you doing way over there?" She stood and brushed off her backside. "Come over here and kiss me."

Chapter Fifteen

T HE MAGIC CONTINUED throughout Christmas Eve. Kat spent every second with Gill. She wanted to form enough memories to last a lifetime. From wrapping gifts to dressing up and serving the staff Christmas Eve dinner, she was the happiest she'd ever been.

When the thought of leaving on the twenty-sixth reared its ugly head, she ignored the sadness and heartache she knew would be coming and focused on Gill and the beauty of the holiday.

Later that night as midnight approached, Kat was in the castle's chapel with his family and friends. She almost lost it. The poinsettias, flickering candles, and wooden nativity set at the altar were simple, yet perfect. She understood why Sophie had wanted to get married here.

Kat glanced at Gill, who sat beside her. This was where she would…

Don't go there.

He held her hand and sang Christmas carols. His voice flowed through her, wrapped around her heart, and gave her a great big hug. After the service, he'd wished her Merry Christmas and kissed her goodnight.

If only time could stop…

Christmas day was just as special. From eating a buffet breakfast to opening stockings to handing out presents. She hadn't been part of a big celebration in years, and though this family wasn't hers, she pretended it was. And Gill, too.

For today.

In the sitting room, surrounded by his mother and friends, he gave Kat a gift wrapped in red paper and tied with a silver bow. "This is for you."

She'd given him a pirate ship ornament, a book on pirate lore, and an eye patch as reminders of the pirate prince who plundered and stole her heart.

Kat untied the bow and then ripped off the paper. She lifted the top off the box. Beneath the neatly creased tissue paper was a folder with a photograph of the African savannah on the front. "What…?"

Smiling, he leaned toward her. "Open the folder."

She did. And gasped.

"What is it?" Queen Louise asked.

The words blurred through Kat's tears. He'd known what the perfect gift would be and given it to her. She was touched, shaken, and if she hadn't known he was the one for her, she did now. She cleared her throat. "It's a travel voucher for airfare and a tour of Africa."

Rowena's mouth gaped. "Now that's a present."

"An extravagant one," Queen Louise said with an incredulous stare.

Kat's heart overflowed with love. She looked at Gill. "I don't know what to say."

"You don't have to say anything." He leaned closer and kissed her.

Right there in front of friends, family, and the staff. The day was pure bliss. Perfection.

But on the twenty-sixth, it was all over. The magic had ended. Santa hadn't delivered a happy ending. No miracle had appeared.

She had to go.

A forlorn look on his face, Gill stood inside the airport. He held onto both of her hands. "Stay in Alistonia. Stay with me."

"I can't." Kat wouldn't meet his gaze. She couldn't. "Your mother has other plans for you."

"So? I'm making my own plans for the future. Ones I hope will include you. There's something between us."

"There is, and maybe if you were just some guy with a meddling mother, it might be different, but you're a crown prince and she's the queen. Things aren't that simple."

"I choose you. I will always choose you."

Those words confirmed what she knew in her heart. She would never hurt him, Sophie, and Jacques. "That's why I have to go. Your family is finally back together. I won't be the one who comes between all of you."

"That would never happen."

"It will if I stay."

"No." The word echoed.

Oh, sweet prince. Kat wanted to believe as he did, and let him convince her to stay, but she couldn't. "Look at what happened with Jacques."

"That was different."

"Are you sure about that?" she asked.

"I…" Realization dawned on his face. "You're right. It's not different. Jacques wanted to pick his own bride—the Church, but Mother didn't agree. She wants to pick my bride, too, instead of letting me choose my wife. But this isn't a hopeless situation."

"I'm sorry, but it is."

"You might as well take your knife out of your suitcase and stick it in my heart. That's how you're making me feel right now."

She struggled to keep herself together when all she wanted to do was fall in a heap at Gill's feet. But she was leaving because that was the best thing for him and his family. She hoped he understood that someday.

Tears stung her eyes, but she looked up to keep them at bay. If she started crying, she might lose what little strength she had left.

She squeezed his hands. "The one thing Sophie has shown me over the years is the importance of family. I always thought there was this perfect family, one that met every statistic, and that lived happily ever after. I longed to be a part of that kind of family because I thought I'd missed out. But I see families differently now. They are real, changing like the seasons, and far from perfect. Families take work and effort. Some people aren't cut out for that effort. Others are, and they thrive.

"Your mother is a meddler. But she interferes because she loves you. Parents, even meddling mothers, need be a part of their children's life. I won't come between you and her."

"Is there nothing I can say to change your mind?"

Kat took a deep breath. "I-I'm sorry. I wish things could be different."

"Me, too."

"I can't come between a family. I just can't do that knowing what it's like to have parents, but never have them part of my life. I won't do that to you or Sophie." Kat stood, rose up on her tiptoes, and kissed him gently on the lips. "Goodbye, Gill."

THE DAYS PASSED slowly, miserably, for Gill. Out in the stable, he sat by the nursing puppies. "Good job, Mama."

The name suited her. She took good care of her little ones. The pups looked more like round balls of fur than dogs, but they seemed to be changing every day. Of the six, four had homes waiting for them once they were old enough.

Gill thought about keeping one himself, but he decided

to give Mama a home at the castle instead. He had to do something to make Max happy. The dog acted miserable. No appetite. No desire to do anything but check on Mama.

A puppy squirmed between two others to eat.

He snapped a photo with his cell phone. Sophie would want to see this. And Kat...

Gill missed her. She was on his mind constantly. He wondered if her being gone was the reason Max was acting like he'd lost his best friend. Gill felt as if he had.

His mother entered the stall. She touched his shoulder. "You're enthralled by those puppies."

He wanted to shrug away from her touch. She was the reason Kat had left, even though he wasn't without blame.

If he'd had more backbone or could walk away from his duty...from the throne.

But he knew how he'd felt when Jacques had done that. Sophie deserved to live her life. Still, Gill didn't know if he could continue like this.

His mother moved closer to the puppies. "They remind me of you when you were little. All you wanted to do was eat. Day and night."

"That's what babies do."

"I know. I had three of them." Her gaze lingered on the puppies and Mama, and then she turned. "Rowena is leaving today."

"She should have left the day she turned off my cell phone."

"We'll find you another princess."

"No, we won't." He stood. "I want Kat."

"She's a strong woman."

"That's the nicest thing you've said about her." He looked at Mama taking care of her little ones. "Did you know one of the reasons Kat's so strong? Her mom and dad weren't a part of her life. They dumped her with her grand-parents to pursue their research and died in Africa. They're buried there. That's why I gave her that plane ticket and tour. Not so she could take a vacation, but so she could see where they'd lived and visit their gravesite. Maybe that will give her some closure with her parents."

His mother covered her mouth with her fingers. "So that's why…"

"What?"

"She mentioned something to me about not wanting to come between us."

"She meant it. Her grandparents raised her and taught her the value of family. But she said she never really under-stood it until now. Family means everything to her… including a family that isn't her own."

The agony in Kat's voice the day she'd left had matched the sadness in her gaze. He'd fought to hold onto her, until he'd realized she'd made her decision, and, although she'd been physically present to say goodbye, emotionally she'd already left.

"I love her. I want to marry her. Only her."

"You told her this?"

"Not in so many words, but I think she knew what I was offering."

"A princess like Rowena is perfect for you."

"She's your definition of perfect, not mine."

His mother arched a brow. "You're telling me Kat's perfect?"

"Far from it, but we're better together than we are apart." He'd said this much; he might as well say it all. "I love her. I believe she loves me, too. But she left anyway."

"Because of me."

Gill wasn't going to deny his feeling. "I'm trying to devise a plan, but I keep running into a stumbling block."

"What's the block?"

"You." The word tasted gritty in his mouth. "Kat won't come between you and me, because if I had to choose, I'd pick her."

His mother's eyes widened.

He'd never known her to be speechless, but she seemed to be now.

She opened her mouth and then closed it. "Your sister would make a fine queen. She's a remarkable woman, but Alistonia will thrive with you wearing the crown. You're the perfect combination of your grandfather, your father, and myself. Our country needs you, Guillaume. What do you need from me?"

"I want your blessing." That was his only hope. "Without that, I don't stand a chance with Kat. But it must be sincere, and you must agree to willingly accept Kat as my wife and the future queen of our country."

NEW YEAR'S EVE at the animal hospital wasn't as busy as Kat thought it would be. Midnight was approaching, and she was crying again. In her office, she dabbed her eyes with a tissue.

This was crazy.

She hardly ever cried, but since she got back from Alistonia, it was all she could do.

The hair beneath her surgical cap itched. She hadn't been on duty long enough to be tired or sweaty, but she removed her cap and tossed it on her desk.

A knock sounded. Jojo opened the door. The vet tech wore grey scrubs with pink cat paw prints all over them. "I have coffee and a hug."

"I'll take both."

The cup of coffee went on the desk, and Kat went into Jojo's arms. "Will I ever get over this?"

Him.

Something squeezed at her chest, as if those muscles had constricted suddenly. That happened whenever she thought of Gill. Being home should have brought her peace. Her routine should have brought her a sense of normalcy. Her work should have kept her mind and heart occupied.

"It'll take time." Jojo gave her a squeeze and then let go.

"I need to see if those test results you wanted are ready. I'll be back."

"Thanks."

Kat took a deep breath and another. Nearly a week had passed, but Gill was still there—on her mind and in her heart and in her dreams when she could fall asleep.

She missed him, Max, Sophie, Mama, the puppies, and the staff, especially the prim and proper Jennings who was in charge of everything and treated the puppies like royalty, Isaac who'd taught her so much and become her friend, and sweet Liv who made Kat feel like a princess.

Those people had made her feel like she belonged. Like she was one of them.

Still, she believed in her heart of hearts that she'd made the right choice for everyone involved.

Herself, included.

Gill needed to be with a woman who wouldn't drive a wedge between a mother and her children. Yes, Kat wanted a family of her own, and she wanted one with him, but she wouldn't destroy another family to get one for herself.

Queen Louise was meddling, devious, and overbearing. She parented opposite from Kat's mom and dad, but if Kat had to pick between the two parenting styles, she'd choose the queen's.

For all Queen Louise's faults, she loved her children and wanted what she thought was best for them. Kat might not agree with the queen's methods, but she hadn't deserted her children, ignored them, or disappeared from their lives. Not like Kat's parent's had.

That counted for a lot.

Queen Louise, Gill, and Sophie had shown Kat that family and work weren't mutually exclusive. Something she'd never realized until her trip to Alistonia. Running an entire country—albeit a small one—didn't stop the queen from being a mother. A helicopter one at that.

As a child, Kat had created a world in her mind where parents needed to make a choice between work and kids. As an adult, she'd clung to that belief. That was easier than admitting her parents hadn't loved her more than their research. She knew better now and had come to terms with that, but she would never make the same choices her parents made. She could have both a career and a family.

And would.

If she ever fell in love again…

Not going to happen, a voice cried out.

Her phone vibrated.

A text message must have arrived. She'd had a few tonight but hadn't read any yet. She pulled her phone out of her pocket.

Sophie: *Happy New Year's! Fiji is wonderful. The resort is divine, but it would be more fun if you were here. Hugs and love!*

Kat laughed. She typed a reply.

Kat: *Happy New Year to you and Bertrand. I doubt he'd appreciate my company on your honeymoon, but thank you for the thought ;) xoxox*

She checked the next message. This one was from Jamie.

Jamie: *Glad you're home. I'm spending my money on puppy supplies. Cheaper than alcohol and women.*

That made Kat laugh.

Jamie: *Can I convince you to visit and teach me how to be a good doggy daddy? Friend helping friend. Enjoy the new year!*

Oh, sweet Jamie. She typed a reply.

Kat: *Buy whatever you want, but your puppy will need food, water and your love most of all.*

Kat: *You will be a great doggy dad, and I am here to help you anytime. No more vacation days left, saving for Africa.*

Jamie: *Africa? I'm in. Just tell me the dates. I'll be there.*

And she knew he would be.

Another knock sounded. "The test results are back. They confirm your diagnosis."

At least Kat still knew what she was doing here at work.

"Take your time, but there's a patient in Exam 2," Jojo said. "Dog. No temperature. Not eating. Sounds gastro related."

"Thanks." Kat glanced at the time. Almost midnight.

She slipped her cell phone into her pocket. "I'll be right there."

She walked to the exam room, knocked, and entered. She made sure to close the door so the dog didn't bolt if he were unleashed.

"Hello, I'm Dr. Par…"

The words died on her lips. Gill and Max stood in the exam room.

Her heart slammed against her rib cage.

She blinked.

He was still there.

The dog barked. The cone was gone. His tail wagged, and his paws pranced against the tile floor.

Shaken, Kat bent and rubbed him as she tried to control her emotions. "It's so good to see you, Max."

The dog soaked up the attention.

She looked up at Gill. He looked handsome in his navy slacks, leather coat, and boots. Who was she kidding? He'd look good in anything he wore. "What are you doing here?"

"Max isn't eating. He misses you. I miss you, too."

Kat straightened. "You flew all this way—"

"To see you." He took a step forward and then stopped. "I want you to understand that I heard what you said at the airport, and I've thought about it and you nonstop since then. I can't stop thinking about you. I love you, and I'm not going to live without you."

She drew back. "Excuse me?"

"Which part don't you understand?"

"All of it."

"I'll start over, but first…" He pulled out his cell phone and pressed a button. The song they'd danced to at the wedding—the one he'd called *our song*—played. "I love you. I'm not sure when that happened. But it did. I won't lose you. I can't. So the only solution is for us to spend the rest of our lives together. Is that better?"

Air whooshed from her lungs. "I…"

He crossed the exam room and held her hands. His touch felt oh so right, even though she knew this could never work out. No matter what his intentions. But she wanted to hold onto him for as long as she could.

"You, Dr. Kat Parsons, are the woman I love. The one who makes me smile and laugh and get annoyed when you challenge me to be better. And you do challenge me. Every single day. I don't want that to change."

"I won't come between you and your mother. I know what it's like not to have parents be a part of your life. I won't let you hurt the way I have."

He embraced her and brushed his lips against her hair.

She wanted to stiffen, but her body betrayed her and sank against him.

"I can't change what happened with your parents. I wish I could, but I promise you won't come between my mother and me."

"I want to believe you."

"Then do." Gill raised her chin with his fingertip. "I spoke with her. Sophie was part of the conversation via long distance if you need confirmation. My mother may have antiquated ideas when it comes to love and marriage, but she's not stupid. She has seen the error of her ways and has given us her blessing. I knew if I came here without that, I didn't stand a chance of winning your heart."

"But you always win."

"Not with you, but this time, I hope I will because I can't imagine my life without you. This week gave me a glimpse of that, and I don't want to live that way ever again."

The longing in his voice caressed her heart.

Love wasn't perfect or easy. Finding a job in a foreign country wouldn't be either. Add in his mother and his responsibilities and those would make things even harder.

But he loved her. That had to count for something. Okay, *everything*.

She gazed into his eyes. "I love you."

His jaw relaxed. "I needed to hear you say those words."

He kissed her on the lips. A kiss full of desire and hunger. One that hinted of their future together.

Kat leaned closer and soaked up the feel and taste of him. She loved this man who was more teddy bear than beast once she saw through his hard shell.

Outside the exam room, a countdown sounded. Then squeals and laughter.

Gill drew back. "What was that?"

"I think the clock just struck midnight."

"Happy New Year, princess."

Kat didn't think it would take her long to get used to being called that. "Happy New Year, Your Serene Highness."

He laughed. "I'm just here as a man with a dog."

"Who lives in a castle and will someday rule over a country." She winked. "Live with it."

"As long as I'm living with you, I shall." He brushed his lips across hers. "I know you can't drop everything and leave your life here, so Max and I will stay in Cedar Village, and Mama can join us after the puppies are weaned, until you're ready to go home."

Home. Kat shivered with delight. She loved the sound of that.

"Max," Gill called.

The dog trotted over and sat.

A red ribbon was attached to his collar. "What's that?"

Gill untied the ribbon and removed something, but she couldn't see what. He dropped to one knee. "You are the most caring, intelligent, beautiful woman I've ever met. You make me a better man and will make me a better king. I want to be your husband and wake up next to you each morning for the rest of our lives. Will you do me the honor of marrying me?"

She sucked in a breath and tried not to hyperventilate. Her hands wanted to flap like bird wings. "Yes, yes, I will marry you."

He showed her a ring—a large sapphire with three diamonds on either side.

Kat extended her hand, and he slipped the ring onto her left ring finger. "It's gorgeous, and a perfect fit."

"Sophie helped with the sizing."

Joy flowed through Kat. Peace, too. "Thank you."

"The thanks belong to you, my love." He stood and pulled her close. "I never want to celebrate another New Year without you."

The love in his eyes matched the love in her heart. "Or Christmas."

"I can't wait until we spend every holiday together so we can add each to the list, but I know which will be the favorite."

"Our wedding anniversary," they said at the same time.

She wrapped her arms around his neck and pressed her lips to his—a once-upon-a-time kiss, a one-true-love kiss, and a this-is-the beginning-of-our-happily-ever-after kiss.

Epilogue

Eight weeks later…

I N THE CONFERENCE room at Ever After Productions, Brad Hammond tapped his pen against the table. He'd chosen a seat that didn't face the floor-to-ceiling windows. The sunny Southern California weather made being inside difficult.

His film crew—Conrad, Dylan, and Wes—sat around the table. All the chairs had wheels. Any minute, Brad feared the three men might start playing bumper chairs. That was what happened when the day started with a dozen donuts to celebrate their episode's most recent ratings.

"Let's get this meeting going so we can head to the beach to grab lunch." Brad readied his tablet. "Can you hear me, Emily?"

Emily White von Rexburg was taking the call in Alvernia where she lived with her husband Prince Luc and ran his charitable foundation. A former advertising executive, she'd made Ever After's last two reality TV shows—*Honeymoon in*

Paradise and *A Search for Cinderella*—a success due to her ability to cast the right contestants. She also had a killer instinct for content.

After much prodding from Brad, Emily agreed to be a consultant on *Ever After*. He was thrilled to have her continue on the team. Not only was her access to royalty proving to be invaluable, but she was also a cool chick.

"I can hear you fine." Emily sounded like she was smiling. She'd been at the royal wedding in December. Marriage suited her. "How were the numbers for Princess Sophie's episode?"

"Great." Brad scrolled through his notes. "The ratings exceeded network and sponsor expectations. Happy, smiling faces all around."

"Does that mean we get a raise?" Dylan asked.

Wes snickered. "Your raise was the donuts."

"I like donuts," Conrad said.

Brad ignored his crew. "Key demographics watched, and a significant percentage engaged with social media posts. Two of which went viral. They've requested similar type episodes be put into production."

"Congratulations," Emily said.

"Thanks." Brad referred to his notes again. "The key draws were the newborn puppies, Christmas-themed royal wedding, castle setting, and the newlywed couple's two older brothers."

Conrad laughed. "Emily, do you know any royals who

breed dogs and are planning a Valentine's Day, Fourth of July, or Halloween royal wedding?"

"I'll have to ask around at the next cocktail party," she replied.

"We're too late for Valentine's Day, but Conrad's not so far off," Brad said. "The Crown Prince of Alistonia and the Marquess of Darbyton both tested positive with focus groups and received high rankings for likability. Either could carry one or more episodes. Though this time around, we need full access to wedding planning, the ceremony, and the reception."

Wes swiveled in his chair. "*The Search for Cinderella 2* starring Crown Prince Guillaume."

"*The Search for a Queen*," Dylan suggested.

Wes nodded. "Or *The Future King Takes a Wife*."

"*The Tiara Chase*," Conrad offered.

Brad cringed. "Catchy, but too pageant-sounding."

"You're all too late," Emily said. "Prince Gill proposed to the American vet who delivered the puppies, was a bridesmaid, and caught the bouquet."

Bummer. But Brad wasn't deterred. "So no courtship show, but another royal wedding would be a ratings hit. Put a bowtie on the prince's dog, and you've got a cute, four-legged ring bearer."

"What's the holiday angle?" Conrad asked.

Brad pulled up his calendar. "Has a wedding date been set, Emily?"

"Spring or summer is being discussed, but no official date has been selected," she said. "Just remember, you'll have to deal with Queen Louise again."

Brad thought back to the video footage they had of her and grinned. "No worries."

"Viewers love weddings and they love royals, so there could be huge advertising potential with this," Emily said.

A cha-ching sounded in Brad's head. "How would you suggest we approach the engaged couple, Em?"

"Call Dr. Kat Parsons at the Cedar Village Veterinary Clinic in Idaho. She'll be more approachable than the crown prince and could possibly be convinced with the right motivation."

"What would that be?" Brad asked.

"A donation to an animal rescue medical fund or, perhaps, medical research. Though the crown prince might have his own charities. Dr. Parsons would know."

Brad typed on his table. "Sounds doable."

"Unless she says no," Dylan said.

"We still have James, Marquess of Darbyton." Brad read the bottom portion of his notes. "Jamie is a ruggedly handsome adventurer. He's adopting one of the prince's puppies. His mother is American. And he's a future duke."

"He also has a reputation with the ladies," Emily warned.

"That didn't hurt Luc," Dylan countered.

"Or keep Emily from saying 'I do,'" Wes teased. "How does *Dating the Duke* sound?"

Dylan shook his head. "*Marrying the Marquess.*"

"*Royal Bachelors*," Conrad shouted.

Emily laughed. "Sounds like you have two strong possibilities on your hand."

"Yes." A feeling of satisfaction flowed through Brad. He hoped this time they wouldn't be scrambling to put something together. "Let's hope both the crown prince and the marquess say yes to *Ever After*."

Brad couldn't wait to give his viewers another happy ending.

The End

If you enjoyed Christmas at the Castle, you'll fall in love with the next book in…

The Ever After Series

Book 1: *The Honeymoon Prize*

Book 2: *The Cinderella Princess*

Book 3: *Christmas at the Castle*

It's going to be a royal Christmas...

Don't miss the newest royal releases!

His Jingle Bell Christmas by Barbara Dunlop

A Royal Christmas Princess by Scarlet Wilson

Christmas at the Castle by Melissa McClone

Available now at your favorite online retailer!

About the Author

USA Today Bestselling author **Melissa McClone** has published over twenty-five novels with Harlequin and been nominated for Romance Writers of America's RITA award. She lives in the Pacific Northwest with her husband, three school-aged children, two spoiled Norwegian Elkhounds and cats who think they rule the house. For more on Melissa's books, visit her website: www.melissamcclone.com

Thank you for reading

Christmas at the Castle

If you enjoyed this book, you can find more from all our great authors at TulePublishing.com, or from your favorite online retailer.

TULE
PUBLISHING

Printed in Great Britain
by Amazon

81877552R00192